Crushing
the Corset

by

Maryanne Ross

Victorians Unlaced, Book 2

Crushing the Corset

Cover Art by *The Wild Rose Press, Inc.*

The Wild Rose Press, Inc.
PO Box 708
Adams Basin, NY 14410-0708
Visit us at www.thewildrosepress.com

Publishing History
First Edition, 2022
Trade Paperback ISBN 978-1-5092-4046-3
Digital ISBN 978-1-5092-4047-0

Victorians Unlaced, Book 2
Published in the United States of America

She put shaking hands on her hips and demanded, "What do you want with documents? Letters? What do you seek?"

What did he seek? He couldn't help himself. His own long brown finger reached out toward her. She stared at it, as mesmerized as a rabbit before a snake. He touched one of the gold and pearl drops dangling from her ears, her left ear, making it shiver in her lobe.

"My grandmother's," she said in a stifled voice. "Recently departed. To my sorrow."

He released the earring. He looped his fingers under the gold chain at her neck, which ran down into her bodice. His knuckles grazed soft warm flesh; her raspberry lips parted, and she hitched a breath. His fingers stilled. He brushed the tender skin of her décolletage where it swelled just under her collarbone. He bent his gaze on hers. For a long moment he was drowning in blue as azure as the inland lakes of the Victorian goldfields. He plucked the locket from between her breasts, warm from her secret skin.

Those plush lips pressed together. Her chin came up, and a delightful flush lit her face. Her fingers closed over his, perhaps shocking them both. "My mother's," she hissed.

Slowly, he released the locket, picked up both of her hands, and held her fingers in his. He had her complete attention.

Farlan stared at the sole ornament, the diamond ring on her left hand. A spike of some strong emotion lacerated him. "Do you love this man?" he demanded, his voice ragged.

She opened her mouth. And…she hesitated.

Dedication

To all the female publicans who carved out successful businesses—including my grandmother Margaret Isabella McNeil and my sister Bernadette.

Acknowledgements

Huge thanks to my editor, the incredible Eilidh MacKenzie, and everyone at The Wild Rose Press, without whom these books wouldn't exist. My dream would still be just a dream.

Thanks to everyone who has bought, read, reviewed, and promoted *Bouncing the Bustle*—I'm so grateful for your support. A special shout-out to my amazing friends and family, my many book-loving cousins, and to the first readers of *Bustle*, my mother Liz and sister Bet.

Chapter One

March 1881—North York Moors

"Look sharp, men. Lady Luck beckons."

"That flash dollymop!"

Farlan Blackitter laughed, pulled his hat low on his forehead, and gave the signal. Horse and man flew as one. His heart thundered in his chest, and he bared his teeth in a snarl. The blood beat in his veins with a wild joy.

The target carriage trundled around the bend and began the sharp descent under the lip of the moor. Farlan cried the traditional warning, his voice as hoarse and ugly as he could make it. "Stand and deliver!" Throwing his arm high in the air, he fired the warning shot.

The carriage horse reared up, and the vehicle slewed across the narrow track, obscured just there by the overhang. His second man toppled the coachman before he could grip his weapon and dragged him clear, grinning at the man's curses. His lieutenant squeezed to the side of the phaeton. "Hand over your strongbox!" he shouted.

The door smashed open, and a furious young woman burst out. Blue eyes blazed in sapphire fury; red-golden hair shone like freedom; hands fisted on hips.

"Cowards and reprobates!" she yelled, clinging to the open door of the carriage. She stared at each man in turn and then unerringly aimed her vitriol on Farlan. "Depriving an orphan of her hard-won earnings. How dare you!" She looked them all over, and her tone softened a notch. "I can give you a little gold for your sustenance, in memory of my grandfather who suffered greatly in the Clearances, but give you all my money I will not."

Farlan smiled at her, which further ignited her incendiary glare. "We don't rob women," he said. He jerked his head at his men. "But please be so kind as to stand aside while we search your carriage."

A flash of fear moved swiftly over her flushed features. "The document highwayman," she breathed. She snapped her gaze to his lieutenant, who had stepped close to her and made to grasp her arm. She wrenched it away and glared at Farlan, her outrage kindling once more. "Please instruct your men to keep their filthy robbing hands from my person!"

The laugh escaped him once more. He bowed and summoned his best social tones. "You may keep your gold. We will accept, as you suggest, a small donation to keep my men in the style to which they have become accustomed." He ignored his lieutenant's derisive snort. He made his voice as low and coaxing as he could manage. "Please, step aside, while we canvass your phaeton." He beckoned her toward himself.

For a moment, she stared at his fingers as though mesmerized and snapped, "I can assure you there is nothing to find." Nonetheless, she walked cautiously toward him, halting three feet distant.

"Good girl," he said, masking his rasp in velvet.

"Hardly a girl." Her musical voice was dry. "I am a businesswoman. People depend on me for their livelihood." Her chest rose as she sucked in an alarmed breath. She closed her luscious lips with a snap, patently sorry she had revealed as much.

She darted him a glance under her lashes. "Shouldn't you be wearing a mask?"

Farlan gave her a teasing smile. "I did try that but found them quite suffocating."

"Less so than a noose around your neck!"

Farlan slanted her a look. "Why should you care for my useless neck, my lady?"

The young woman's gaze burned him as her vivid blue eyes lingered over his cheekbones, his jaw. Her lovely eyes dwelt on his lips and then flashed back up to his fascinated gaze.

"Someone must point out the danger to you, as you are so careless of that neck yourself." Her tone was crisp, but a rosy blush mantled her soft round cheeks.

He swept her a mannered bow learned in the lush ballrooms of goldrush Melbourne.

He let her watch, her body held stiff and straight, as his men ransacked the interior of her carriage with marked thoroughness. The two highwaymen ran their fingers behind the squabs and lifted the cushions. His lieutenant, holding the gun in one hand, made slashes and rents in the seams of the fabric lining, slipping his hand in to feel behind.

Her driver had been trussed hand and foot, his old eyes speaking murder and vengeance. "Let them!" she called to him. "They will not find anything, and they have promised to remove only a token sum."

Farlan cocked a glance at her. He liked that she

cared for her dependents.

She put shaking hands on her hips and demanded, "What do you want with documents? Letters? What do you seek?"

What did he seek? He couldn't help himself. His own long brown finger reached out toward her. She stared at it, as mesmerized as a rabbit before a snake. He touched one of the gold and pearl drops dangling from her ears, her left ear, making it shiver in her lobe.

"My grandmother's," she said in a stifled voice. "Recently departed. To my sorrow."

He released the earring. He looped his fingers under the gold chain at her neck, which ran down into her bodice. His knuckles grazed soft warm flesh; her raspberry lips parted, and she hitched a breath. His fingers stilled. He brushed the tender skin of her décolletage where it swelled just under her collarbone. He bent his gaze on hers. For a long moment he was drowning in blue as azure as the inland lakes of the Victorian goldfields. He plucked the locket from between her breasts, warm from her secret skin.

Those plush lips pressed together. Her chin came up, and a delightful flush lit her face. Her fingers closed over his, perhaps shocking them both. "My mother's," she hissed.

Slowly, he released the locket, picked up both of her hands, and held her fingers in his. He had her complete attention. She did not regard her scrabbled carriage but watched wide-eyed as he rubbed a thumb slowly and firmly over each of her fingers. Her skin had the softness of youth but was roughened by work for all that. Not a servant's hands, but nor were they the white pallid paws of a wealthy lady.

Farlan stared at the sole ornament, the diamond ring on her left hand. A spike of some strong emotion lacerated him. "Do you love this man?" he demanded, his voice ragged.

She opened her mouth. And…she hesitated. Fatally.

With an abrupt movement, he tore the ring from her finger. "I will take this, then. As you do not value it." He spoke more angrily than he intended, wanting only to treat her with gentleness.

And with that, in two strides he was away from her and, with a magnificent leap, mounted his black horse, wheeled the beast until it reared, and as suddenly as they had come, he and his men disappeared in a swirling cloud of mist.

Asphodel wrestled with the knots tying her coachman. She could hardly understand the coachman's stream of curses and self-recrimination; it was like the clamor of crows, barely any words penetrating the uproar in her head.

Rocking in the carriage once more, Asphodel stared at the empty space on her left ring finger.

****

The Black Hart Hotel
Fangmoor Beck, North York Moors

"Where is your engagement ring, Asphodel?" Her fiancé, Dougie McDonnell, lowered his gray-black jutting brows and pushed out his fleshy bottom lip. "I paid a fortune for that diamond." He clicked his fingers at Maeve to hurry and pour him another ale.

Asphodel fought the pulse of anxiety skittering in her skin. "I…took it off when I was assisting Mrs. Kell in the kitchen with the curd tarts." Her voice rang high and clear, with the undertone of authority she had developed while running this busy and prestigious hotel.

She didn't know why she lied. Perhaps she could still feel the intense molten silver gaze of a wild man, who had touched her with such sizzling gentleness. A lost man, who had treated her with consideration, leaving her with her precious heirlooms.

And instead, thieving the ring.

She couldn't meet Dougie's affronted glare, instead staring around the Black Hart Hotel's pretty bar. The room glowed gold as the setting sun streamed through small mullioned windows. The pub was so popular she not only had tables here in the bar and in the dining room, but also small private tables tucked under the rafters and the staircase and nestling in the window embrasures.

Dougie said, "You will join me now for an early dinner. The dining room, naturally."

Asphodel instead itched to get back to work, worrying about all the myriad things that could go wrong without her watchful eye. "It's a terrible example for the staff, to see the proprietor and her fiancé at rest while they labor." She hated to tarry while the day still had daylight left in it; it didn't suit her quicksilver temperament. "It's such a sunny spring! Farmers and good York wives will have a thirst."

Dougie McDonnell bestowed a patronizing smile on Maeve and snapped his fingers at Wragg. Asphodel cough-laughed as Wragg merely became more stolid, his weathered features blanking to a bucolic stupidity.

Dougie downed his second beer and wrenched himself up from the bar, making his ponderous way to the dining room for his early evening repast. "I will see you there in five minutes, Asphodel."

On the way back to the kitchen, Asphodel watched from the hall as he opened the menu, licking his fleshy lips as he scanned the selections. Asphodel discovered herself hoping he would choke on a fish bone.

She started and quickly smothered the rebellious notion.

He spied her there and summoned her with another click of his fingers. She chose to enter the room, head held high, and pulled out a sturdy chair across from him. He did not even bother to stand, she noted. It was time to assert herself.

"We must cease eating here," she said. "This lovely room is for patrons and guests, not to eat into the profits ourselves or detain my busy staff from the paying customers."

"You are quite wrong, my dear." The fruity laugh and avuncular tones grated on Asphodel's nerves. "When our two families, and our two businesses, are aligned under the law, we should live in the manner to which we will be entitled."

Nonsense. "I'm not sure about that," Asphodel retorted. She paused. Even if the comment riled him up, she had to say it. "A businesswoman should work to improve the business, to invite new customers, attract more patrons, not loll around eating rich food."

"Come, have a little wine." He shook with a fat chuckle. "Relax."

Asphodel gave a quick shake of her head. "No, thank you, not just before the evening rush. This publican prefers to appear sober as she conducts her establishment."

"You are too hard, my dear." His tone sharpened. "When we are married, you will not be concerning yourself with all this."

Asphodel snapped to attention. That clear note of greedy possession in his voice—had he always spoken so?

When the highwayman had taken her ring less than two days before, he'd awakened her from an enchantment. Stupefied with grief after her grandmother's passing, enshrouded in a gray mist, she'd sleepwalked through the weeks, all sound and sensation muffled.

She had only put energy into her legacy, the Black Hart Hotel, which her grandmother had bade her to "hold tight."

Sometime during that fog, Dougie McDonnell had proposed in this very room, saying that her grandmother had desired it so. In a state of numb loss, Asphodel had accepted him.

She studied her fiancé's countenance and person. His coarse-grained skin and thinning hair proclaimed his age, the late forties, a great contrast to her nineteen years. She would turn twenty this June, still a year away from her majority.

His fluffy gingery-brown facial hair partly obscured the red veins beginning to streak across his cheeks and nose. Bright blue eyes lent him a kindly appearance, which she now knew was as false as his teeth. His stomach, stretching an embroidered silk waistcoat, protruded sufficiently to precede him into rooms.

She looked at his chubby, hairy hands, gripping his cutlery and sawing into his dinner. Those fingers would not graze her skin, with a sensuous, delicate touch that called forth fire from her nerves. She doubted those fingers would return a gold and pearl earring or let fall a gold engraved locket, once they had grasped such objects.

He was her grandfather's much-younger half brother, her guardian, and now somehow her fiancé.

What had she been thinking when she accepted him? She stared now in rising horror, which she prayed did not appear on her features. Hopefully Dougie was too engrossed in the second course of duck enlivened with citrus and peas to notice. He inserted a large portion of fatty duck into his mouth and chewed.

Restlessness possessed her. A need for solitude so she could think properly threatened to overwhelm her.

She stood. "Excuse me, sir…" She scrambled for an acceptable excuse.

Before she could speak, he said, "Why do you not wear a corset, Asphodel?" He took a large gulp of his third glass of claret. His eyes roved her body with the same lust he employed preparatory to devouring a large roast of beef.

"I do not believe them either healthful or conducive to work," she answered him shortly.

He smirked in a way which he clearly appeared to believe was a lover-like expression. "I prefer women to appear womanly. Tomorrow you will oblige me by wearing one."

A red tide of rage rose in Asphodel. The highwayman, with his sensitive touch, his vulnerable gaze, and his strength, had suddenly released her from the frozen emotional lake in which she had been held prisoner after her grandmother's death. Now she felt everything too intensely.

"Just because you wear a corset, sir, does not mean I shall wear one." Oh dear. All her guns were blazing. But she noted his blanched cheeks with satisfaction. His eyes narrowed and his expression turned mean, his mouth pursing and his brows lowering.

Undaunted, she leaned her hands on the back of her chair. "I do not *choose* to squeeze my innards in such an unhealthful way. I like to move with freedom and breathe unencumbered. I hardly need a corset, as I am slight"—she looked defiantly at her fiancé's waist—"and even if I did have a larger girth, I still would not wear one, except on formal occasions."

He turned purple. Worried he would have an apoplexy within her hotel if he continued to be presented with her unwomanly form, she turned and stalked away.

****

Asphodel kept the key to her grandmother's tower room close on her person. She took the narrow circular steps two at a time, relishing the freedom of movement and sensation of athletic smoothness. Her heart leaped in her chest with a mad elation. She knew there would be retribution, but for now happiness sizzled within her.

Somehow, she had been frozen, and now she was alive. She remembered how her skin had thrilled to the highwayman's touch, how his atmosphere of danger and his somehow vulnerable gaze had awakened something within her.

"Thank you!" she said fiercely, out loud.

Asphodel sat at her grandmother's small elegant writing table. It was typical of Isabella McDonnell, making do with something small and discreet, but elegant in its proportions and beautiful in its detail of inlaid mother-of-pearl and jet.

Restless again, Asphodel arose and strode around the circular tower room, pausing often to stare out at the vast moody peaks and folding dales. Stars beckoned like glittering wishes in the velvet sky. A fingernail-paring of a pale lemon-colored moon hung on the horizon, so low she could almost reach out and swing on it.

Here in her grandmother's room, the last nights her nana was present came back to her in a vision so strong she reached out fruitlessly for her grandmother's frail hand.

She could almost hear the strong, beloved voice.

That terrible night, the clouds had roiled purple-black outside, making fantastical, sculptural shapes in the twilight sky over the North York moors. The old woman had insisted on keeping this high room, declaring she wanted to survey her domain as she lay dying.

Her grandmother's breathing hitched and labored. "Who's that?" The voice was thready but lucid and with some of her old spark.

"It's me, Nana. Asphodel." She gave the old hand a squeeze. That hand had been her guide, her solace, and her authority, all through her childhood and youth, and now it was as weak and discolored as a cast-off leaf in autumn.

Her grandmother struggled to raise her head from the pillow, grunting with frustrated effort.

"Shh, Nana, shh. I'm here." Asphodel barely held back the note of panic, half standing in her effort to soothe and placate the old woman.

Her grandmother's head collapsed back on the pillow, but her eyes were open now, their cornflower blue a faded version of their original brilliance—eyes, they said, just like Asphodel's own.

"That fool Dougie will be back soon," her grandmother wheezed.

Fool?

"Listen to me, Asphodel." Her grandmother never called her Ash or Asa.

"Yes, Nana. There is only we two here."

"This hotel is yours now. Hold it tight." Her breath was a gasping wheeze.

"But Nana…I am not yet of age!"

"I have appointed a guardian, as is the law. *Don't* let Dougie wrest it from you. Hear me, Asphodel!"

She nodded, squeezing her grandmother's hand, but she doubted the old woman could see her properly. Her own voice was caught in a lump in her throat. She shut her lips on a moan of grief threatening to escape her control. Her grandmother would not approve.

The old woman choked and gurgled, jerking her head up once more. Her breathing was shallow and rapid in her anxiety. Although they had never been physically affectionate, Asphodel stretched out a tentative finger and stroked the wispy hair back from her face, trying to calm and settle her. Her nana raised a shaky hand and held Asphodel's in her soft, weak fingers. Asphodel froze, all her emotions, her senses, focused on that simple touch, trying to hold on to the moment, to keep her nana with her for a while yet. The worn fingers twitched.

"It's Asphodel, Nana. I am here with you."

"As…pho…del. Hold this hotel tight. Hold this

place…and its secrets. *Hear me?*"

The woman gave a rattling breath and closed her eyes, muttering syllables and sounds that Asphodel failed to decipher. She waited. She didn't want to upset the old woman further. But would she ever get a chance to ask again?

"What secrets, Nana?"

But she had hesitated too long. Footsteps echoed on the tower stairs. Her grandmother opened her eyes once more, gazing directly at Asphodel in a purposeful stare.

The door opened, and Dougie bustled in, all stomach and importance. Her grandmother immediately lapsed back on the pillow, muttering and moaning and rambling to herself.

Asphodel looked at her sharply. Did she merely pretend to wandering wits? Or had she in fact talked nonsense this evening? No. Her grandmother had, however briefly, seemed her old fiery self.

Dougie strutted over to the bed and bent over, his corset creaking audibly. He said very loudly, "I'm here, my dearest Belle."

Her grandmother tossed and muttered, her eyes closed. Dougie peered at Asphodel suspiciously from under graying beetling brows. "No change?"

Asphodel shook her head. "I'll stay with her a little longer."

He jerked a nod. "I'd relieve you, my love, but my responsibilities grow. This is a more suitable place for a woman."

His *love*? Hardly. Her grandmother's husband's youngest brother. A remote connection at best. He had never been more than patronizing to her, but these last weeks he had been all false solicitousness. It set her teeth on edge.

Asphodel gave him her best glare, learned from the woman whose hand she still held. He sniffed and backed away through the door in an inelegant rush. Asphodel almost laughed. Coward.

As the sky darkened and lamps in hamlet windows twinkled all over the crests and dips, Asphodel sat there, fingers on the old woman's skin, shivers creeping up her spine.

She stared at the old, well-known face, scanning for clues. Had her grandmother been lucid? Or rambling?

What secrets?

And then two nights later…

It had been very late. The hotel was quiet; even the most enthusiastic drinkers had stumbled home. The walls seemed to ring with all the different voices absorbed over the years, breathing them out in ghostly whispers and creaking sighs.

The staircase ascending to the tower room was wreathed in shadows and pools of darkness. Asphodel kept stopping every few treads, looking over her shoulder, listening hard. Nothing. But she had a feeling her grandmother wanted her…

Asphodel opened the door to her grandmother's room and stifled a shriek.

A dark figure stood there, bent over her grandmother's bed. Asphodel stared, a terrified scream pressing to burst out as she clutched at her own throat. The stranger saw her and straightened, allowing Asphodel to catch a glimpse of her grandmother.

The old woman was awake, half propped in the

bed. Something passed from her grandmother's shaking hand to the dark stranger's firm grasp. The flickering candlelight glimmered on the smooth cream surface of a letter or document. The letter disappeared into the stranger's pocket. He bowed, turned, and strode toward Asphodel. His hat was pulled low over his eyes, a dark muffler obscured the lower part of his features, and a many-caped carriage cloak swirled around his form. Brilliant eyes scorched her.

She started back in fear and then realized he wanted the doorway. She let him pass, her back pressed to the wall, heart thundering in her chest.

The image of the letter was impressed on her vision. One word only of the direction was clear, caught in the dim yellow beam of the candle: *Trustee*.

Her grandmother crumpled down in her bed. Asphodel leaped forward.

The old woman breathed harshly. "Hold the Black Hart tight, Asphodel."

"Yes. Yes, I vow it."

"I named you, as your mother lay dying. I named you Asphodel, for my favorite wildflower, back home in the Scottish Islands. The Hebrides. My tiny, bright star. Hopeful as the sun."

"I know, Nana."

They were the last words Isabella McDonnell ever uttered. The old woman closed her eyes and slumbered. In the wee hours, the old woman's spirit and strength departed with her mortal body, leaving just the waxy, frozen shell.

Asphodel was alone.

****

Asphodel snapped back to the present. "That fool,"

her grandmother had called him. "That fool."

"Oh, Nana," said Asphodel, stroking the writing table. "Why didn't I listen to you properly? It's me that is the fool."

Asphodel paced some more.

So why had her grandmother made her grandfather's much-younger half brother her guardian, if she considered him a fool?

What had Isabella said? *I have appointed a guardian, as is the law. Don't let Dougie wrest it from you. Hear me, Asphodel!*

Dougie had told her he was her legal guardian. Isabella could well have meant the exact opposite. And now he was also her fiancé. A greedy man, more than twenty-five years her senior. *How* had it happened? And why on earth had she said yes?

Dougie had told her that it was her grandmother's dearest dream to see them united in marriage, with him to take care of Asphodel, and their businesses supporting each other. That was why, when Dougie proposed to her—offering "a merger"—she had blindly agreed.

With this hotel on the North York summits—currently owned and managed by her—his small textile factory in Pickering and his nearby farm, stocked with Rough Fell sheep, they would be secure from the poverty that had driven her grandmother's family from their Scots island home.

"Oh Nana! Why did I believe him? I knew you wanted me to be safe, but marry Dougie? Surely not! Did you really make him my guardian? What *did* you want?" A voice like her grandmother's brushed her mind. *Read the will again.* She did not recall seeing that phrase there, making him her guardian…and now Dougie had possession of her grandmother's legal papers.

Asphodel stared sightlessly out at the darkening sky. Thank all the stars the highwayman had held her up and woken her from her grief. *Just in time.*

"If I am Dougie's ward, I am legally in his power, and now thanks to my stupidity in believing he spoke of your wishes, I am bound to become his wife."

Bound because she was a woman of honor. You had to keep your word in business, or you could fail fast and spectacularly. Did that mean she had to go through with this marriage now?

Imagine the scandal if she did not. Jilting her legally appointed guardian. *If indeed he was.*

And worse! Could the resulting scandal hurt her beloved Black Hart Hotel? Her grandmother's legacy to her? Her nana's great trust?

Asphodel was about to turn away, when a light sparking in a deep expanse of blackness stretching to the north caught her eye. It winked where there was no business for a light to be: in the old Blackleech Castle, reputedly cursed and haunted, long abandoned to fall slowly into ruin and decrepitude.

She stopped thinking about Dougie and fastened her curious gaze on the flickering light, appearing and reappearing as if someone moved around. Her heart smacked against her ribs.

The owner was long dead.

And the Blackitter heir was long missing.

So who, or what, was out there?

Chapter Two

March 1881—Blackleech Castle, Fangmoor Beck

Farlan Blackitter stubbed his left big toe on a fallen bit of masonry, which jarred his left leg. He wobbled, overbalanced, and landed heavily on sharp-edged rubble. He cursed robustly. His lamp flared as it flew through the darkness. The tinkle of breaking glass was like the smashing of new hopes. The small flame extinguished. Darkness swallowed him.

Normally, he could see like a cat in the dark, and he took his athletic agility for granted. He *never* fell.

"You are a fool, Farlan Blackitter!" His gravel voice echoed in the darkness. No wonder he had tripped, dreaming like a loon of a woman with red-gold hair as sparkling as a sunbeam. A glorious woman like that could have nothing to do with him—or at least with the man he had been. The man he had thought he was.

Now? It all depended.

Despite his bruised left hip, his heart soared and his mind sang. The skin on his hands stung where they had been scraped raw. He wiped the seeping blood on his trousers. More scars for the collection.

He pulled his cloak from where it had adhered to a twisted piece of metal, grimacing at the sound of tearing, and gingerly pulled himself to his feet. He waited until his eyes adjusted to the darkness. It was far from the first time he found himself in a dangerous place with no light—but he didn't especially care to be reminded of them.

All that was behind him now.

As long as he could find the papers...and beat the family curse...

He picked his way through the heaps of broken stone, fallen statues, wild overgrown gardens, and long-obscured pathways to the rear of the ruined Blackleech Castle, cursing himself fluently all the way.

He managed to arrive at the small back kitchen with only a knock or two to his ankles and more scrapes on his boots. He grinned ruefully. Where was a valet when you needed one?

By contrast to the rotting disarray and neglect outside, the small kitchen was clean, tidy, and comfortable. Kitchen shelves and the wooden table gleamed in the firelight. A box of vegetables collected from the overgrown kitchen garden waited by the stone sink. A fresh bucket of water, pulled from the pump that morning, waited for cooking and washing. That had taken a mort of effort! Getting that bedamned pump working again. So many essential things that a gentleman's education did not provide... Lucky for him he'd had plenty of the other type of education too.

And he needed his insalubrious schooling in his current quest. He would not achieve his ends, overcome obstacle after obstacle, with gentlemanly manners and notions of fair play. No, this would be a street fight. His speciality.

And now he had seen a vision of loveliness, of tart North York womanhood, her sharp tongue whipping his interest as much as her creamy cleavage and plum pink lips. Those celestial blue eyes! That strawberry hair! That feisty temper.

Farlan stood aimlessly in the kitchen with a foolish smile sliding over his face.

An amused Irish brogue nearly ripped his ear off. "What's the point of hiding out here if you insist on lumbering through the wreckage shouting and cursing and smashing things like a great lummox?" His second man, the ex-jockey McEvoy, shouldered him out of the way and began assembling knives, vegetables, and several rabbits, preparatory to whipping up one of his infamous game stews. "What's got into you, Lord Blackitter?"

Farlan laughed. "You only call me that when you are cross. And it's Baron Blackitter, Lord of Blackleech to you."

"Don't care what fancy construction you put on it. I like the sound of it, you know. Me! From the stews of the wild Australian goldfields, cooking and lookin' after the horses of a lord! And all those years you never said a squeak."

"I didn't know. And it wasn't relevant."

"I suppose not. Scouting for Her Majesty in those dense New Zealand forests. Brawlin' and diggin' for a living on the Ballarat goldfields."

"I'm yet a highwayman," Farlan reminded McEvoy. "With my neck in a noose if I don't find those papers. They don't hang barons." He snatched a piece of carrot, narrowly dodging McEvoy's cleaver. "And the brawling was largely confined to yourself, with me paying the fine to jump you from the bails the next morning!"

"Well, you're handy with your fists when need

calls, even if you scam otherwise now, *my lord*."

His lieutenant Gentleman Jack darkened the doorway. Jack ducked his head under the lintel—far too low for his lean height—and sauntered into the kitchen.

"Good evening," Jack greeted them in his rich mellow tones—the very tones he had schooled Farlan in during his youth. Like Farlan himself and McEvoy, he wore tattered ex-military garb. They had found the fabrics and line of the garments stood up to the hard wear demanded by their lifestyle. Jack flipped two pistols with the verve of a music-hall showman. He folded himself down at the table and began to clean and prime them.

"Here's your real lord, born and bred," Farlan said to McEvoy. "I was only born."

"The infamous black sheep. Compulsory in all the best English families," agreed Jack, squinting down the barrel of one of the pistols. "Complete with reprehensible friends"—he gestured with a showman's wave to Farlan—"and undesirable Irish acquaintances who harbor revolutionary notions."

"I'm still doin' the cookin' and the muck work, aren't I? Still under the hammer—no revolution—yet," McEvoy muttered with an evil sneer.

"Merely practicing my aristocratic duty and attempting to keep you in your place, my lad." Jack shot a look at Farlan. "What's bothering you?"

Farlan plastered a relaxed grin on his face. Or so he hoped. "Merely having to endure the witty banter of you both."

"By all means," said McEvoy, "go and sit yourself up there in that dusty dining room, and I'll fetch ye yer buttered crab and roasted swan."

"I'm not sure ex-jockeys with dubious pasts are the usual footman stock," Farlan countered. "Perhaps I'll just eat here in the kitchen. At least I won't fall from a missing wall or choke on cobwebs."

Jack said, "You do need to cast away this highwayman game and reassume your identity and title, and soon. You must practice being in polite society once more."

"Why so? And what if the old man decided to embroider a final fantasy tale for me before he met the real devil below? I may be no baron at all."

"Come now, my friend. People take one on face value. You must act, live, and breathe Baron Blackitter. There must be no doubt in your audiences' minds, nor your own, for a long con to germinate and come to fruition."

"I may be Baron Blackitter in truth. I need the papers. I was only ten when my grandfather rushed me away to the Victorian goldfields, as you know. It was only as he lay dying that he impressed on me the need to return here and claim my birthright. He insisted. *Claim my birthright.* He said he had saved me from the Blackitter curse."

"Do you remember this place?"

"Something very like, anyway. I remember the rough heights and grassy dales, the smell of the air and the horned sheep."

"A boy's memories would be of the outdoors."

"I remember running madcap through a grand old castle—but that doesn't mean I'm a baron's son. Might be his by-blow."

Farlan poured them all a frothing dark ale from the barrel. "Being here is making phantoms in my mind; I recall shades of our hasty and secret departure in the dead of night. Years before that, a hawk-nosed man whom I called father."

"Assume the title and role. Begin your repairs. Look at this place. No one has claimed it in your absence. Who will gainsay you?"

Farlan shrugged. "I have a mania to hold the proof. We knew so many men on the goldfields with stories of family wealth and titles back in the old countries. My grandfather was a romantic and a storyteller. He could have been inventing all this."

McEvoy interjected, "Come now, Farlan lad, we've bin over this. But by all that's holy, I'm in agreement with his nibs for once. Give up this quest for documents. It will all come to naught if you are caught and hanged."

Farlan said, "My grandfather told me with his last breath that he loved Isabella McDonnell at the Black Hart Hotel." A deep swallow of malty dark ale cooled his tight throat. "That fierce old lady gave me a packet she kept safe for the old devil. No Blackitter testaments."

"And now she is passed."

Farlan nodded. "That inn hides more secrets." He flicked froth from his upper lip. "So we search travelers linked to the hotel."

McEvoy snorted. "It ain't the goldfields, my lord. Gills hereabouts hide their sparkles and files safe in cottages. Stone mansions. Not in their carriages."

"They might, if they have stolen papers to keep close." He quirked a grin at the little man. "It's a fine lark! And we're hard men to catch."

Jack Darnley's brows twitched up. "And the new

proprietor?"

Farlan shrugged. He had an idea about that…but he kept it close. He would indulge his curiosity tomorrow. "I am yet to discover that," he answered shortly.

"Crackbrained," marveled McEvoy. "Stop the crazy fool, Gentleman Jack. Before we all swing. He listens to you, the devil knows why."

"Because I schooled him to a gentleman when he was a lad and young man. It's a shame an old lag like yourself refuses to absorb a little culture."

"Put a plum in me mouth and sound like an English? I would betray the music of the auld country. Here, better put this dinner in yer mouths instead."

They took his advice and fell to eating. Farlan had to force the food down. His usually healthy appetite had deserted him.

He waited until he could be alone in the upstairs bedroom so he could take his dream out and enjoy it.

Except his dream had changed.

Instead of seeing himself reclaiming his birthright and restoring Blackleech Castle, a pair of bright sapphire eyes as blue as a summer sky in a lovely face swam in his mind. In his imagination, she let down her tresses of yellow topaz hair, and he threaded his fingers through the silky strands.

****

The stranger chuckled. The rumbling murmur barely rippled the warm drone of the bar. If Asphodel hadn't been straining her ears so hard, she would have missed it. The low laugh was so warm and contagious it summoned an answering smile of her own.

She paused in her work and cut a glance over to where he leaned his long sturdy length against the wall in the dimmest end, in the shadows. He was listening to the old York lawyer, who had been disbarred long ago for his unscrupulous defense of villains. The lawyer could charm a stone. She almost envied him.

The stranger twisted his head toward her. Under the deep brim of his hat, she caught the mercurial gleam of silver eyes. The shadows striped his features, like prison bars. His long curling black hair hung free of its riband today, half obscuring his face. His chiseled chin shone black with short bristles. Her fingers unaccountably itched to feel their rasp.

One of the farmers demanded her attention to adjudicate in a stubborn argument regarding Swaledale sheep. She answered them teasingly, keeping the mood in her hotel light, but her entire awareness focused on the stranger as he peeled himself from the shadows and came toward her.

She almost spilled the ale she pulled from the tap.

That dark hair, those eyes, that particular mocking quirk of the mouth, that athletic movement—the man had held her at gunpoint a bare two days before.

Her cheeks warmed. How dare he come here?

He stood close to the bar and leaned in toward her. His eyes sparked, and his long mouth twitched up. "There could not be so many businesses—nor businesswomen—on the untamed moors."

He had come to find her then! Her blood spiked in her veins. "You would pay for your ale with my own gold?" she hissed.

He laughed again, and the sound warmed her, despite her warring emotions.

She said, tone low, "If I can recognize you, so might others. You will be caught."

"As you have been caught." He opened his clenched fist for a moment and showed her the ring.

Asphodel flashed a panicked look around the room. Her patrons might appear bucolic and immersed in their country concerns, but they missed little. Dougie could saunter in at any moment. "Give me that!" she breathed.

He said, tone low and private, "One wearies of holding up coaches for sport. My talents crave variety. I have a mind to rescue a beautiful, trapped damsel." He closed his fist around the ring.

Asphodel swelled like the parson's lady faced with a hobbledehoy, rude ripostes jangling in her mind as she traded glares with him. She hardly knew what to shout first. The word "beautiful" echoed in her mind like a bell.

She deliberately calmed herself. He sported with her, that was all, as men in their cups were sadly wont to do. Even the staid farmers allowed themselves a modicum of very mild flirting. It put them in charity with themselves as they returned to their wives and farms, until those sensible Yorkshire hearthwives cut them back to size once more.

"Which is the man who gave you this ring?" the highwayman asked. His silky and caressing tone wrought shivers on her skin; it was as though he stroked her with those long, tanned fingers.

His timing was impeccable.

Her fiancé, Dougie, rolled into the bar. Asphodel flashed the highwayman a warning glare and put her chin up.

"Asphodel!" Dougie said imperiously. He cast a fulminating look at her figure. He flipped up the panel into the bar as though he owned it and strode toward her, laying a thick-fingered hand directly on her waist, which remained defiantly uncorseted. His coarse features purpled, and he pouted like an angry baby. He jerked a thumb toward the door into hallway.

Asphodel stiffened and suppressed a sharp retort. They were in full view of her customers. Suddenly she saw Dougie very clearly. The highwayman's presence had dissipated the fog she had been floundering in. Her cheekbones ached, and she squeezed her fist on the beer pump: *how* had she allowed Dougie to speak to her so, treat her thus?

She quashed her rage. "Hello, Dougie," she said, mustering a polite tone. "I am working at the present moment. Perhaps you will like to relax in the garden bar. Wragg will bring you—"

"*You* will bring me food and a restorative. Wragg will serve in here. It does not accord with my notions of the behavior of my affianced bride to continue exposing herself as a working publican." Dougie was enjoying working himself into a passion, and the farmers watched, their eyes sparkling with this unexpected entertainment.

"Dougie," she replied quietly and widened her eyes at him, nodding to the room. She wanted rid of him. Her uncle must not suspect what the stranger held in his fist.

"I will expect you directly," Dougie announced plummily and stalked from the bar.

The highwayman still leaned his muscular length against the bar.

Asphodel could not look at him. What would he think of her? She fussed with glasses and cloth until she could no longer resist the magnetic lure of the man. She rested her hands on the bar, raised her eyes, and matched that mercury stare. The brigand neither mocked nor derided. Instead, he regarded her with a steady, assessing gaze. His face was warm with concern.

Asphodel swallowed.

The highwayman said softly, "I lay my sword at your service, my lady. Such a fat dragon should not be long in the slaying."

Asphodel smothered her laugh in a pretend cough. "You go too far, sir. Please, return me my ring. This instant."

The highwayman studied her. His teasing grin danced across his features. "In time I shall give you another. You will like that one better, I assure you." He stood away from the bar, preparatory to leaving.

Asphodel put her chin up. "Ha! You imagine a great deal about my feelings!" Her riposte won her an amused silver glint and a mocking curl of his lip. She said quickly, "What is your name, dragon-slayer?"

"Farlan…" He hesitated and glanced outside. "Crow."

Asphodel noted the one black bird perched on the old crabapple tree outside, staring in with its one yellow eye like a harbinger of doom. A crow. She had no doubt the stranger had borrowed his name from the fell bird.

The stranger wouldn't be the only one with secrets who spent their money in her grandmother's hotel.

He was the one who most intrigued her.

Her attention was dragged away from his departing form. Maeve jerked a pointed chin. Her new client had arrived.

Asphodel took a breath, inhaling strength from her familiar hotel, her world. Word-pictures took so much out of her, but people needed her. They seemed to find such solace and refreshment after a session—so how could she have the heart to deny them?

Leda was a woman of middle years, neatly dressed, worried, biting the edges of her lips. Worn knuckles showed white where she clutched her reticule. They both pretended the woman sought help with budgets and accounts. Asphodel often assisted with those too, but they all came for something else—her word-pictures.

Asphodel set Wragg to tend to Dougie and calm his rage with stalwart moors placidity. She ushered her client to the sweet alcove under the stained-glass window, which looked out into her flower garden. The little alcove was away from the general hubbub of the back bar, where conversations could not be easily overheard. She could do her word-pictures for her clients but still keep an expert eye on proceedings.

Asphodel still grieved for her grandmother. Her absence was such a hollow in her life. She hardly knew if she could summon the energy, the vital piece of herself needed to give her customers confidence and courage. The total immersion into their personalities, hopes, fears, and worries.

The client sat, and Maeve brought tea and a plate of fat rascals, the delicious Yorkshire rock cakes studded with dried fruit and nuts.

Asphodel took the woman's hand, preparatory to doing the reading. Tiny hard calluses and seams of scars ran down Leda's fingers and right thumb. Her hands and arms were covered in small, healed cuts.

Asphodel knew they were typical weavers' marks, caught in years of operating the spinning jenny in the Yorkshire textile mills.

The clients' hands told her so much even before they spoke. Callused laborers' hands. The small burns of a cook, the scar patches stretched and shiny, smooth and sensitive. The soft white hands of the rich, although here on the desolate peaks, even rich folks' hands often revealed a very different past.

"I am a weaver," Leda said. "Making fine clothing at the McDonnell tweed factory over there in Pickering." *Dougie's factory.* Fervor rang in her client's voice. "I have taken a very risky step. My sister weavers and I have spoken of going on strike. The price of piecework must be raised, or we will starve!"

Asphodel tried not to let the frown show on her face. Dougie paid slave wages? Asphodel clasped her client's hand more firmly. "How very brave of you all. There is strength indeed in unity and sisterhood. Women alone can be so vulnerable."

She paused, pushing back the urge to tremble. Her own aloneness hit her with renewed force. This hand in hers was so visceral she was jolted back to the last time she had held her beloved grandmother's hand, in the topmost bedroom of the hotel tower. She could almost feel those weak, age-spotted fingers, urging Asphodel to do her will, even as she lay dying. Tears built behind the wall of Asphodel's pride. She forced her mind back to the present, to focus only on the woman before her. There was work to do. Someone needed her.

Asphodel said, "There will be no charge for today. And later, you will please enjoy your midday dinner here in my hotel."

The woman tried to jerk her hand away, but Asphodel held on. "Now, if you will, tell me all about yourself."

Asphodel allowed herself to sink into Leda's story, absorbing all that was said and unsaid. She allowed her senses to open completely to every impression. The woman's emotions became hers too: the fierce pride, the struggle for independence, the determination. Her fear and self-doubt.

The woman was hesitant at first, and then her story poured out. Poverty and pride, aging mother and five children. Husband long gone—missing or dead. She was the breadwinner, dependent on her work, but also proud to do a fine job of work.

A common female story for the times: proud, brave women quietly going about their business, supporting families and parents, keeping everyone fed, everyone clothed and educated. Keeping everyone safe.

Finally, Leda's story stopped spilling out like a spring downpour and slowed to a trickle. Her shoulders and arms relaxed with relief.

Then Asphodel told her story back to her. This was her gift. She didn't understand it herself, but apparently it gave people strength, hope, and cheer. So she kept doing it, and the small extra income was very welcome. Even if she did waive the fee more often than not.

Asphodel told the same tale back to her client, but now the story highlighted the client's unique abilities. Her courage. Her determination. Her fierceness. Her extraordinary organization skills, her talent. As she spoke, the weaver's head rose higher, and her eyes sparkled. By the time Asphodel ushered her over to a small table for her midday dinner, the woman walked straight and tall, re-energized for another tilt at the labor that was life.

As for herself, Asphodel was exhausted.

She would visit the tower room and imagine her grandmother, while she wrestled with the problem of Dougie—a problem that was becoming as intractable and dangerous as a fen boghole. A problem of her own making.

****

A misshapen shadow lurked at the bend in the tower stairs. Asphodel's skin fizzed, and her heart banged hard in her ribs. She jerked back, hands clenched. She knew every trick of light and shade in this hotel, and that shadow had no business being there.

The stranger stepped out from the alcove.

She was still open from her client reading. All her senses flew to him, half shadowed as he was. His personality clanged into her with the force of a bolting carriage, closed in and hard, overlaid with a shiny, mocking veneer to fool the gullible. Mystery shrouded him like a cloak, fitting tight to his form, tailored to his broad shoulders, weighing on him. A crack sundered him, buried deep within, roiling with monsters to torment him through the watches of the night. Self-control, tight as a coiled spring. *Secrets.*

"Have you come to complete your robbing and plundering?" Her voice shook with fright. She strove to master it. "My hotel is full of men who will gladly escort you to the magistrate—as you so evidently wish." There. That was better. "I hear tell there are those men who would seek their own destruction, bent on an unstoppable path to ruin."

He laughed, and the shadows around him seemed

to shatter and dissipate. Perhaps he had just moved more into the light filtering from the single stair window. "I have met such men, many such men. I am not of their company. The very opposite, in fact." His voice rumbled deep-toned and amused. His gray eyes shone clear in the half light, intent on her face.

While Asphodel pondered his words, he took two steps down. She had to bend her neck to gaze up at him. He squeezed his large shape past her, not touching, although the heat from his body radiated into hers, scented with open air and heather. He had gained proximity to the tower stair door which led back to the hotel and thus into the street.

He turned back to her. "Your hotel?"

His shadowed face, his lean height, his intent dark silver stare gave her a flash of memory. The night her grandmother lay dying…the stranger who took the paper…had something of this highwayman's presence.

She marshalled her resources. "How came you on this tower staircase, sir? This is a private part of the hotel, not open to the public. What do you want here?" And more softly, "Why do you dally with me?" He should not be here, alone with her.

The stranger stepped up three stairs back toward her, favoring his left leg, limping a little. He towered over her once more. The highwayman stretched out a long arm and took her chin in his long, strong fingers. He bent his head and regarded her steadily. His gray eyes darkened to molten mercury, and his mobile lips parted. His presence enveloped her like a thick moor mist.

"I would not *dally*, if the world was a right place. You interest me. And it seems to me you are in need of protection."

His breath tickled her cheeks, and for a mad moment her blood raced. *Was he about to kiss her?*

Instead, he growled, "Tell me again. Do you love that bumptious fool?"

Asphodel battled the myriad emotions which coursed through her: her leaping heart, her tingling skin, her desperate curiosity. She sought for that strong streak of practicality which defined her. She bethought herself of her grandmother's legacy—*survive*. Protect the hotel. It gave her the strength she needed.

She jerked her chin from his grasp and took two steps backward up the staircase. "Perhaps you will oblige me by returning with me to the public areas below and explaining your presence in this tower? In case you are in any doubt, I forbid you this tower again. Should I find you here, I will summon the magistrate."

Asphodel hardly knew if she was pleased when his expression hardened back into a sardonic mask, creating cold distance between them. "Well done," he gritted. "A creditable performance. I almost believe you."

Sparks of fury ignited in Asphodel. "I am heartily sick and tired of men speaking and behaving toward me with patronizing condescension. You may believe it, sir. I am a woman of my word."

An arrested expression crossed his face. "Even if that word is a promise to marry a grasping blunderbuss? To waste yourself on a greedy bladderwrack?"

She snorted a laugh before she could restrain herself. He had summed up Dougie magnificently. But then she sobered. "Even so." Curse the highwayman. She was in a bind, and he knew it.

Which all went to remind her. "You must leave. This is my private tower. That greedy bladderwrack—my esteemed fiancé—will come to seek me soon; I am astonished he has not done so already. He must not discover you here."

The highwayman's eyes warmed, and the strong planes of his face tightened.

Asphodel's traitorous heart fluttered in response. She exhaled a shaky breath.

He said, "I do not like to leave you in the clutches of that man."

"I am not in his *clutches*," she responded tartly.

His voice was soft and low, a gritty murmur. "Are you not?"

They gazed at each other for a long moment, time suspended and every sound stilled.

The highwayman added, "You claim this hotel is yours. You are rightfully proud of that fact: it is a fine establishment, well patronized and well ordered. What of your marriage? After that? Surely you know the law? When you marry that puffed-up buffoon, it will all be his, to mismanage, spend, alter, and destroy. The capital and the income."

The highwayman's words were like bullets of cold truth piercing her heart, one fell shot after another, straight into the bullseye. He did not relent. "And he will own *you*. He will have the right to your body and to control and direct your behavior. By law."

Asphodel opened and closed her mouth, but the words tangled in her throat. His words were blows raining down on her, flush hits on her will, her pride, her independence. Her knees buckled, and she fell against the wall. Her heart thundered under her ribs, and she couldn't breathe. It was true. It was all true.

"You do not garnish your words," she managed to gasp.

He grinned without humor. "I exist in the real world. The here and now. Whatever romance lived in me as a youth has been blasted away."

"Why should you care?" She pressed her hands on the wall behind her, the coolness of the stone on her fingertips anchoring her.

"Because each time I have set eyes on you, twice before, the blood leaps in my veins and I rejoice that I am alive. It is like sensation returning to numbed limbs, painful, tingling, and lively."

He stopped abruptly. His eyes flashed, and his lips tightened. In the half dark, it appeared as though he reddened. With embarrassment? With fury? "I have said too much. I have no claim on you, but I ask you: wait. Wait a little. Put off the date."

Asphodel swallowed against a thick throat and licked her dry lips. She summoned what strength remained to fight him. "You are very interested in my concerns? You still have not explained why you should be so."

"I…I cannot. Not yet. I ask you for time. Can you promise me that?"

"For the sake of your deadened heart that finds itself stirring to life? Oh, how fascinating are these functions and feelings within you! Well, I have no such issue. Of what interest can your sensations be to me, pray?"

She hardly knew why anger bubbled. His querying upset her organized, calm world, summoning questions she had been content to quash. Yet she craved more emotion from him, more detailed expression of how she made him feel. This breathless, skittering anticipation felt new and wonderful. No one had ever said such things to her. She hungered for more.

He stiffened and averted his face. Hurt. She hadn't meant—

"Asphodel!" called an imperious tone faintly from somewhere in the hotel. She came to herself with a start.

"Greedy bladderwrack," muttered the highwayman. He grinned, and Asphodel tried, valiantly but unsuccessfully, not to share his smile.

"Go back to your harsh reality, Mr. Farlan *Crow*," she said, allowing him to perceive that she knew he had not told her truth.

His mouth quirked up in acknowledgement of the hit. "Bravo!" he murmured. He turned and, in a smooth movement of shadow, glided down her tower stairs. Light speared and slanted across the stone steps as he opened and closed the bottom door, and then she was alone.

"*Asphodeeellll!*"

****

Later, pacing in the tower room and staring out at the great starlit sky, Asphodel could not put the highwayman and her grandmother together. It did not make any sense. How could the dark stranger that night be Farlan Crow? Why would her grandmother give papers to a highwayman? Had she misinterpreted or misremembered what she saw that night?

On the tower stairs, the stranger said he had seen Asphodel twice before: robbing her and then in the hotel? Or did he refer to the night Isabella lay dying?

She must be mistaken. And yet…

Asphodel halted in her pacing; the lights flickered in the abandoned Blackleech Castle once more.

Chapter Three

March 1881—Blackleech Castle

That ten-year-old boy running headstrong through the castle and tangling in the landscape, filled with vital life, still breathed inside him. Farlan strode the high moor, absorbing the sight of dawn turning to golden day.

Brisk air, rich as fruitcake, stung his nostrils, as he reacquainted his eyes and mind with the twisted sandstone ridges, lush dales, and tinkling creeks—*becks*—of his birthright.

It was all so strangely familiar—and yet, not. The smell of peat, the lonely shriek of a curlew. Threads of trailing mist making the black-faced sheep appear to be floating on the dawn-damp heather.

Dry lightning flickered in the distance. Under the crack of jagged light, the black castle reared into the sky like a fist. Blackleech Castle.

Its broken, lonely facade called to him. A ruin, a heap of crumbling castle, and yet his. Something that needed fixing in its form and its spirit. A shout echoed in his mind: *Mine! This land, this castle, this name, is mine!*

His thoughts flew to his grandfather, Forley Goforth Blackitter. An inkling of what Forley had given him, had sacrificed for him, rose as though to choke him. His grandfather had been a wily old adventurer, but he was the only family Farlan could remember. The old man had been crazy as an eel, leading Farlan a merry dance through his childhood and youth. Farlan had loved every minute of their riotous life on the goldfields.

The old man's deathbed confession had been quite a shock.

His grandfather—how he must have missed all this, if he was indeed the third baron of Blackleech. What a tale that old man told Farlan as he held the wiry old claw and wept unashamedly.

Farlan had promised him. A deathbed promise.

"Here, lad." The old man lay dying of a life well lived: a few stray bullet holes, a grumpy liver, the wasting disease. The old man's vitality still blazed in his dark silver eyes—the same eyes Farlan saw whenever he chanced by a mirror to shave.

"We've had some times, haven't we, lad?"

"Aye, that we have, sir."

"And you've had the education of a gentleman. I saw to that! Listen to you now; you'll be able to ponce about with the best dressed amongst us."

"Better late than never, sir," Farlan answered mock gravely.

"I'm dead now, my boy."

Farlan stirred uneasily. He bent and kissed the old man's brow. "Nonsense. You are as indestructible as the devil himself."

"Not this time." Forley Blackitter suddenly flopped back on his pillows, wheezing and gasping for air. A gray pallor tinged his cheeks, and a blueish color ringed his mouth.

His grandfather gripped his wrist. "Listen to me. I know not whether I've wronged you or kept you alive. You'll forgive me though?" His voice was urgent, his expression intent.

"There's nothing to forgive. What are you talking about, Grandfather?"

"I traded your birthright for your life."

"Grandfather?" Was this a dying man's ramblings and mumblings? Or something true?

"The Blackitter bane. The heir in every generation meets an early death. When your father was killed in that carriage accident, and your mother too, I…couldn't bear the idea of losing you. I surmised that more than an evil fate threatened."

Farlan sat on the edge of the bed. In all these years, he had never heard anything about a family curse. Or heirs.

The old man coughed. Blood spotted the handkerchief Farlan held to his lips. When he could speak, Forley said, "You must return and claim your birthright. Baron Blackitter. Blackleech Castle built high on the North York moors. It is ours, and double damn the Blackitter curse." The old man wheezed while he clutched Farlan's hand. "You aren't some soft white lord. You know how to fight and survive now. Go back and claim what is yours."

"The moors," the old man said now, and his voice was a thready whisper. "What I'd give to see and smell my home again. To set eyes on my lovely Isabella one more time…"

That was about the sum of it. Soon after, the old blackguard lapsed into incomprehensible mutterings. Farlan soothed him as best he could and held the withered old hand in his own as the old man slipped away to where his grandson could not follow.

He had made that old man a sacred promise on his deathbed.

The scars on the backs of Farlan's hands whitened as he clenched his fists to the broken castle in salute.

He *would* be the fourth Baron Blackitter, Lord of Blackleech Castle and Fangmoor Beck.

Even if it killed him.

****

"Have you heard anything about Blackleech Castle recently?" Asphodel asked Wragg. She was breakfasting alone in her tower room, enjoying the sunlit peace of the early morning. Wragg had come up to stir up the fire and bring more logs. It might be early spring, but the morning air still held a winter chill.

Wragg half straightened, his left hand in the small of his back. "Just the usual, ma'am. Hauntings, groanings, and murderous screams. Strange shadows and vengeful spirits." Wragg said this with a deadpan expression and voice.

Asphodel laughed, although she wasn't entirely sure he joked. "Mysterious lights? Weird shouted curses?"

"Yes, ma'am. Theys too." Wragg regarded her with a gimlet expression. As he turned to go, he added, "There is allus a Blackitter at Blackleech Castle. There will allus be a hawk-nosed, iron-eyed Blackitter in Fangmoor Beck."

Asphodel stared after him. "Well!" she said to the empty room. Then she remembered Wragg was of those who had rowan witches' posts either side of the hearth fire in his cottage, engraved with their crosses against witchcraft. She had them here in the little downstairs bar.

She resumed her breakfast and mentally ran over the busy day ahead.

Asphodel rose from the table and looked out upon her grandmother's world. The dawn sky blushed as pink as a summer lily. The heathlands stretched ahead in their spare beauty, brown and yellow and black, frowning over the wet fens far below.

Asphodel's heart soared. She was alive! Grief was finally beginning to peel away like last winter's chilblains.

A merlin winged away across the heather toward Blackleech Castle, silhouetted like a broken tooth jutting from the terrain. She could make out the shape of the once-famous gardens, no doubt an untamed wilderness now. Her grandmother's prohibition rang in her mind. "Never set your foot there, lass."

She was not inclined to disobey her grandmother now. But Asphodel was a grown woman, almost at her majority. Her grandmother had never explained *why* she did not wish Asphodel to venture into the old castle and its extensive grounds and gardens. They did need fresh herbs for the kitchen, after this long winter…and a few early blooms would be so lovely…

She was definitely *not* putting together the sudden lights in the night and the surprise appearance of the handsome stranger…

Before she could change her mind, Asphodel hurried into a walking dress and pelisse, sturdy shoes, a bonnet, and thick gloves for her hands. The sun outside looked bright enough, but she knew the dawn wind would slice at her skin and bones like a frozen blade.

Blackleech Castle loomed a mile north. Asphodel carried a small basket for the pilfered herbs and flowers. She stretched out her legs and strode along, glorying in everything that heralded spring on its way: a line of baby ducks following their mother to a farm pond, early wild daffodils peeping amongst the heather, lapwings swooping and tangling together in a joyous dance against the periwinkle blue sky.

Tall fences and ornate cast iron gates enclosed Blackleech Castle. Asphodel paced partway around the perimeter until she reached the side entrance, also set with tall iron gates, and peered through, avid with curiosity. She couldn't see much. Just the eastern turret of the castle jutting into the garden with high arrow-slit windows, ramshackle doors, and a long balcony.

She pushed at the gates, rattling them and tugging, to no avail. Everything was far too high to try and climb, even for a limb of the moors such as herself. She would have to retrace her steps and then walk to the west.

The south-facing front entrance was very grand indeed, with a large circular driveway and formal garden beds completely wild and overgrown, yet somehow retaining the bones of a sleeping grandeur. Asphodel pushed her face into the gaps in the locked, chained, and padlocked front gates and stared into the property.

The castle towered high and spread wide through the grounds. Ornate pillars decorated the front entrance above steep, crumbling stone steps. Mullioned glass windows refracted and distorted the light. Climbing plants ran amok all over the building, lacy tendrils reaching up toward the roofs and prying into window frames. One whole wing, the west, appeared to have half collapsed, and rubble scarred the garden on that side. There was a palpable air of neglect and decay, made worse by a flock of ravens choosing that moment to fly low through the grounds, cawing their deathly warnings as they flapped their sawtooth wings.

Asphodel shuddered. Ravens meant death or profound change. Isabella had once held Asphodel's hand when she was very young, and said, "I saw the ravens before the factor came, to send us from our home on Leòdhas. Many died. When the raven calls to you, pay attention. Death comes, or profound change. The raven calls, and in that flash, you see your *soul self* as it truly is. The future is change, and living in your true self is power."

Seven-year-old Asphodel had asked, "What does that mean, Nana?"

But her grandmother only laughed and said it was Scottish nonsense that couldn't survive on the York barrows and mires, which had their own fancies and fairies. "The stories here are different from ours." And she refused to say another word, until next time the fey mood caught her.

Despite the ravens, Asphodel looked eagerly around her. Bright blooms peeped amongst the lush long grass. Clumps and hedges of dense herb bushes sprawled every which way. Perhaps if she went farther west, toward the collapsing wing, the high perimeter fence might also be weak and crumbling.

The fence was intact, but the side gates seemed more damaged and bent. Asphodel put down her basket and pressed herself against one of the gaps—there! Her head was through! She wiggled and managed to squeeze her shoulders through, then pressed her breasts painfully against the bars until her top half had popped through the gate, almost leaving her bodice and camisole behind. She impatiently wrenched her dress and undergarments back over her décolletage back to a seemly level. Her bottom presented quite a struggle for while—there was no decreasing that roundness!—until finally with a huge contortion her whole body shot through the gate, and she fell in a most ungainly fashion on the grass beyond.

She was on the other side! Asphodel brushed herself down and ignored her hurts, staring wildly around her. She would worry later about how to get out again. Maybe there was another way from this side.

Gravel paths snaked through the grounds, although they were almost completely overgrown with herbage and moss. The castle towered above like a witches' lair, far more damaged than appeared from outside. Crumbling stone left gaps in the roofline and upper walls like missing teeth. The roof slates frowned low and slid over crumbling eaves. From somewhere Asphodel could hear the slow drip of moisture, as though the process of wearing away everything was well underway. The stone itself had perhaps once been honey-gold but was now dank with slime and mold where the roof sagged.

Asphodel shuddered. This place would be terrifying in a storm. Low clouds were collecting overhead to enhance the somber mood, although strong, straight golden beams of sun still slanted down from the heavens, highlighting a patch of purple crocus here, gleaming on bright daffodils there.

Hyacinths. Look at them—spreading in luxurious

abundance through swathes of the lush, long grass which she assumed had once been gracious lawns. Rosebushes like tall thin trees towered against the sides of the castle as high as the second floor. They would be utterly lovely in summer. Hedges of sprawling box and ungainly yew had burst out of their topiary into their own grotesque figures. They looked like weird people assuming bizarre postures in the untamed garden.

Asphodel stopped to smell purple, pink, and white hyacinths. Heavenly! She would pick a huge bunch before she left. Bending right over, she pulled the grass stems apart to find more treasures—red and yellow tulips, like drops of blood and cups of gold.

Was that a sound? She straightened in a rush, looking around her. Was that a shadow *moving*? Back into deep shade of the unpruned trees lining the driveway?

She froze, except for the thoughts stuttering in her head and her heart kicking against her ribs. The ravens. They had warned her. Why had her grandmother forbidden her this place? What secrets did the ruined Blackleech Castle hide?

Was she about to find out?

****

He had given himself away and frightened her into the bargain.

It was the sight of that rounded, delectable bottom, irresistible as pudding, poking up out of the hyacinths, that had enticed him closer. Breaking his rule.

At first, he didn't recognize the woman who was the possessor of that lovely rump, but when she straightened and looked around, his heart jolted in his chest.

Just like the first time he had set eyes upon her, the blazing spirit in her expression nearly knocked him over. He hadn't recognized her as she pressed herself through that gate, most likely because it wasn't her face that had him riveted where he stood.

Initially, he had struggled to suppress his mirth as her watched her. He hadn't felt so much merriment in years. Her determination. Her wriggles and contortions. Her pushing and pulling, and the final pop, falling through the bars in the gate like a cork from champagne.

But somewhere in the middle of her struggles, he had become possessed by a flaming desire so fierce—and so unwelcome—that he had been utterly paralyzed. He was transfixed by the beauty of her soft white curves and broadsided by her splendid resolve.

To expose her to his presence would endanger her as well as him. He should fade away into the gardens, like a whisper or a passing thought. That would be best for both of them.

Farlan could not make himself do it.

Her lucent hair had become disarranged and hung in long curls, shining with strawberry fire in the sunshine. His fingers twitched, and he inhaled sharply. She had hastily bundled it up in an arrangement more than a little askew after pressing herself through that gate. A smile twitched at his lips.

It was the girl from the carriage. The proprietor of the magnificent Black Hart Hotel. Isabella McDonnell's granddaughter. Not a girl. *A woman*.

He must not speak to her, not here. He was on the wrong side of the law, for the moment. The last man for a woman such as she.

The courage she had displayed on that day he had held up her carriage! He admired her. Possibly…even…had he fallen a little in love with her as she faced him down and told him what she thought of him and his men? Calling them cowards! And then offering them "a little gold for your sustenance, in memory of my father and grandfather, but give you all my money I will not!"

She was beautiful, and lovely, and sweet. Her spirited approach to life called to him like a siren song.

But it was too late.

Unless he found—

His brain stopped. Of their own volition, his feet moved. They walked toward her, gravel crunching loudly with each step.

"You!" Her voice pitched high with shock. She squeezed the hyacinth stems she held in her hand, looked down at them in confusion, and then dropped them. She swiveled to face the gates, patently searching for escape, whirled and stared toward the castle, scanning its entrances and balconies. Looked back at him, her brilliant blue eyes wide, pink lips parted. Her entire body was poised to flee.

He said, "I would speak with you."

They both heard the rasp of untrammeled desire.

Chapter Four

March 1881—Blackleech Castle

His voice rang as deep and musical as she remembered from the day she first saw him. "Allow me to facilitate your escape. Perhaps in a more dignified mode of egress than your ingress."

A laugh danced in his words, though his face remained perfectly grave and polite—except for a teasing twinkle lurking in those clear gray eyes.

Hot prickles needled her all over like she had fallen into a giant needle case. "You saw me squeezing through those gates?" A searing flush heated her cheeks, her neck, her heaving chest. "You watched? And did nothing to assist?" She took a long, calming breath. "How extremely ungallant of you, sir."

He bowed and—the devil—actually *grinned* at her. "You are correct. Most ungallant. But in my defense, I was spellbound—fixed in place—quite unnaturally incapacitated—with…" He swallowed and visibly reconsidered what he had been about to utter. "Extreme mirth."

"*Mirth?*" She replayed in her mind squeezing her breasts through the gates, almost losing her bodice, the struggles to get her plump behind through, and then her fall onto the ground. Goodness knows what she had displayed during the process, or indeed when she fell.

He read her mind. "Only a pair of luscious, creamy breasts popping over their constraints. Plump buttocks wriggling in the most enticing way. And a good length of slender, shapely leg. I could almost resist, and then that same bottom was poking up and twitching so enticingly amongst the hyacinths that I could no longer keep myself from introducing myself to their owner, improper though that may be."

She glared, speechless and mortified. His simmering focus flayed all her defenses. That hungry, needy look in his eyes, the urgent shape of his mouth as he described her body and movements…a different kind of heat burned under her skin. Thrills spiked and cascaded in her leaping blood. Her skin tightened like a ripe fruit.

She had never felt so naked and exposed.

Nor so beautiful.

"I was not aware that I was not alone," she managed to say in a constricted breath.

His iron gaze gleamed like tempered steel. "I was glad to make your acquaintance on the York highway." He smiled at her, warm and beguiling. The wretch. She fought to maintain composure.

"When you removed my engagement ring from me."

His face, warm and amused moments before, stiffened and became truly grave this time. "That was not well done of me. Come into the house, and I will return it."

"No, I thank you."

"Ah! Good news! You do not wish the ring returned? May I hope that the engagement is sundered?"

"Why would you hope such a thing?" She tapped her fingers against her waist, pretending she did not wait feverishly for his answer.

He stepped closer, until he almost touched her. His eyes never left hers. A new blush mantled her cheeks, but she refused to look away. His gaze darkened. He looked at her lips and then her waist.

"Surely you will not tie yourself to that excuse for a man. He is a greedy, bullying, pontificating barnacle. He has no appreciation for a fine woman."

They stared at each other. She was drowning in a silver lake, humor like sparkles of sunlight glinting at her.

"And you do?" *Why had she said that?*

His face shuttered. "I do indeed. Appreciate. Unfortunately, circumstances proscribe me from offering more." His voice was clipped, regimented, controlled. Something military in his background? Command. No-nonsense tones. Able to face stark facts as they came to hand.

The planes of his face lengthened in a kind of sorrow. His dark crimson mouth compressed and released. His lean, athletic frame bent toward her. He smelled like warmed honey and heather. Long lines of muscle ridged his arms, sculpted his middle, and pressed against the cloth covering his long thighs.

Asphodel blinked. She was sinking into word-picture mode when she needed to remain alert. She coughed and said, "I declined your invitation to the house. Perhaps you would condescend to bring the ring to me here, prior to assisting me to leave these premises."

His eyes blanked; she could not deny it. A flash of

frustration darkened his countenance, followed by something bitter and resigned. "I will never harm you," he rasped.

She took a breath, inhaled some sass. "Said he, mere minutes before strangling the foolish damsel, who had ventured into the beast's lair."

His laugh exploded, summoning her own smile. "I comprehend. But perhaps, on another occasion—you will permit me to tell you a story."

"A story? A romantical tale full of fabrication, no doubt!" Yet she itched to hear more.

His velvet, deep-water voice tickled her skin like the sound of the wind in the trees. "It is an adventure story."

"My favorite, indeed. And is there a young and dashing hero?"

"The most dashing, I assure you. It is story of a lost will, a missing heir, and a stolen inheritance."

"Is there a feisty heroine already in this tale of suspense?" she breathed.

"This story is not over. There may yet be one."

Their eyes met and held.

****

A veritable goddess. Here. She had sprung like a nymph from his riotous garden, from his disordered imagination, tempting and utterly delectable. He must remove her from the Blackitter grounds before his men saw her, and yet he yearned for her to tarry and tease him, just a while longer.

"Who are you, sir?" Her round cheeks bunched up, and an imp of mischief gleamed in her lovely eyes. She made a show of studying his features, which sent his blood pricking and hurtling in his veins. "Would you say you have a hawk nose?"

What? "I hadn't considered it. Does a hawk nose please you? If so, then yes, I have a hawk nose." He smiled as she smothered a charming giggle.

"I have no feeling about it either way," she responded, waving an elaborately careless arm in the air. Her azure eyes sparkled at him from under long black lashes. "I perceive an iron-eyed stare, in addition."

"May I hope this too is to my credit? An iron-eyed stare. Yes, I believe I may offer you that." Farlan lowered his brows and narrowed his eyes in his best iron glare. He was rewarded when he elicited another giggle from Asphodel.

She met his gaze directly and her smile fled. "I have heard these described as Blackitter traits. Farlan *Blackitter*!"

He was dumbstruck. How well his name sounded in her mouth, issuing from those pink plump lips!

He hesitated.

Mischief possessed Asphodel, perhaps engendered by the sunny day.

Before he could respond, she asked in conversational, drawing-room tones, "Have you always been a highwayman?"

Farlan choked and recovered himself. "It is a recent choice of occupation."

"Necessitated by…?"

"It is no worse than many other occupations I have assumed over the years. Goldminer, soldier, physician…"

She persisted. There was a fascinating mystery here. "One answers an advertisement, perhaps?"

"One does not." Farlan seemed to be wrestling with himself, dark brows frowning mightily. She could tell—with just a little prodding—he could be persuaded...

A small dirty figure bounced up from the garden.

Asphodel took an involuntary step back. Billy! Dougie's carriage boy. A pulse of fear smacked into her. She gripped Farlan's arm, hard. "Dougie!" she hissed, agitated. Then she looked harder at the lad. "Why is your arm in a sling?"

"I can tell you, Miss Asa," Billy said. "Us was there."

"What? What are you talking about, Billy? And what are you doing *here*?"

"Back to the stables, Billy." Farlan spoke gently to the lad, giving him an encouraging push.

Her head spun from one to the other. "Wait!" she commanded.

Billy hopped from one foot to the other, positively beaming.

"Do you mean, Billy," she asked, "you were there when Farlan became a highwayman?"

"Yes, miss. Fine walloping his lordship give our Dougie."

Farlan interjected, moving his body between Asphodel and the lad, "Miss Asphodel doesn't want to hear your tales, Billy. There's dinner in the kitchen for you."

"Stop!" She narrowed her eyes at Farlan. "A low move, my lord. Almost guaranteed to make the lad disappear. But I've been here in Fangmoor Beck longer than you."

She put her chin up in a regal manner. "His

lordship is being bashful. I rely on you to tell me this fascinating story, Billy. And then you may have your noonday dinner."

"Was a reet mill, miss. Mebbe I's cack-handed, or Dougie just mardy mooded, for he was gi'ing us a fine braying with whip."

Asphodel's eyes widened in their sockets. "Dougie McDonnell beat you with *his whip*?" Fury built in her like a storm.

"And then His Lordship Blackitter here comes a-ridin' fast round edge of moor, and he draws out gun and shoots whip right outta Dougie's fat hand!"

Asphodel snorted a laugh. She shared the lad's admiration. "What happened then?"

"Dougie says I'm his to beat if he wants. So his lordship asks, all gaffer-like, if I'm his son? And Dougie calls us grimy urchin and says he is publican and mill owner and us his carriage tiger. Dougie's face was that purple, my lady, he was like to blow apart."

"Go on."

"So his lordship here tells us to run along home, so I tell him I ain't got no home, only Dougie and lately stables at Black Hart Hotel, miss." Billy tugged the curl flopping over his forehead with his good hand. "I mighter been bit teary and snotty, miss, coz Dougie had bin whipping me that hard. It's that or starve I tells the lord here."

"Definitely snotty," added Farlan, clearly enjoying Billy's vivid tale now he was unable to stop it.

"Sorry, sir."

"Go *on*, Billy! What happened then?"

"Lord Blackitter tells me I got new job with him, looking after his horses. And I get meals three times a day!" Billy's mouth was such an *O* of surprised wonder that even Asphodel laughed.

"I likes workin' with McEvoy here at castle, miss, but lord here makes me wash *every day*!"

"That will be good for you, Billy. Now, the highwayman part of this remarkable tale, if you please."

"Then the lord looks like he's bin hit by lightning. He announces, grand as you like, 'I am the Document Highwayman,' and bows like king to Dougie McDonnell. He tells us to explore every inch of carriage for papers. He holds gun on that fat lobcock whiles I does as his lordship asks."

Billy grinned. "Sir says to keep money I find for all the wages I missed, and did old Dougie splutter and choke!"

"Did Lord Blackitter find any papers?"

Billy clamped his mouth shut, and his eyes widened in alarm. Asphodel didn't miss Farlan's quick shake of the head.

"He shot his gun at ground at Dougie's feet, and that made that shabbaroon shut up. His lordship tells him never to mistreat a child again."

Asphodel enquired in a dangerous tone, "And how did Dougie take that news?"

"He said he would make his lordship regret this day, miss. That he would have the law on him soon as burp. But the lord here, he just laughs. He scoops us up on the horse along with the heavy chest we pinched from the carriage, and we gallops off over the hills. And us bin here ever since, miss, and I belong to the lord now."

Asphodel nodded. "A vastly amusing tale, thank you, Billy. Tell me, who set your arm?"

"The lord, miss." Billy jerked his head at the highwayman. "Dougie twisted it bad."

"Away off to your dinner now."

When the lad had vanished once more, she regarded Farlan with horror. "My great-uncle whipped his tiger?" She would never call him her fiancé again. She struggled. Managed to speak her fear. "My uncle saw your face? He will have the law on you. He is friends to magistrates and all manner of powerful men."

Farlan reached out and twined one of her long ringlets around his finger. He tugged it gently, somehow sending a rush of sensation spiking through her, despite her terror.

"I am flattered by your concern." Sardonic. Curling lip.

"Farlan Blackitter, that was a mad thing you did," she began. "But a brave and good one. Thank you. How could I have no idea?" She shook her head. "But I knew Dougie can be narky and mardy, as Billy says. Did I think he behaved thus only to me?"

Farlan wiped a tear from her cheek with a gentle fingertip. "I cannot abide the ill-treatment of children. If indeed I am the b—" He checked. "A local landholder, then I will—"

"If this is your castle and you are a Blackitter," she began impatiently, "then you must be…" Asphodel's mouth opened. She stared at Farlan, who was looking most concerned, shaking his head at her.

She finished in a rush of words. "The lost heir! Baron Blackitter in the flesh!"

"Please." Farlan seemed to be struggling with a strong emotion. "I may be. I don't know the truth of it myself."

She stared in confusion.

"Before you go," he said, abruptly changing the subject, "what think you of a physic garden?"

"A physic garden?" Asphodel's mind struggled to catch up.

"An herbal. To make compresses, salves, teas, and other cures for minor and seasonal ailments." He touched her arm. "Perhaps you will allow me to show you the lovely walled herb garden, sadly overgrown."

Asphodel stopped. She said, her tone acerbic, "No doubt an herbal is useful in your profession, Farlan Blackitter. To patch up bullet wounds and the like. Because it would be impossible to call the local surgeon."

"Luckily, I am physician-trained. It seemed an honorable and necessary profession, after what I had seen men suffer—" He cut himself off. "I patched so many injuries and physicked so many plaints that the formal learning was a joy to me."

Now he had her shocked attention. "You are full of surprises," she said softly. "Show me your herbal then. Do you know how to tend it?"

He led her around the castle, patently on the alert for something or someone. A man of mystery, this.

After a few moments, he answered her. "My life has not been the sort in which one learns settled activities such as gardening. If I find someone to plant and tend the physic garden, then I do know how to wring medicines from plants."

"Where are you leading me, Farlan Blackitter? *Baron* Blackitter? Didn't you just say I must flee from here?"

"Here. Just in here." He gestured through an

ancient garden doorway. Watched her as she whirled around in delight in the scented garden.

He said, his voice as earnest, "I beg you. Please. Keep my name to yourself."

"I will trade your name for my ring."

Oh dear. He could willfully misunderstand her riposte…

"That has a pleasant sound to it. My name for a ring." And then in one stride he was close to her. He touched her chin. Laid his fingers on her cheek. Her lips parted. Her breath huffed in her throat.

Slowly, giving her time to move away, he lowered his mouth onto hers. He pressed there, lightly touching, testing, and tasting her shape and softness.

He made a groan in his throat that melted her. And then her hands grabbed his waist, and he gripped her hips and pulled her close. He deepened the kiss, exploring, plundering, savoring.

He tore his lips from hers. He stared at her, breathing hard. "I must not. I am a highwayman!" He trapped her gaze. "Not forever—and not for long. I promise. You must be gone from here." He placed a warm hand in the small of her back and ushered her from the herb garden.

"Please allow me to unlock these great gates for you," he said. "I recall myself just in time—this is not a safe place for you to linger. My lieutenants must not find you here. Here!" He bent and madly picked swathes of gorgeous-smelling hyacinths, pink, purple, blue, and white, until even his large white-scarred hands were full.

He carefully loaded the flowers into her basket and waiting arms. "I must ask that you tell no one that you have seen me here. I apologize for demanding your secrecy, but it is of the utmost importance."

"Are you afraid you will be captured by the law, sir?" she asked boldly, her heart stuttering once more.

He sighed and smiled at her again. "Yes. That too."

She waited demurely in the Blackleech Castle grounds while the mysterious silver-eyed, sweet-tongued highwayman produced the key to the gate. "It is not safe for you to return here."

She treated him to her best regal glare. He bent close and gazed deeply into her eyes. His lips hovered close to hers, and then with the lightest of touches, like a spring promise, he kissed her again. Stepped back and inclined his body in a graceful bow.

Her lips parted. And then she shrugged on the businesswoman, turned, and strode away toward her own domain.

Before she reached the Black Hart Hotel, she stopped and touched her tingling lips with a trembling fingertip.

****

Farlan paced the ruined grounds of Blackleech Castle, trying to walk off his restless thoughts and calm his fevered blood. Now there was even greater urgency to find the papers. Without them, he was a highwayman, with the specter of a noose around his neck.

He had so many specialized talents, honed into him since he was a child, burned into him by life and death situations, survive or perish crises.

He had found Isabella McDonnell, the woman his grandfather adored, but too late.

"I loved that wicked, charming old sinner, your

grandfather," old Isabella said to Farlan on her death bed, on that dark night of the soul. "Ah well, no doubt I will be seeing him again soon. Look after my granddaughter, Farlan Blackitter. Promise me! For the sake of the love I bore your grandfather. She has nobody else, except a pig who would disinherit her."

He promised and took the papers the old woman thrust at him from a secret compartment in her bed head. It took the last of her strength.

He turned, and his eyes lit on Asphodel, staring stricken in that candlelit room of death. She stood there, slight and slender in a white nightgown, her shape revealed and concealed by the lacy layers in the candlelight. Her hair hung down over her breast and back in long yellow topaz curls. Her eyes glowed blue as a dream; her lips were parted, rosy and plump. She looked like an angel, a phantasm of his feverish brain.

He stared for one long moment while his entire world tilted on its axis, and then he rushed away, thoughts and emotions pummeling his brain. In that very moment, the first time he ever saw her, he fell deeply, impossibly in love with her.

He always kept his promises. The promise of protection for Asphodel Quick.

He just had to work out how.

The woman in that room was also the blazing goddess who refused to be waylaid by a highwayman. He had put it together, about being a businesswoman on the moors, and then haunted the hotel despite the danger of being recognized as the document highwayman. He had been unable to tear his eyes from Asphodel Quick.

And then today! Hell! Those lush curves, almost

but not quite exposed. Her beautiful rosy blush when she realized she was not alone. Her sparkling joy in the flowers. His body had turned traitor, burning for him to touch her, kiss her, take her…every lustful instinct aroused.

But how did he dare to touch her? He was much older than she—twenty-eight—and damaged from the wars. He had never known a mother's love, had not experienced that softness and care. His sexual experience was short, hot grapplings in various occupied villages with willing damsels who loved a soldier.

That fiancé of hers! Was he seeing him through a prism of jealousy? He wanted to punch him until those false teeth flew out and that fat stomach doubled over. How dare he speak to Asphodel in such a manner.

He couldn't bear the thought of those greedy hands grasping for her—

She was in some kind of trouble. He could feel it—all his soldier's instincts screamed at him. Her grandmother had hinted at it too, and he didn't at all like what he saw between Asphodel and her fiancé.

He had to keep on the high toby—how else to discover what he sought? And yet he had to remain uncaptured. He had promises to keep.

Damn the traps. If they caught him, he would be powerless to watch over Asphodel.

Farlan went into the castle and upstairs to his room. He opened his battered steel chest and removed the envelope of old papers stolen from the strongbox in Dougie McDonnell's carriage. Dougie must be frantic to get these back.

Asphodel's birth certificate. She was nineteen,

born in June 1861.

Another torn document, a faded, creased title to a business—owner Donal McDonnell. Half the paper was missing.

The third was the title deed to the Black Hart Hotel.

The documents he sought so desperately had not been in Dougie's papers. *Damn it all to hell.*

He studied a yellow envelope containing a thick yellow paper given to him by Isabella McDonnell on that dark night. He drew out the document and read it again, although its contents were imprinted on his mind.

The paper gave him great power but would immerse him in a terrible coil.

It was the legal guardianship paper for Miss Asphodel Quick, naming Farlan Blackitter as her lawful guardian.

Chapter Five

March 1881—Black Hart Hotel

A lanky, brown-eyed stranger in worn military garb of an unfamiliar style was subjecting her to intense scrutiny. When he strolled to the bar to buy his ale, Asphodel said, "Really, I'll have to rename this place the Highwayman's Head!"

Farlan's lieutenant grinned at her. "I trust your coachman has recovered fully?"

"Except for the savage desire for vengeance burning in his stubborn Yorkshire heart."

"He will enjoy cosseting that grudge. It will keep the old fellow amused and lively."

Asphodel swallowed a laugh and gave him a look from under her lashes. "You are inspecting me?"

"Someone must care for the lad."

"The 'lad' being the large, muscular, and competent Farlan Blackitter?" She swallowed and put up her chin. "He has no one to love him?"

She tried not to show her fascination with the answer to that question and busied herself about the bar. When the stranger did not reply, she stilled and gave him the benefit of her full wide-eyed stare.

The man finally replied, "Aye. The lad is a brave one and true. He has a great and loyal heart." Asphodel noted he did not quite answer the question.

"Are you warning me? Or merely inspecting my person or my premises with the intention to rob and plunder?"

The man laughed and held out his hand. "I'm Jack Darnley, known to many as Gentleman Jack for my unfortunate aristocratic antecedents."

Asphodel shook his hand, and they traded banter for a few minutes. She took her chance to indulge her overpowering curiosity. "How did Farlan Blackitter get those scars all over his hands? I surmise he has had an adventurous life, but they hold a story, I'm sure. I am almost afraid to ask…!"

"He got those scars saving his men when a goldmine collapsed, back in the Victorian goldfields. He dug those men out with his bare hands. Every man was saved." Gentleman Jack glinted at her. "He is a brave lad, but it left him with a strong aversion to dark enclosed places."

"He was in my tower staircase!"

"He tests himself. He practices overcoming his fear, making himself subsist in dark places until I drag him out, sweating and shaking. He is determined to best it." Jack smirked. "And perhaps he had good reason to be there."

Asphodel tossed her head. "How dreadful. And courageous too."

Jack half turned his back and covertly examined the men in the room. Worry flickered on his face. He said, voice low, "He must cease this highwayman lark before he is captured. Prison, for him, with its small, dark cells…"

Asphodel gasped. "I understand! Poor Farlan!"

Jack laughed. "He will survive. Trouble slips off

that lad like oil on water." He turned back to her and leaned in. "If he can find his papers and become baron in truth, a draughty open castle is exactly the right home to make him feel comfortable!"

Asphodel laughed too, but a worm of worry burrowed in her mind.

Fear of small, dark spaces. Prison. Enclosed dark cells.

****

That afternoon, the entire hotel froze for one complete second. This was a temporary community formed of assorted individuals, and Asphodel knew she had become its brain and beating heart.

So, like a beehive in spring, all buzz and action, it had sensed danger to its queen, and everything and everyone paused, for a one solid tick of the clock. The background hum of conversation and work resumed, but it had been enough to warn her.

Her legal guardian, the child-beater Dougie McDonnell, barged through the heavy front door of the Black Hart Hotel. She smiled as he struggled with the ponderous oak doors. It took at least two beats before the doorman, Iain, gave his muscular assistance. She must remember to reward him later.

Dougie McDonnell. A friendly name—an impression as false as his padded shoulders. Like many bullies and tyrants, Dougie pretended heartiness, while eyes as flat as stones looked around him to spot his next advantage or his next victim.

She stood still and watched him. He was a corpulent man, expensively dressed, assuming a calculated charm of manner as deceptive as his corseted waistline. Pronounced whiskers hid his cruel mouth. He was nothing like his half brother, her grandfather, who had blessed them all with his humor and kindliness while he lived. This brother, younger and envious perhaps, had nothing but vitriol running in his veins. She knew it now. *Too late.*

Asphodel avoided his kiss, turning and walking briskly to the back bar. Her neck tickled with awareness. She swept a glance under her lashes. Farlan Blackitter's forceful gaze glimmered from the shadows.

She had gone to the bar, almost without thinking. His vital presence cocooned her in warm safety—despite his highwayman's ways. But it was not safe for him. He should not be here. It would only be a matter of time before someone recognized him. She imagined small dark prison cells clanging shut on his vibrant, laughing face and terror engulfing him.

Dougie followed her in full bluster. By the mean look on his face, she had need of all the strength she could muster. She inclined her head to the bartender, who brought over a bottle of good red wine and two glasses.

"Those weavers! Think they can best me! I'll fire the pestilential lot of them!"

Asphodel poured him a glass of wine and practically shoved it at him. "They need a living wage," she replied mildly.

"They need to be disciplined. They are women. They should be tending to their families, not ruining the economy with their pranks and whims like a lot of blasted harpies."

A tide of temper rose within Asphodel. "Women make excellent businesswomen. We are craftspeople and deserve to be remunerated properly. You would not want inferior work."

"My factory is the pride of Yorkshire! McDonnell Tweed exports its quality garments to London's elite and even to the new gold-rich in Melbourne far away in the Colonies. Those blasted women will break me." He guzzled most of his glass. Asphodel topped it up.

"These upstart women are a threat to business. I'll call my friend Westgarth, the magistrate, and we will soon see who is on top and who is underneath."

Asphodel winced at his description. Nothing to do but endure him. In a year and a half, she would attain her majority, and she would take immense pleasure in barring him from her hotel. Once she had worked out how to free herself from this unwanted and untimely engagement.

He drank two more glasses. "Well, my dear, to business."

His false-friendly leer spiked her instincts alert. She cast an involuntary glance over to Farlan Blackitter. He loomed in his shadowed corner, emanating anger and danger. He met her eyes and gave her a grim nod. Reassuring. She was safe with him. Something in her uncoiled a little.

Dougie smirked and asked, "Would you like to go to the hotel library, my dear? I have news of a private nature I wish to impart."

Asphodel racked her brains. What could that mean? She didn't want to be alone with him. He made her feel soiled. "We will be fine here, Dougie. This window embrasure is my office."

Dougie looked around him and squirmed a little. He put his meaty, damp hand over hers. She tried to bear it, but her flesh crawled. She tugged her hand away and wiped it on her skirts under the table.

She flicked a glance to the corner of the bar. A pair of burning eyes were practically scorching a hole in her guardian. She repressed a grin.

"My dear, I have always cared for you." His yellowed teeth bared in a simpering smirk that sent her guts roiling.

Asphodel swallowed revulsion. "Sir, I am sorry to hear about your factory, but you must pay workers what they are owed, you know. Now, good day, I have work to—"

His arm shot out, and his fist closed hard around her wrist, squeezing the slender bones together. His face reddened, turning even uglier, were that possible. Asphodel tensed. She sensed movement from the far corner.

Dougie's voice slithered in a sneer. "You are a young woman, too young to know how to manage an important hotel such as this one. You need guidance."

"I thank you, Dougie, but I do not need guidance. My business is very successful. I had an excellent tutor in my grandmother, the famous Isabella McDonnell. Look around you. Now, may I get you something to eat?"

Dougie's face flushed crimson. "I remind you that I am your legal guardian. It doesn't matter what you think."

"I will have my majority in a little over a twelvemonth."

Dougie slammed his spare fist on the table. From the corner of her eye, she saw Farlan Blackitter start forward. She would not have him reveal himself for her sake. She shook her head at him. He stepped back, his whole frame alert and wary. She faced her guardian.

Dougie said, "It is time you were married, my dear. You must name a date."

"I am still grieving my grandmother."

"The mourning period for grandparents is six months. We are well past that date."

"Isabella was more of a parent to me, sir."

"This is Fangmoor Beck. Rules are different here on the moors."

"Indeed they are. I have no wish to be married at present." Asphodel snapped the words. She shook her arm free.

"And yet you will be."

"Why the unseemly haste, Dougie?"

"Unseemly? Unseemly for a young woman such as yourself to be imagining you can run this hotel. Why, Prince Albert Victor and his brother have stayed here! You will run it into the ground with no notion of profit."

"I have no problem with figuring, sir. I have been doing the accounts for my grandmother for five years now, since I was just fourteen years."

"Ridiculous. I am your guardian, and you will not be allowed to run amok as you have been. It is not seemly. This family wishes to rise in the world."

Asphodel studied him. His forehead shone with oily beads of sweat.

What ailed the man?

"Are you feeling liverish, sir? Perhaps if you imbibe less wine and take more water, you will find your thoughts less disordered."

He snarled, "I need resources to underpin my tweed factory while these infernal strikers are raising havoc. We must keep the asset in the family."

Two beats. Asphodel's head tilted to the side. "*Pardon?*" Had she perceived his meaning? He wanted her hotel profits immediately—by marrying her forthwith. A cold hand clutched her heart.

"I can perhaps…advance you a sum to defray immediate costs…"

Dougie smirked. "I don't need your sums. This place needs strong management. You cannot be permitted to do as you like any longer. You are becoming a disgrace to womanhood. That sharp tongue of yours can be put to better uses." Asphodel blinked.

Dougie seized her lace collar in his clammy fist and pulled her to him. She could smell wine and the bacon and eggs he had consumed for breakfast.

"As soon as I can arrange it with my friends, Mr. Wilbur Westgarth the magistrate, and His Excellency Bishop Snelling, *you will marry me.*"

Asphodel jerked from her chair, her hotel whirling and fragmenting around her. She clutched the table with white-knuckled fingers.

Dougie's voice lashed. "And put that ring back on."

She squared her shoulders. Went back to work.

She avoided the highwayman's stare for a long minute, her skin tickling with awareness. Unable to stop herself, she finally sauntered over. Pretended to check his glass. He regarded her steadily with that molten steely gaze.

"Begone," she breathed. "And thank you."

****

Two days after the Blackleech Castle encounter, early evening danced in rose and gold on the pub windows.

Asphodel had been half distracted all day, responding to requests with random comments that startled her staff or finding herself in reveries, halfway in a room and unaccountably unable to remember what she had intended to do in there.

The handsome highwayman's warm presence. His gentlemanly manners. That compelling attraction that he somehow exercised upon her. Did he feel it too? She could not be sure, changing her mind every half hour and exhorting herself to focus on her work instead.

He may, of course, be merely amusing himself, or ingratiating himself with a young woman who he believed rich, or foolish, or both. She blushed as she recollected what he had said about her person: creamy breasts, plump wiggling bottom, long and shapely legs. But something inside her thrilled and delighted, all the same. She loved the dark, hungry look on his face as he had described her. His Blackitter iron stare. His famous Blackitter hawk nose. She wanted his greed and hunger for her again.

And there was that other inducement: the story he had promised her, perhaps regarding the mystery of his true identity. She had to use all her willpower to stop herself rushing back.

She idled in the kitchen as the staff were doing the evening meal prep. How was he caring for himself? How could he find sustenance and warmth? Asphodel continued on her rounds, ensuring all operated smoothly, managing a thousand little queries, making innumerable decisions. The rhythm of this hotel was like the beat of her heart, the pulse of her own blood.

She sensed the hiccup in the smooth flow of the

hotel when Douglas McConnell pranced in as the bells of St. Mary's church tolled six o'clock. Her spirits sank, and her flesh shivered.

He stalked toward her and grabbed at her left wrist, turning her hand painfully to check for the engagement ring on her finger. "Where is that ring?" he hissed. "Find it and do not remove it again."

With the same hand, he clutched at her waist, squeezing and pinching her flesh. His hand travelled up toward the underside of her right breast and nudged it until her flesh wobbled.

As he did, a bolt of nausea gagged in her throat. Revulsion crept over her shuddering skin. She stepped away in the pretense of facing him more fully, disengaging her person from his touch.

He said, his voice a lecherous hiss, "Where is your corset?"

"That is not your concern. We are not wed yet."

"I am your guardian."

One that manhandles his ward and abuses his power.

She declined to join him in the evening meal, intending instead to catch a quick snack in the kitchen. Told him she had work to do. She turned away as a peevish, malignant expression twisted his features.

In the shadowed, cozy back bar, she rubbed the empty place on her ring finger while she gazed at the massive bunch of hyacinths placed in a great urn on the bar, scenting the air with color and perfume in place of the usual drunken invective and blasphemy used by some of her patrons.

****

Night cloaked the hotel windows in inky darkness.

Candles and lanterns glimmered reflections of the convivial company within.

Dougie had been imbibing great quantities of claret in the back bar, snapping his fingers at the waitresses and talking loudly. At one point, he treated the bar to several stirring Scots songs which a number of the patrons joined in with, until there was a general air of festivity and good humor. People even came racing in from the elegant front areas of the hotel, keen to celebrate and join in the songs.

She didn't mind Dougie when he was like this, cheerful and gregarious. His singing voice was quite good, strong and rich. She even joined in a chorus, clapping along.

So it was a surprise when the last patrons were leaving and Asphodel was only thinking of her bed, that Dougie propelled her into the hotel library.

A pulse of warning trembled in her veins. She glanced around. Neither Wragg nor Iain stood nearby. Still. Dougie had been jovial and expansive all evening, in fine fettle, singing and chatting with the patrons.

The Black Hart was *her* hotel. No harm could befall her here.

A huge fire crackled in the fireplace, and a tray had been laid with wine and biscuits.

He poured her a glass of wine. "It's time, Asphodel my dear, that I sample the goods before I buy."

Sample the goods? Excuse me?

To buy time, her shocked emotions striving to awaken her numbed brain, to give him a chance to mean something innocent, she said, "You eat here every day and drink quantities of the best brandy." She stood firm while Dougie imbibed a large swallow of wine. "I deny you nothing."

He leered. "Nothing? There are some goods that I must try before too much longer."

Asphodel misliked the expression on his face. Surely he wasn't suggesting…?

"Dougie. It is late, and you are elevated after your singing. I must be up early, as usual, so excuse—"

"Not so fast. I am soon to be your husband—to love and *obey*, hmmm?"

Asphodel tried for levity. "Perhaps we will have different marriage vows! I am not sure those vows are quite to my taste!" Well, that didn't work. Dougie looked like thunder. Oh no. Was he going to turn into a nasty drunk?

"Dougie," she said, her voice as low and dangerous as she could make it, "I am accustomed to removing from *my* premises those gentlemen who have become somewhat high-spirited… I will not hesitate to call Iain and—"

"You little trollop! Come here!" Dougie made a clumsy grab for her. Asphodel danced out of the way. This situation was becoming entirely distasteful. She should have him thrown out and hope he did not remember in the morning.

"I demand my rights!" he exploded.

"I beg your pardon?"

"My rights. When we are wed, you will be my property. You will oblige me as I desire. You will be my property, as will this hotel, and the children of your body."

Asphodel backed away from him, horror coursing through her veins. "I…I have changed my mind."

Dougie looked at her and leered triumphantly. His

faced twisted into an expression so evil, so knowing, that he resembled one of the gargoyles from the roof. "Ah, but you cannot *change your mind*. I am your guardian and have legal control over your person and your possessions. This hotel is mine, in effect—it is only yours in trust."

Lightning exploded in her vision in a blinding flash. "You want the hotel. And marriage to me will give it to you."

He sneered. "Not just the hotel, my lovely, although it needs a man's touch to manage such an important business. Don't underrate yourself. You may not be the most beautiful woman, but you have the charm of youth. I've had my eye on you a good while now. When we are married, you will trot to my whip fast enough."

...not the most beautiful woman... Despite her revulsion, the barb struck somewhere tender.

Asphodel shrugged on her strength, armored herself with the mental image of Isabella, her grandmother, the former proprietor of this hotel. She knew this. She just needed the tact and firmness required to manage a nasty drunk.

"Dougie, you are top-heavy! Quite disguised. I will not continue this conversation. I bid you good night."

He staggered to the door and stood with his back to it, barring her way. "It's time you realized who is in charge here, Miss High and Mighty."

His expression changed, turned to a simper. "Come now, there's my sweet little Asphodel. Give me some of your smiles. I have always thought you a pretty little thing. Ah, you are tired from working so much and afraid of the marriage bed, are you not? Dougie will take care of you. Come here now, my dove."

He took two steps and reached for her. She stood there, stiff and frozen as he put two fat hands on her shoulders. "You have only me now, Asphodel. So long as you keep to my rule and do as you are bade, we shall muck along together nicely."

He bent his face to hers. She could smell claret and meat, sweat and age. His voice slurred. "And take note, little Miss Ice, I am your guardian. As such, I pronounce this marriage the only one I will countenance! No other union shall be approved. Heh heh!" His lips landed on hers with a squelch. He seemed to be sucking and slavering over her lips.

She could abide no more.

Not caring how roughly she treated him, she hooked a foot around his right leg, pushing him suddenly with all her strength with her left hand, and succeeded in unbalancing him. She squeezed through the door and sprinted for the tower room staircase. He cursed as he creaked to his feet and lumbered after her, uttering threats and imprecations.

There was simply no way he could catch her, drunk as he was, as she sped up these narrow twisting stairs, but her heart hammered within her.

She burst into her grandmother's room and turned the key in the lock. For good measure, she added a table and heavy box.

His heavy steps lumbered up the stairs. He alternated commands and curses when she refused to answer him or respond to his shouted orders. He hammered on the door, which shook and shuddered in its hinges, but the door was strongly made, and it held.

"Very well," Dougie slurred. "The door to the

tower staircase will be locked, until you come to your senses."

What? What on earth was she to do? She could not marry this monster. And he threatened Isabella's beautiful creation—her inheritance. She stayed tense by the door, listening to his steps slowly receding, and finally the lower door slammed into place.

"Oh, Nana," she said to the cold night air. "How can I get out of this debacle and save your hotel too?"

Asphodel spent a sleepless hour or two turning plans over and over, only to reject them. Dougie was her guardian. She could make no decision without him. She could not refuse to marry him.

He was friends with magistrates and bishops. She could not properly manage the business if he wanted to put a spoke in her wheel. And apparently, under the law, he could even make good his threat and lock her in her tower, like a fairy-tale princess.

She was in trouble.

A pair of intense silver eyes floated into her mind. She was not entirely alone.

Asphodel rushed to the north window and watched the flickering lights appear and disappear in the old Blackleech Castle.

Who was he, Farlan Blackitter? The rightful heir of Blackleech Castle? Or someone else? Something else wriggled at the edge of her consciousness. The stranger the night Isabella died. Those eyes…

No. Imaginative nonsense. She must retain her sharp sense, lest these imaginings distract her from her intention of making this hotel the best it could be, of continuing the proud tradition begun by her grandmother of female ownership.

Asphodel did a rapid calculation. Only March. Still fifteen months until her majority and full ownership of the hotel. Could she survive that long? Create delay after delay to the marriage date? It didn't sit well with her honest, impatient temperament. She would rather face Dougie down and have it out with him. But could she succeed in arguing him out of it? He wanted the hotel.

Surely Dougie couldn't keep her locked up in the tower for fifteen months?

It sounded like the law, made by men, would support him. *In trust.*

It was true she had nobody now.

She looked again at the flickering lights. Or did she?

A mad idea possessed Asphodel's brain.

She waited. Waited until Dougie had likely imbibed yet more alcohol and fallen into a stupor. She waited until the old hotel had stopped its creaking and began settling back into its haunches for the night, until the thin crescent moon had risen high in the sky and the sky was studded with brilliant stars. She waited until the night hummed as quiet as it got here on the lonely reaches, with the scream of the curlew like the screech of her own fear and frustration.

She needed help as she had never needed it before—and her own grandmother had some kind of connection to Blackleech Castle. It was a sign.

She dressed quickly in warm clothes and carefully locked her tower room door behind her.

Chapter Six

March 1881—Fangmoor Beck

Asphodel crept down the tower stairs, stepping on the edges of the treads to avoid making creaks. No doubt Dougie still lurked in the hotel somewhere, dirtying, disarranging, and wrinkling one of the best guest rooms. The door leading from the tower into the hotel was indeed locked. How dare he!

Cleansing rage wiped her fear away. She took out her master keys and very carefully unlocked the door and stepped through, fastening it again behind her.

Swine. She racked her brains for a plan to rid herself of the man, but so far, nothing sprang to mind. Perhaps when her brain stopped circling, panicking, and buzzing like a fly in a bottle, she would think of a plan. She was *not* leaving this hotel to him—perhaps that was his plan. To frighten her into abandoning it. Never. She would not yield Isabella's life work, her sacred trust.

This was just a hiccup.

She had to find out the extent of his power over her. But who could she ask?

She smiled grimly to herself that she was seeking help from a highwayman, a man outside the law. But his solidity reassured her. His deep voice lent her courage. And when he looked at her…as though her protection was his aim. He radiated capacity.

And who else would not be surprised by a midnight visit by a hotel-owning minor in a scrape?

Asphodel shut the side door of the hotel behind her and stood, one foot poised over the paved entrance. Nighttime on the moors was no gentle picnic. After the setting of the sun, drawing-room rules no longer applied—or even less than they did in the day. If someone should see her!

She could turn back and try again to reason with Dougie. Maybe he had just been drunk.

Ha! Give that plan up now.

Asphodel draped a heavy cloak around herself which sported a deep hood, which she drew over her hair and much of her face. She put her chin up.

She prayed to her grandmother's old Scots gods, if there were any here, and kept her eyes forward and her senses on high alert.

****

Asphodel shook with cold and fear by the time she reached the ruined Blackleech Castle. The nighttime paths were so different to the day! So full of shadows and weird shapes. She had jumped in fright often and had hidden herself in shadows five times until an imaginary danger was past. Her joints were so stiff with terror, she could hardly bestir herself to keep walking.

But now, there was another insurmountable obstacle. How could she find the highwayman? And now she was here, what on earth did she think she was doing? How would he interpret her visit? The way he looked at her…! And perhaps her own motives…his fingertips sizzling over her skin, that dark mercurial gaze, even the crack in his deepest self.

She almost returned to the hotel.

But the thought of Isabella, her hotel, and the revolting Dougie turned her back to her current purpose.

Asphodel stood at the gates, hands on the bars, peering in. *Locked out*. She had half expected him to have left the gates unlocked for her in case she wished to visit and pick flowers once more. *But it is night!* Despair curdled her stomach. He would not leave the gates open then! He must hide from the law.

"Sir!" she called softly. Nothing. Everything was still, dark, and quiet here.

What was she doing? She knew nothing about him.

Dougie, she reminded herself. I need help. *My freedom is at stake. My living. My inheritance.*

"Sir! Ring thief!" Nothing. She became more emboldened, more desperate. "My Lord Farlan Blackitter!"

Asphodel squeezed herself through the gates on the broken western side once more. Perhaps because she was tense with fear, the entire procedure took much longer.

She jumped and squeaked as a hand clamped around her mouth and pulled her tightly into a hard, muscular body. She could smell him, and she relaxed, a very little. It was him. Man and sweat with notes of honey, heather, and a faint sweet tinge of hyacinth.

"Were you followed?" The gravel voice was a rumble in her chest, a breath on her ear.

She shook her head. Her voice did not seem to want to come out.

He spun her around, keeping his firm, hot hands on her shoulders, looking down into her face. His lips clenched in a grim line. The planes of his face cut sharper in the cold moonlight, as though he were made of marble and not a flesh and blood man at all. But the heat of his body enfolded her, and the steady rise and fall of his chest calmed her rushing pulses.

He quirked up an eyebrow. "I imagined I had given you more than sufficient hyacinths? But I suppose it is a very large hotel."

A strangled laugh escaped her.

"I am in trouble," she whispered.

Both black eyebrows elevated. He stared at her hard and then stepped back. A wash of boredom blanked his features.

"I told you this morning that there is danger here," he snapped. "This is not a game. I will not be part of some elaborate taunting of that fiancé. Give him up or stay where you belong."

Asphodel gasped. Her cheeks smarted as though she had been slapped, or thrown bodily into a freezing fen, to half drown in thick, choking peat water.

She swiveled to run back to the hotel. Willed herself to stop. She turned back to him, her nerves pricking with panic.

"Somehow, you have you put a finger most perfectly on my trouble. Sir...my very liberty is at stake. My business. My life."

Marble-man surveyed her, hard and cold. "Why come to me?"

"I have no one," she whispered. "And something about you... Oh, I am a fool!"

She kicked a tulip, which wobbled and snapped back on its stem.

"Not a fool. You have excellent instincts. Come, perhaps you will condescend to venture into the house.

There, I will give you a warm drink, and you will tell me your story."

She hesitated. Once inside—would she be in his power? Escape one tyrant only to fall into the clutches of another?

Nobody knew where she was.

She stared at him. Tall. Broad. Shadows gathering around the planes of his face in the moonlight. Those eyes—midnight silver under strong straight dark brows. His hands. Brown, long fingered and broad, and somehow both calm and gentle, like a musician's. The hands of someone who thought about things. Who cared. He wore the scars to prove it.

There were times in one's life when one simply had to trust one's instincts.

She put out her palm. He took it in his rough warm one and guided her toward the house.

Every sense focused on that sure, careful grip. Nerves jangled up her arm. Shivers skittered on her skin. They went around the crumbling west side of the house, stepping over fallen bricks and stone now overgrown with weeds. In the bright moonlight, Asphodel could see perfectly well, and she had always had good night vision. She jerked her forearm away.

"Hold onto my hand. I would not see you fall."

She hesitated and then retorted, "It's not that kind of fall that most concerns me."

He barked a laugh, and his full attention snapped back to her, a grin curling his wide, mobile mouth. His voice sank in a soft, vibrating caress. "You are safe with me."

"More's the pity." The errant words escaped her. He swung around and drilled her with a flare of silver.

Whew! Those eyes were brilliant!

He studied her for an intense moment, then said, "Come," and recommenced picking his way around to the rear of the crumbling mansion.

The highwayman stopped to light a lantern hidden behind rubble and closed the aperture to a slit. As they walked, the light bobbed—the light Asphodel had spied from her tower window.

Farlan Blackitter wrenched open a side door of the castle, and they stumbled through hallways lined with gold-flecked wallpaper, peeling now in long strips. Gaps in murk and rubbish revealed discolored patches of black and white patterned floor tile. Pale squares along the walls marked the places of missing paintings, although there were plenty left, with subjects strangely illuminated in patches that the mold had missed.

They reached a heavy door. Her guide pushed it open to reveal a kitchen, a servants' room, with a large scrubbed table, shelves of china of all descriptions, heavy pots and pans hanging from beams, and a shining floor covered in muddy boot prints. Thankfully, a large blaze crackled and roared in the hearth. The warmth hit Asphodel like an embrace.

He gestured to the table, and Asphodel sat gingerly on a chair and looked around some more.

He made her a cup of tea from the hissing, battered kettle swinging on a hook and poured in a solid slug of whisky from a flask.

"I don't need that."

"Drink it." She shrugged and took a swallow. The laced tea tasted wonderful and warming, burning right through down to her toes.

He sat down and regarded her. "So you are old

Isabella McDonnell's offshoot."

She put her tea abruptly down on the table. "Her granddaughter. *Her heir.* That hotel is *mine.*"

His brows quirked up. "Except that…?"

"Yes. You have it. There is an *except.*"

He waited, never once taking his eyes from her.

"I am a minor. The hotel is held—in trust—by my guardian. Who is also…is also…my…"

"That man put a ring on your finger."

"Yes." She gulped some of her tea and whisky, the burn of the alcohol making her toes curl.

She made a decision. "It is most dishonorable to criticize someone for one's own mistakes. Weak to complain when the fault is mine. But I am in trouble. Bad trouble."

"Yes?"

"He didn't just put a ring on my finger. There is a collar around my neck, chains on my wrists, and he wants to put a *corset* around my waist."

He smiled. That was, if a quirk of the lips and a dent in one corner of his mouth could be called a smile. "Shocking, indeed." His voice was coldly amused.

Asphodel's skin heated. "You think I am being petulant or missish. But you saw him today! Heard him speak to me like so!"

She lifted her hands to grip her temples and studied him. The teacup rattled as she banged her hands on the table, harder than intended. "But I will not argue or plead my case with you. If you will not help me— though indeed I do not know what I expected you would be able to do, in any case—then I will take my leave of you."

He slammed a hand down onto hers, pinning her to

the table. "I did not say I would not help you. Explain, if you please."

"I made a mistake, I know that. I was grieving. My nana had appointed him my guardian, and when he said she wanted us to marry—I don't know, I was in a kind of fog of grief—I somehow said yes. At least, I must have because I wear his ring!"

The highwayman looked pointedly at her bare finger, and she managed another shaky laugh.

His eyes sharpened. "You do not recall?"

She answered with some temper, born mainly at frustration with herself. "I was possessed by a numb grief of mourning. But I have been wearing his ring, so can I suddenly say I was mistaken?"

"Can you not?"

"He wants me to name the wedding date very soon. He wants to secure the hotel. He wants to leach it of profit, nay, grab any money he can get his greedy hands on."

He turned her hand over and thoughtfully, gently, traced the lines on her palm.

"And he…and he…wants…"

The highway man glared like a fury. "He wants?"

"To…*sample the goods*." She rushed the words. Now that she was safe, shock sliced through her. Hot tears gathered behind her eyes, and she sucked in a gasping breath.

Farlan Blackitter leaned into her. He stretched out a long finger and delicately, like the kiss of butterfly wings, wiped a teardrop away with his fingertip. Her lips parted. It was all she could do to hold in the flood of frightened tears.

Then he stood and paced around the kitchen,

running his hands through curling hair already in disarray. "You must be married to another. Secretly. No, no, that will not do. The marriage must be public to save you."

Asphodel stared.

An idea tickled in her mind. The idea grew within her and blasted across her brain as though angels blew trumpets and all nature cheered.

"What an excellent notion, Farlan Blackitter!" She smiled. "I will marry *you*!"

He stopped in his pacing, and his eyes grew large, and his mouth opened and shut.

"Are you addled in your wits?" he roared. "You cannot marry me. I am an adventurer, and you are a property owner. You know nothing about me."

"Are you refusing me, Farlan Blackitter?"

"Yes, I am refusing, damn it! I am—not fit to be your husband."

"I think I am the best judge of that."

"Yes, you have a truly excellent record of selecting your fiancés!"

"Ouch! Well, that was a low blow." She smiled at him, and his expression softened.

He came and sat down again. "Asphodel Quick. A beautiful name. Unusual, but it suits you."

He picked up her hand and kissed each of her fingertips. His lips were soft and warm. Each time they touched her fingertips, small bright shivers travelled from her fingers and right through her body.

His voice was quiet again as he said, "Asphodel, don't torment me with such a delicious offer. My name is under a cloud. My inheritance is in question. I cannot offer you what you deserve."

The kitchen flickered with the lantern's golden beams and the ruby flames dancing in the hearth. The whisky sent Asphodel both mellow and slightly silly—which might go some way to explain her precipitate marriage proposal to him. Or maybe it was that she floated outside of time and her normal life, enclosed in a safe, warm, glowing bubble with Farlan.

"This is a terrible question. But what stops you?" she whispered. "From claiming your inheritance? And offering me—"

"I fear what I may yet have to do."

If she had expected anything, it was not that.

"First I must discover all the true facts of the case. I have only snatches of unreliable childish memories to go on, plus one or two other clues. I am seeking evidence of my claim."

He broke off abruptly. "You see—I am not a suitable husband for you."

"You do not desire to see me constrained in corsets, I'll wager?"

"You wager, do you?" His grin was pure evil. "Then you would lose your gamble."

Asphodel stared at him but could not quite discern his meaning. She said, "In any case, we are undone. My guardian says he will not condone marriage to any other, and under the law I am a minor and so need his consent."

"But he cannot force you to marry him, can he? If you merely stay unwed—although you seem to me the troublous sort that should be married on the instant to protect you from further mishaps of your own devising!—then you will attain your majority and you will inherit as your grandmother McDonnell intended."

"Somehow he will try to force me. I know it. I just cannot ken how."

Farlan ran his hand through his thick dark curls, his brows drawing together.

She added, "My guardian believes me locked in the tower room at this precise moment."

He laughed, loud and musically. His face brightened, his eyes as merry as any man's she had ever seen. Perhaps that was what he had looked like before all his troubles beset him.

He clipped out, "Surely you have friends? Staff? Admirers?"

She didn't want to admit to no conquests. She snapped, "I have been busy, caring for my grandmother, running the business. Who has time for admirers?"

His eyes glinted at her. The lids lowered, and his penetrating stare practically sizzled her where she sat. "I have risked my own venture because I so dearly wished to see you again, Asphodel Quick, after our most instructive first meeting on the highway. And especially after your unique but appealing visit to my current abode." He waved a gracious arm.

She blushed at the memory.

He smiled at her. "It is dangerous for me to be seen, you understand, but I have also ventured into your premises to make a particular friend. A friend of my own grandfather, who used to drink there, years ago. He was indeed there."

She thought for a moment. "The lawyer!"

"Yes. He has suggested to me a nugget of political and legal information which may be relevant to your situation." He poured more whisky into both their cups.

"Don't look at good Scots whisky like that! It won't bite you!"

"I'm not so sure of that. I proposed after one small measure. I feel nervous about what I may do after two shots!"

His laugh bubbled through her, his body relaxing and his eyes glowing like the silver moon reflected in a twilight fen. "I refused you, didn't I?" He gripped her fingers. "I am your friend, Asphodel. You are not alone. You have me."

"And you have me," she answered him. She was never more sure of anything in her life—as sure as she must hold the hotel in honor of Isabella McDonnell.

He said, "Listen to me, Asphodel. The lawyer, Sean Donegal, told me that there is great debate in Parliament. Sometime in the next year or two, a new bill is likely to be passed. A new law."

"Does it permit highwaymen to marry heiresses, then?"

His chuckle warmed her. "Not far off. It is called the Married Women's Property Act."

She stared at him. "That sounds intriguing. How does this help me?"

"You are not at all slow, Asphodel. Concentrate. Ask instead how does it help your fiancé to marry you *before* the passing of such an act. Currently in law, all of a woman's possessions and earnings become her husband's on their wedding day, with limited exceptions."

"And after this act?"

"A married woman's property remains her own."

Asphodel gasped. "The utter fiend! He is doing his utmost to dispossess me! Farlan, how can he behave so?

Surely there are rules for guardians too?"

"Yes, my little hyacinth, there are rules. But you are a woman of property and of business. You are aware, no doubt, that there are rules, and then there are other rules for other men."

"Yes. Dougie is friendly with the magistrate, William Wentworth, and the bishop, Reverend Snelling."

"Then indeed he is likely to have very different rules applied to him."

"What is the matter? You look very grim?"

"Only that he could have me arrested on sight, should he suspicion who I am."

"Farlan Crow. The document highwayman."

"Yes. As you say." Weariness rippled in the shadows of his eyes and chin. Farlan rubbed stiff palms over his cheeks. "When I am in your establishment, you must not show, by look, word, or deed, that you know me or have ever laid eyes on me. Are we agreed?"

"Every good publican remembers her clientele. You have visited more than once already."

"Then maintain polite detachment. Speak or look at me seldom."

Impossible.

She summoned a wicked smile from somewhere amid her fear and rage. "Simply maintain that secretive style, and we will come about." Asphodel had found no solution to her pressing problems, yet the idea of him close by here at Blackleech Castle and in the Black Hart warmed her more than the whisky. "And *thank* you!" She twisted her fingers in her lap. "When could I expect… No! I am sorry. You must come when you are able."

"I will attend the Black Hart Hotel as usual this week. But now—I will escort you home."

Chapter Seven

March 1881—Fangmoor Beck

Farlan ghosted Asphodel along the dark nighttime lanes. They drew close to the hotel, and he barred her way with a long, solid arm. His body held still as he listened to the night, his arm resting against her collarbone, warm and protective. He slid his arm around behind her, and a large hand cupped her shoulder. She relished his body heat and solid strength.

He released her, and Asphodel unlocked the side door into the back bar. They bustled inside, laughing under their breath and bumping hips and arms, brushing fingers. As though he made any excuse to touch her.

Could he be attracted to her too?

All tender thoughts dropped out of her head and her smile jerked into dismay when she saw what waited for her.

They regarded in appalled silence the enormous chain hooked onto one side of the low door which led to the tower stairs. It was not stretched across the door and locked, but all the hooks and attachments were in place to thoroughly secure the door.

"Your guardian intends to lock you in?" Farlan asked, his deep voice a ripple in the quiet of the hotel.

"It appears so." Asphodel's cheekbones tightened. "Can he—can he indeed treat me thus?"

"It is behavior that few gentlemen would condone, but yes, *if* he is legally your guardian, then I imagine he may have the right in law to discipline you as he believes is needed. Sean Donegal warned me of something like."

They both stared at the chain.

Asphodel said, her tones flat and disgusted, "Discipline." Her stomach clenched, and she tasted bile in her throat. "He is a blackguard." She shrugged her shoulders back. "He will *not* treat me thus." A glow lit Farlan's eyes, as though he approved her courage. She basked in his warm approval.

"Would you like me to remove it for you?" Farlan's mock-polite tone darkened to grim and implacable. "Or better still, shall I remove the bladderwrack entirely from your life?"

"Oh, I don't know what to do!" Asphodel rubbed her hands down the front of her skirts. "Yes! Get rid of the ugly, terrifying thing." Her mouth curled at the corner. "The chain, I mean." Her voice lowered. "It may be far more difficult to get rid of the other."

Uneasy suspicion shocked her. "But why has Dougie not locked it, if he believes I am asleep in my tower?"

"Would you permit me to accompany you to your room?" Farlan asked. His black frown promised thunder. His face was as stiff as if he had never smiled or laughed in his life.

"It would be more appropriate for you to wait here, if you would, while I investigate." Asphodel turned to him, put her hands on his arms. "But I would much rather you came. I mislike this. Why *has* he not locked it?"

Farlan ran a hand over her hair. "I will come." He looked down at her. "Asphodel, I will *always* come." He ran the fingers of both hands along the edges of her jaw, touching lightly, sending smalls shivers through her. "You do not need to be afraid of that man."

He took a small metal tool from his pocket and, with a few jerks and a final wrench, removed the chain from the wall, placing it in a pool of shadow. "Come. Let us see what bogey awaits you."

They crept up the stairs together. Asphodel was amazed how silent he was, how stealthy and light footed. He seemed a ghost or a shadow, blending with the shadows and the small sounds of the old hotel. She remembered his fear of dark enclosed places and glanced back at him. A sheen of sweat glistened on his forehead and hollows danced in his cheeks, but his body marched upward, radiating determination.

They paused at Asphodel's grandmother's tower room door, now Asphodel's bedroom. She put out a hand to the door, but Farlan enclosed it in his and gestured for silence.

A sound smote the night. A small snore. Coming from her bedroom.

Farlan opened the door.

There, stretched out in her bed, mouth open and snoring, lay Dougie McDonnell.

Asphodel's hand flew to her mouth to smother the gasp she could not quite suppress.

What? Had he come up here and somehow gained admission to her room? Found some keys or forced the lock? Asphodel looked at the door. It bore scratches, and the metal parts of the lock had been bent out of shape.

The look she gave Farlan was pure terror.

She couldn't escape Dougie even in her own hotel, even in the locked tower—her safe refuge.

He had come here seeking her and had forced the lock into her private domain.

It was a violation. She was in deep, deep trouble.

With only a wanted highwayman to help her.

"Shall I eject that buffoon for you, my lady?" asked Farlan, his voice grinding the words into gravel.

"No. No. Come away. I will call Iain and Malcolm, the bar manager. They served my grandmother faithfully and will assist me now. You must not be seen to aid me, or Dougie will find a way to discover that you are wanted by the law and then compel the authorities onto you."

"Don't concern yourself with me." Anger simmered in his voice.

She shook her head at him. "I could sleep in another room tonight, but I believe it is best to expel Dougie forthwith, with witnesses. Who knows what Isabella hid in that room. I have not fully explored it…it is still too sharp, the grief, when I touch her things…"

Farlan reached out a fingertip. Touched her cheek. Asphodel inhaled.

She said, summoning brisk resolution, "We will pretend Dougie was in his uppers and did not know what he did. That is best."

Farlan was a shadow watching over her as she went downstairs and woke Iain the doorman and Malcolm the bar manager. Apparently satisfied that Asphodel was safe between the two large Scotsmen, the shadow softly detached and faded away as they clattered up the stairs.

Two large, enraged Scots woke Dougie and roughly bundled him out of the bed, scolding him in deep musical voices for his poor behavior in entering Asphodel's room.

"For it is not the right thing at all, man," said Iain. "Ye should know better."

Dougie staggered as he pulled himself from the floor, disoriented and shaking his head groggily. His bloodshot gaze fastened on Asphodel lurking in the background, and his cheeks purpled. He pointed a finger. "She is my fiancée," he spat.

"She," said Malcolm, in the calm, strong voice he used to persuade stubborn drunks on their way, "is an unmarried young woman, and you know verra well that you do not come in here without her permission." He cast a glance at Asphodel. "Or even *with* her permission. 'Twill not do at all. This is a respectable hotel."

Dougie scrunched up his face like a spoilt child about to tantrum but was no match for the hard-muscled bodies of Iain and Malcolm, who half carried him to the door.

Asphodel cast a look around the room. Had he ruined it for her? Despoiled her sanctuary with his evil intent? Was it polluted with shades of Dougie now?

She caught movement out of the corner of her eye and swiveled to stare at the north window. There, a shape was forming on the glass, like a frosty apparition. Asphodel stared. Her heart leaped into her mouth. It looked like…?

"Iain. Malcolm," she called. They looked up from where they were none too gently beginning to bump

Dougie down the tower stairs. "Look there. Is that a— shape—on the glass?" Her voice dropped to a whisper. "A woman?"

"By all that's holy!" hissed Malcolm. He dropped Dougie and stepped a pace back into the room, his eyes starting from his head, and his brows almost disappeared into his hairline.

"It is herself! She walks!"

Iain came back in, dragging Dougie. He gasped and coughed out, "*Isabella!*" He slapped Dougie hard on the face. "Look there, man. The old woman is watching o'er her granddaughter. You don't come in this room. You don't lay a finger—"

Dougie wrenched himself to his feet, and his eyes veritably popped from his head. In an instant, he was stumbling through the door and cursing and bumping down the stairs. The two large Scotsmen still stared at the apparition as though it were Macbeth's ghost at the feast.

"Thank you," said Asphodel. They both seemed to awaken from their trance, told her to call them whenever there was need. Iain said, "We will all keep an eye on you, lass, for the old lady's sake and your own. It is her wish, we can see."

When Asphodel was alone in the echoing quiet of the tower room, with only the night skies and the frosted shape on the glass for company, she said, "Isabella? Nana!"

As she watched, the frosty shape thinned and then dissipated.

She was alone once more.

Except now she had a highwayman, a doorman, and the bar manager to help her. Yet Dougie had all the weight of laws written by men and powerful friends who were magistrates and justices to see his rights were upheld.

What had she done?

And how could she hold on to her rightful inheritance and escape the clutches of that…of that…*fiend*?

An urge to recite prayers possessed her, to decontaminate her beloved refuge. Somewhere within her, she found the answer.

Looking out into the clear, starry night, she remembered an old song her grandmother used to sing when Asphodel was young. Using the sweet tones of her singing voice like a cleansing incense, she sang the old Jacobite air "Skye Boat Song" and walked the edges of the room, until she felt that her grandmother had re-established her powerful no-nonsense presence and the taint of Dougie had washed away.

****

Asphodel worried and fretted for two days while running her hotel with her usual accomplished aplomb. Would Dougie appear and create a scene? Would he bring his odious magistrate friends? Or worse—would he bring a preacher and insist on their marriage forthwith?

By the early on the third day, a Wednesday, Dougie had failed to appear, and Asphodel had half begun to relax. While bringing the freshly pressed newspapers to one of her wealthier guests, she was struck by a brilliant idea.

It might be considered cowardly, but it would have the effect of delaying the inevitable argument and scene until after she made a definite and irrevocable move.

The more she considered it, the more she liked the idea. During the morning, she gave her orders about managing the bar to Malcolm, who winked at her in response, the cheeky man, and hurried to the stables, where she harnessed her favorite horse, Whicker. She would gallop posthaste to the small post office in Pickering, seven miles distant.

She greeted the postmistress.

There, she placed a personal advertisement in very large type, for display in the post office window and to be printed in a week of newspapers. Asphodel winced at the cost quoted but believed that it would be worth every penny:

The engagement subsisting between Miss Asphodel Quick, granddaughter of Mrs. Isabella McDonnell (dec.) and heiress to the Black Hart Hotel, and Mr. Douglas McDonnell, youngest brother to Mr. Donal McDonnell (dec.), is hereby sundered due to irreconcilable differences. Miss Asphodel Quick wishes to announce a prior claim on her heart and has therefore released Mr. Douglas McDonnell from any obligation from this day forth.

Asphodel's heart thundered in her chest, but her spirits soared aloft into the blue day. On the glorious ride back to the hotel, she laughed with happiness. Dougie had become such a millstone, such a fearful, towering giant in her mind. And now?

She had thought out a clever strategy and boldly acted on it. She had formally de-engaged from him in a way that the entire world could witness. He might—and likely would—rant and rave, but she could put up with a little of that. Because at last *she was free of him*!

As she crested the hillock in the bridle track and

picked her way down the steep descent, a deep shadow crossed her path. A great black horse and, astride him, a tall man with hat pulled low and coat flying out in the wind.

"Stand and deliver!" the man cried, his voice hoarse.

Asphodel checked and restrained her startled mount from bolting over the heather. She held her ground; a dark suspicion entered her mind. "You already have my ring, bandit," she shouted.

The man's laugh carried on the wind to her. He tipped his hat back. A familiar pair of gleaming gray eyes shone with mischief. His lips, sculptured and mobile, twisted in amused invitation. With wanting.

"You think I will be content with another man's ring?" he replied. His thighs squeezed his horse, and horse and man stepped closer until he brooded less than a yard distant. His intent steely eyes pinned her. She was rooted to the spot like a vole under the fierce gaze of an eagle: spellbound, half terrified, half exalted.

His eyes raked her up and down. "No sidesaddle then?" he asked, his voice a caress. "You look like a moorland goddess, fierce and free, astride your mount like a force of nature." His expression burned her. It hurt to maintain the stare between them, but she could not avert her gaze.

"I was not expecting to encounter a highwayman with a concern for the proprieties," she answered tartly. "Or to be the least bit concerned by them."

His laugh warmed her through. "In that case, you will not care if I steal something else."

Asphodel stiffened, but her whole body thrilled. A spear of heat stabbed her down where she sat the saddle and pulsed there.

The highwayman brought his horse closer. He reached out a scarred hand and touched her upper arm. "I would taste those luscious raspberry lips," he said, his voice a croak.

Asphodel put two fingers lightly on her own lips. "I am unused to idle flattery," she responded as valiantly as she could. She made a tremendous effort to counter his words; all her heart craved was to hear more of such sweet remarks…and for him to suit actions to the words.

He reached out and selected a curl dangling over her shoulder. "Flattery implies my words are not truth," he answered. "Or that I desire something, which is true." He twined the ringlet through his fingers. "Look at this unique vivid tint. The color of sunrise, of gold glinting in a stream, of precious chrysoberyl."

"What—?" Asphodel cleared her throat and looked blindly down at the primroses nestling in the heather. "What is it that you desire, sir?" She forced her gaze up and locked eyes with him. The hot blush mantled her cheeks, but he would not best her in this exchange. "You wish to secure a piece of my hair?" She hardly knew how to go on. He was so strange, so much fiercer and bolder than other men she knew, and yet so gentle with her.

"A piece of you. To begin with, certainly." He quirked a feral grin. "This," he hissed on a breath, and then he leaned in and held his lips close to hers, so close, the heat of his body cocooned her from the breeze, his breath tickled her lips, and his deep-brimmed hat overshadowed her riding bonnet.

And then, at last, he kissed her.

His outlaw lips touched hers. He pulsed with want and need for her; his strength, held at bay, tested her desire, her willingness. His lips pressed gently and drew back. She waited, everything in her focused completely on him, his presence, his heathery Farlan smell, the warmth of his mouth on hers.

When she did not pull back or protest, suddenly he reached out and pulled her to him, lifting her bodily from her horse and placing her in front of him. His arms encased her in his heat and strength. His mouth took hers, tasting, plundering her with his lips and tongue.

"Asphodel," he murmured into her neck, and his voice was a groan. His breath heated the hollow under her ear. His hands pressed against her breasts, sending spiky arrows of desire shooting straight down her body.

His large strong hands gentled under her jaw, and he held her face as he kissed her thoroughly again.

"I want you," he said. "In every way. But this is not the time."

He slid down from his horse, still holding her in his arms. Standing, they pressed against each other. Sensation fizzed under Asphodel's skin.

"I ask you, keep that finger free of rings for me."

Asphodel swallowed and battled to regain some semblance of rational thought. "If that was a proposal," she snapped back, "then I've had better." She swung herself back onto her horse and, without looking again at the highwayman, kicked her heels into her horse's ribs and galloped away off over the muddy track, bent over its back.

Well, that was a lie.

His kiss had entirely claimed her.

And she had claimed him right back.

****

Predictably, the next day, Dougie arrived in an absolute storm cloud of fury. Barely even waiting until he had cleared the vestibule, he commenced yelling and cursing. He stood, legs apart and hands gesturing dementedly, eyes bloodshot with temper, calling down plagues on Asphodel's head.

Asphodel, Iain, and Malcolm practically collided in the doorway, running to cut off the disturbance at its source. The two men moved to manually pick Dougie up, preparatory to throwing him bodily out onto the entrance yard fronting Hawkmoor Lane.

"Now, man, that will do!" said Iain, his voice as gray and implacable as the cobblestones he was about to fling Dougie on. "I will not hear you speak to the lass like that."

"I am not *the lass,*" Asphodel inserted neatly into the rising storm. "I am the proprietor of this establishment, and everyone under this roof behaves in a respectful and couth fashion. Or else!" Holding his furious gaze, she made an abrupt cutting motion with her hand across her throat.

Dougie moved forward, prevented from reaching her by two sinewy Scots forearms barring his way.

"Bitch! Unnatural woman! I will have you removed from management of this establishment! Incompetent! Unfeminine in every way!"

"Being feminine is not an attribute to which I uniformly strive," she said, her voice drier than a beck in summer. "Indeed, I am persuaded that you must consider me unfeminine due to my very competence in managing the Black Hart." Having delivered that blow, she glanced around, aware of the growing crowd of interested onlookers, some of whom were beginning to exchange coin and scribble notes in their betting books.

Asphodel smiled grimly. "But as you did me the inestimable honor of offering for my hand—" An audible snort from Malcolm almost made her laugh despite her mounting annoyance. "Please Dougie, let us discuss the situation with calm and rationality."

"Our personal affairs will be discussed in private."

In private. Her mind shouted a warning like the discordant clanging of bells. Her skin shuddered, reliving Dougie's thick fingers clutching her person and his wine-scented breath in her face last time they met in private, in the library. He had been top-heavy when he threatened and assaulted her.

And then—breaking into her tower room, waiting *in her bed.* Every cell crept with viscid revulsion. *Billy.* She would never forget nor forgive Dougie's brutal treatment of that child. His own carriage tiger.

The highwayman had saved her, woken her, challenged her to leap into life once more.

The clustering onlookers' eyes shone with avid prurience. Oh dear. She clicked her tongue, undecided. She itched to have Dougie thrown out to the roadway, like the flotsam he was—but would he then return with his powerful friends and wreak vengeance on the Black Hart Hotel? She feared the power he held over her.

What choice did she have?

Asphodel turned and stalked through the bar, down the long, carpeted corridor, and toward the expansive library. Dougie's thumping feet shadowed her. Her skin prickled as if he breathed into her collar.

At the library door, Dougie hissed, "Alone." His fleshy lips turned down, and his heavy-lidded gaze gleamed with malice. "Or perhaps I shall have one of the hotel staff charged with theft. That wench Maeve."

She jutted her chin. "You would not get far. All my staff are scrupulously honest."

"My good friend, *the magistrate*, would perhaps find one of my keepsakes in her possession."

Asphodel squinted at him. *What could he mean?* Later, Maeve could explain if there was any truth to Dougie's claim. A surge of protectiveness rose within her. He would not harm her staff.

She squared her shoulders. Her own decisive action had engendered this scene. Perhaps she owed him this last discussion. She would have it out with him and then be rid of the man.

A shame their final scene would be in the library, one of her favorite rooms, filled with books, fresh flowers, and mellow light. She didn't want it polluted by shades of her guardian.

Too late now.

She cut a glance at Malcolm and Iain, standing solid as the oak door on either side.

"Please. Wait outside, if you would."

"Are ye sure that's wise?" asked Iain in his deep gravel voice.

"Probably not, but I owe him the dignity of privacy to discuss this."

"You owe that leech nothing," replied Iain but subsided into a frowning, glowering statue planted to the left of the library door. Malcolm took up position to the right.

Goodness! Clearly her staff disliked Dougie's overbearing ways as much as she did.

"Come in, Dougie," she said pleasantly, nimbly

stepping through the door before he could press his body against her. As he entered close on her heels, she turned to him, temper snapping from her like darts.

"*Great-Uncle* Douglas," she began.

"I am still young, barely into my forties." He preened himself in the old mirror over a side table.

Asphodel snorted.

"Very well, very well! Barely into my late forties, still vigorous…"

"I cannot…"

Dougie walked to the sideboard and poured a large whisky, which he gulped down. He poured another and drank half. He turned to Asphodel. He came toward her, so Asphodel skipped behind a large comfortable chair.

He reached over and took her hand. "Please, lass." His voice was husky. "Forgive me. I admire you so much that I forget myself, forget what is due to a fresh young virgin like yourself. Please. Say that we can try again."

A small stab of guilt pierced her. Dougie's pale blue eyes pleaded now. For a moment, she wavered. He was born in another age and struggled to assimilate her modern notions. Dougie was her only family left, here on the moors.

…and what use was a handsome, teasing highwayman, wanted by the law?

She came from behind the chair. Dougie was a businessman. They would discuss their situations in a sensible manner.

Then Dougie put his thick, sausage fingers on her breast and squeezed.

Asphodel shouted a curse worthy of the back bar and jumped back.

The images burst again in her mind, flashing red as danger lanterns: predatory Dougie waiting in her bed, the chain across the tower stairs, designed to steal her very freedom…

"All right, lass?" Malcolm called through the thick door.

"For the moment." How she yearned for the highwayman's elegant fingers and gentle touch, the intelligent gleam in his eyes. His hardness and gentleness all at the same time.

Dougie lunged and grabbed her, forcing his wet lips over hers, kneading her right buttocks with his left hand. Repulsion shot through her, and her flesh shrank back as if she had touched a hot stove. She pushed at him, but he held her fast.

A tide of rage erupted within her, burning determination and courage into her veins.

"What is it?" he said thickly. "Another man? I'll have the scoundrel whipped." He aimed another sponge-like kiss on her face.

"I'm sorry, Dougie." She wrenched herself free, panting as lightning flashes of fear and fury snapped and sizzled in her vision. She struggled to control her shaking voice. "We will not suit. I am surprised you cannot see it yourself."

He reached for her. Asphodel dodged neatly and sucked in a hasty breath. She gritted her teeth. Her eyes widened in utter astonishment as Dougie guzzled more whisky, slammed his glass onto the mantelpiece, and launched into ranting speech.

"As your guardian, I am not approving marriage to any other. You will marry *me*."

She faced him down. "This isn't the dark ages with

me trapped in your castle. You are in *my* castle, and it will not be for much longer!"

"When your bully-men aren't around, you might find yourself compromised, my dear—and worse—and then you will find yourself glad to have *anyone* marry you! Don't expect me to be generous then! I was prepared to treat you with devotion, but now I see what a minx you are! You must and will learn to be obedient. You will exist to make me happy. A wife's duty is to her husband, in every respect. Rape does not exist in marriage."

A cold hand gripped Asphodel's heart. "Are you *threatening* me, you scoundrel?" Her stomach flipped over. "You don't frighten me. You make me *sick*!" She walked to the door.

His voice flew after her like a club. "I hold the whip hand, my dear. You will be declared incompetent."

"You won't be able to prove it! Everyone knows I am *extremely* competent!"

"Try and prove that from inside the asylum!"

Asphodel gaped. Suddenly, a torrent of fell images rushed through her appalled brain.

"*What* did you say?" Her mind clamored and clattered like hail on a tin roof. "If you need money, I can advance you some, if that is what this insistence on marriage is all about!"

"I don't need your advance. You *will* marry me."

"You cannot compel me!"

Dougie came close, sickening her with his stale perfume and rotting breath. His voice was soft and poisonous. "Oh, but I can, my dear. There are places to put an obstreperous ward. The Harrowlick Lunatic

Asylum awaits women who refuse to obey their menfolk."

Asphodel's mouth formed an *O* of horror. "Those places are vile!"

"You'd be better with me, don't you think? You have a time limit, my uppity little miss. One week."

He pushed past her and stomped out of the room. She listened to the sound of him cursing her men fading through the hotel and the brief flare of carriage noise from the lane as he opened the front door.

Asphodel stood in the library for a few more moments, her limbs trembling with shock and emotion.

This room had been one of her favorites. She tried a few quavering bars of the "Skye Boat Song," to cleanse it of Dougie's presence, but only a strangled high-pitched noise squeaked from her tight throat.

He couldn't, could he?

Terror slammed into her, like a metal suit lined with agonizing iron spikes closing over all her dreams. Her mind spun, whirling uselessly, a wheel on a broken axle.

Slowly she folded over the upholstered chair, nothing more than a wilting fens flower.

She put her hand to her mouth as her stomach jerked, to hold in the retching.

Chapter Eight

March 1881—Fangmoor Beck

Asphodel screwed all her courage into appearing calm and unaffected while her brain whirled in turmoil and her stomach stuttered and roiled with extreme anxiety. She smiled at Malcolm and Iain waiting outside the library—she hoped it was a smile— thanking them and sending them back to work.

One week. One little week. That was how long Dougie said she had before she must marry him.

Marrying Dougie—how could she, now? He was a monster. She shivered. What a lucky escape she had had. Imagine if Dougie had not revealed his true self; indeed, if Farlan had not appeared like an enchanted prince disguised as a highwayman and broken the spell which had her sleepwalking through her days since her grandmother's death…

He had certainly woken her. From the moment she set eyes on him, from the moment she heard his quiet voice, his laugh, the touch of his fingers on her body, it was as though she had woken up to sun, to music, from a strange gray land in which she had been wandering, lost. Snapped her right back into the living present, into her own visceral body, into smell, and touch, and hearing. Back into her mind.

Outside the library door, Asphodel stood for a

moment.

Just for that second, the hotel rested quiet, a frozen moment. The peace of the grand old building seemed to bear her up. Its special Black Hart smell of beeswax and woven woolen rugs, whisky and ale and trickles of pipe smoke. Flowers and laughter and happiness.

The walls exhaled all the dreams and songs that had ever been dreamed and sung by hopeful people finding solace, or community, or peace under its high roofs. The hotel was as much a social creation as bricks and mortar. Her grandmother had made a place where people came and visited again; when once they ate a grand meal, enjoyed the service and the quality rooms, with a choice of bars to suit, they spread the word and returned.

This was her grandmother's great gift.

Asphodel walked dreamily through the spacious high-roofed hall. A long carpet runner welcomed her feet, holding and cushioning them. Glorious botanical prints by the renowned female botanical illustrators Elizabeth Blackwell, Marianne North, and Anne Pratt glowed from the walls.

In the spaces, ancient maps of the York moors villages hung amongst vivid etchings of wildlife—short-eared owls, red grouse, water voles.

All anchoring her to place.

Asphodel peeped into the main bar and waved a cheery greeting to the various groups: conversing around the long main table, relaxing in armchairs before the open fire, perching on stools near the bar, and debating on benches lining the magnificent front windows, colored patterns from the stained glass creating harlequins of their faces and clothing. All was quality, all was discreet, offering luxury and comfort.

Shadows lurked in the small back bar, hiding those who preferred to dwell away from the brighter lights of the rest of the hotel.

The dining room was a masterpiece of tasteful paintings, elegant furniture, soft piano music, and floral decoration.

Where the hall branched into the main bar, a large portrait of her grandmother hung. It was painted when Isabella was fifty-two, six years before her death. Her salt-and-pepper hair was plaited in complicated braids and pinned up in a coronet. Her old face gleamed vivid and alive, her blue eyes bright with intelligence, humor, and schemes. Her chin jutted up, held in the proud carriage Asphodel had always known.

"Nana," whispered Asphodel. "What a sorry pickle I am in. I tried to pay attention to everything, but I didn't pay enough." She gazed into her grandmother's painted eyes, seeking advice, direction, and solace. "Help me, Nana."

Asphodel, feeling foolish, traced the outline of her grandmother's hand and placed her hand flat on the canvas, as though she could reach through the paint and canvas and touch warm, living flesh. She closed her eyes and imagined…did that hand move softly under hers? Was it clasping Asphodel's hand in her work-worn one? She could almost imagine it had the texture of skin, the feel of flesh warming under hers, a faint squeeze of the fingers. When Asphodel opened her eyes, she looked ruefully at the old face and then at her hand. She frowned in puzzlement.

Where she had placed her hand, the old woman's hand was no longer quite underneath her own.

Asphodel stared. Did the old woman's hand now point toward...the tower staircase? She had looked without always seeing at the painting every day since she was fourteen. Was she sure where the painted hand had been?

"Oh, Nana. You always did tell me to stop dreaming."

But Asphodel stared at the painting for a while longer and then gazed toward the tower stairs. Slowly, as though she were sleepwalking or forcing feet through sinking sands, she stepped toward them.

At the tower door, Asphodel blinked herself from her trance. She had work to do. The Black Hart needed her. She did not have the time, nor mental space, to waste on fancies and weakness. Her own grievous need for her grandmother was creating phantoms in her mind.

****

The moon shining in the north window woke Asphodel. She felt happier than she had in a long time, as though somehow her grandmother's spirit had infused her dreams. And indeed, there were traces of tears on her face, and a lingering sense that someone had been calling her, as though from far away, faintly, the echo vibrating the air in the room as though on a mysterious wind.

Did someone call her name? Was that why she awoke? She listened intently for an age but heard nothing but the usual sighing of the old hotel and the breathing of its timbers.

A bolt of alarm snapped her gaze to the door. After her recent Dougie experiences, she had to be careful, but the door remained locked with the large trunk wedged against it.

"Asphodelllllllll." Thready, faint, barely sound.

She sat bolt upright in bed, pulling the covers up past her chest. The wind suddenly beat against the tower walls and windows, like a thousand pebbles thrown against the glass. It rattled like hail, but the sky out of all the windows shone starry and clear, despite shredded white clouds racing the moon.

Asphodel leaped out of bed.

She stood, looking wildly around in the silver half-light. Something compelled her to the bureau, to begin rifling through its contents, grabbing handfuls of papers, glancing at the contents and strewing them on the floor, faster and faster. In a kind of possessed whirlwind, she pulled out drawers, opened cupboards, wrenched boxes out from under the bed. Shivering in her transparent cotton and lace nightgown, she stood on the trunk and ran her hands over all the panels in the room, feeling for hidden sections, listening for hollows.

She looked up, and there, against the glass, the frosty shape of a woman—her grandmother—had formed once again—and yes! It was pointing…toward…

Toward the headboard of the bed, just behind it, the wall behind it.

Asphodel was possessed of a strange, frantic strength, impelled by a weird force, as though the moon's beams powered her. Somehow she pulled the huge wooden bed away from its moorings and heaved it to the side. Frenetically, she tapped and banged at the wooden paneled walls behind the bed head, and suddenly…!

A hollow sound.

She tapped and prodded and pulled. She pinched her fingers in wedges in the carved woodwork and broke two nails trying to prize sections out.

Nana! Asphodel hissed at the frosty shape on the glass. *What am I looking for? Where is it?* But the image seemed to waver and melt, leaving just the trace of a face and then a sad smile, like a ghostly clown.

In her more lucid moments, she knew that in her extremity she was imagining things. She so urgently needed her grandmother's help and guidance that she had conjured it there. But a small part of her mind and heart believed with all the force of hope and need and desperation.

Over the next few days, whenever she had a moment, she came up to the tower room and searched.

The room looked like it had been burgled.

But still she found…nothing.

And then, when she did find it, it was nearly too late.

****

The old, yellowed papers were tied in a blue silk ribbon. Tiny black cursive script flowed across the parchment in a formal, elegant language so filled with rodomontades and digressions and qualifiers that she could barely make any sense of it.

Legal papers. And her name flashed within them.

She had tapped and tweaked and pulled and pried at the wood panels across the walls, inserted and torn fingernails in carved roses and snakes, banged panels and pressed floorboards. Finally, she had examined the bed itself, the great high four-poster bed in which Isabella had slept and now herself.

The papers were tightly rolled in a special cavity

engineered in the front left post of the bed, close to Isabella's pillow but away from sight of the door and window. Ingenious. Asphodel had found a faint star-like flower scratched on the inside of the post: a symbol her grandmother had used in letters—a kind of stylized asphodel flower which grew in the Outer Hebrides and here in the fens. It meant herself.

Asphodel pressed the flower, and with a tiny click, part of the bed post had opened on an invisible hinge, revealing a long cylindrical cavity. And in the cavity were the papers.

Asphodel shook as she stood there, with fear, with excitement, with the giddy notion that she *had* seen her grandmother's painted finger point to the room, *had* seen her grandmother's image in frost on the glass. *Not* her imagination. Urging her to seek, to search, unrelentingly, and now, at last, to discover.

"Why, Nana? Why the big mystery?" Asphodel knew there must be danger and duplicity somewhere in this. She must be careful. Guard the papers as carefully as had Isabella.

A knock on the door. She stiffened and froze, the papers clutched in her hand.

She prayed it wasn't Dougie, not yet.

"Asphodel. *He* is asking for ye."

Everything in her relaxed. Only Maeve.

"Which *he*?" It came out as a snap. Asphodel breathed in preparatory to an apology, but it was not needed.

Maeve understood instantly. "Not that lummox Dougie McConnell. The other one. The tall, silent one with the shoulders and the eyes."

Asphodel smiled to herself. Could it be?

She opened the door, still cautious, not entirely feeling safe—Dougie could have compelled Maeve after all, and Asphodel would hardly blame her. The man was terrifying. He could be loitering near, waiting for her to open the door, ready to pounce.

She breathed out. Only Maeve, with a wicked glint in her eye, and a very saucy smile. "He wants a reading, he *says*."

"Thank you, Maeve. I will be down shortly." Belatedly, she caught the barmaid's interested stare at the papers she still clutched in her hand. Foolish! What if Dougie had been there? All might have been lost. "Return to the bar if you would." She smiled her brisk manager's smile and gave an encouraging nod. With a last stare at the papers, the maid turned and flounced back to her bar.

Asphodel shut the door. Him, here! Wanting a reading. Did he really, or was it just an excuse to see her—to watch over her? It gave her a warm, glowing kind of feeling. It thawed the ice of feeling so alone. Interest tickled up her spine. She would give him a reading.

Asphodel carefully returned the papers to where they had been secreted so cleverly and effectively for so long. Later. She would try to make out their sense and meaning much later tonight. She stared hard at the bedpost. Did it look a little shinier now? Using her embroidered handkerchief, she cleaned and polished all of the bedposts and a variety of other woodwork. There! Hidden in plain sight. Unless someone took an axe to the room, she would be safe.

She looked ruefully at the grubby cloth. It would be useless now to try to tidy herself with it! She poured a little water from the jug on her washstand into its dish, washed her hands, and scooped a little water and splashed and brightened her face as best she could. She smoothed and tidied her long bright mane of hair into a large fluffy roll on the crown of her head.

She couldn't help herself. She pulled on her lightest, laciest chemise and added loose stays that still boosted her bosom into two pale mounds. She added a rather more lower cut dress than usual, a cool blue, whose silk swished and clung to her form.

She went downstairs to do her reading.

****

He leaned against the bar in the dark back bar, saturnine, glowering, focused. Twinges tickled down her skin, a current raced in her blood, her breath quickened. Her breasts swelled, her nipples peaking and sensitive under his dark silver gaze. The apex of her thighs heated and tingled in a peculiar and wonderful sensation.

His gaze locked on her as she strolled toward him, her head carefully high and dignified, her back straight and chin raised. His mobile lips curved into a half snarl, half smile, like a hungry wolf disguised as a man.

"Maeve says you wish for a reading." Businesslike. No nonsense. But that was not how she would speak to any other person asking for a reading. She heaved in a breath, released it. Sought for compassion. Gave a small smile.

His direct gray eyes shone as clear and lucid as water in the fen. His gaze challenged her for long seconds, then lazily, slowly, scorchingly travelled from her face, to her collarbones, to her soft, trembling skin on the top of her breasts as they pushed at her neckline.

His eyes fixed. Her breath came faster and strange heat slid along her veins. His eyes measured her waist, her hips, her skirt, her boots peeking beneath.

His face softened as he looked at her and then tightened in a kind of pain. When their eyes met once more, his were dark and haunted, flaring with desire and desperation. Then his expression shuttered.

"Come," she said, and now she did not pretend compassion. He carried pain within. Somehow her readings allowed people to recognize that the pain they carried, often for many years, was not their pain at all but the shadows and echoes of others' burdens. That it was sometimes much easier than people suspected to put down that load, to deliberately cast away that pain, to refuse to accept the shape imposed by someone else. She knew too that people only took on others' pain or strange ideas through love, or fear, some kind of strong emotion and attachment, even if it was hate.

All she ever did was reflect people back to themselves; and in themselves, they found the answer. Some people took many readings to peel away strong and stronger layers of protection.

Farlan, no doubt, was of this variety.

She took him into the tiny private parlor off the back bar where she took the clients most damaged.

She sat him down facing the tiny round ornate stained-glass window through which he could see the patch of garden bright and blooming with spring flowers, to cheer him, and to cast light on his face. Not that she needed to see, exactly; she sensed people's real messages through tone and atmosphere and body language and a sort of extra sense, a sense that linked into clients' emotions and pain.

But her own face in shadow was better. The client focused on their own feelings, their own words. She slipped behind the small table and sat in the seat just under the window, facing him.

Farlan regarded the garden outside for a long moment. When he looked at her again, all the ghosts were back in his eyes.

She took his hand and began.

Chapter Nine

March 1881—Black Hart Hotel

Asphodel clasped his hand in hers. Farlan sat in silence, his lean frame still, watching her with hawk-like interest.

He wasn't one of those bursting to talk, who, when given just a few kind words and full listening attention, poured their story out like a dam released, a boil lanced, words spurting bitter or grief-sodden or anger-fueled, spraying her, and she couldn't help it, breathing it in, absorbing their burdens through her skin, into her dreams, there to torment and torture her. That was the price—she gave them something of her own clean heart and took some of theirs inside her.

Fanciful! In truth, a swooping mix of emotions rioted within her—the prickle of fear, the pull of fascination—about Farlan. *Baron Blackitter*.

"How are you?" Farlan said. His low voice hummed through her veins. "I came to see if that flotsam who calls himself a man has inconvenienced you."

Dougie's meaty paws and sloppy lips flashed in her mind.

"I'm well. As you see," she replied shortly. "You are here for a reading, so we will engage in one."

He cocked a brow. "The York lawyer informed me

you offered such things. But they can be of no interest to a hardened outlaw such as myself." A smile flirted on his lips.

She tore her gaze away with an effort. "There are eyes in this hotel, highwayman. If you use my readings as an excuse, then you must subject yourself to one."

"I am beyond any kind of redemption, I fear. Even—especially—in my own mind."

"Nonsense. This is the object of my readings. People curse and belittle themselves for many years, often with the critical voice of another who will not leave. They carry ghosts and scars within them. Somehow, I draw much of it out, like poison from a wound."

Farlan had stopped smiling. "And where does this poison go? You absorb the wounds, the self-hatred, the despair of others? Until you crack from the weight of everyone else's pain?" His strong warm hand stroked her forearm back down to the tip of her third finger. She hitched a breath.

Asphodel made an effort to smile and make her voice light. "I am strong with the strength of a moorland flower who bends with wind and snow, allowing it to slide away. I fly with the wings of a lapwing, the cold wind filtering through my feathers. I have my grandmother's spirit in my heart and her blood strong in my veins. When a client tells me their story, yes, it is a burden, but I gain strength too when they find their own force inside."

Farlan's eyes burned molten mercury. His scarred hands gripped hers.

Asphodel took a deep breath and fought for serenity and calm. Detachment but passionate interest.

Suspended judgment. She had to get rid of herself, her own strong feelings—she was in the way like a massive balloon—or the magic wouldn't work.

So she talked, pitching her tone soft and low and soothing. Farlan wasn't ready for questions, but soon, when her voice and presence had lulled him, she would begin to ask them. She would use his nom de guerre in this hotel, where the walls had ears.

"You are searching, Farlan Crow, for something important to you. You exist in layers, and you are hiding most of yourself in those layers. You are in danger. You carry damage, and fear, and violence, and attract it fatally toward you as a whirlpool sucks in all around it. You have seen much, and it has hurt you."

Farlan's face was open and vulnerable, his brows raised in surprise, until he shut himself up again.

"Why did you request this reading?" she asked.

Silence. "For pleasure of holding your hand," he responded, very quietly. "And gazing, uninterrupted, on your lovely face and soft bright eyes."

Asphodel breathed in. "Your life has been difficult, that such an activity as holding my hands is rare enough to be appreciated. Not many women. Not much softness. Little leisure."

He released her hands and rubbed his hair and face. "Yes, perhaps that is very evident. The years tell their story on worn skin, on damaged body, in the scratch of my voice."

"A soldier?"

"A weapon."

"Hmmn?"

"I can hide, hunt, kill a man with just my hands or with an improvised weapon or any knife, bow, whip, gun, lash, or even poison. I can live unaided in the bush for months. I can follow orders to the grave and beyond."

She stroked his hand and listened as he sucked in a breath. She said, "Who did this to you?"

"The English army, rot their evil souls."

Asphodel rose and strolled away to the little back bar, returning in moments with water, two small glasses of her grandmother's best single malt whisky, and a half-filled bottle. She smiled at him and gave him the drink.

"Let's go back," she said. "Tell me about when you were happy. The time you remember, when life was glorious and golden, and the days were not long enough, and every morning was filled with excitement for what the day would bring."

He crooked the side of his mouth at her. "You have asked me, unerringly, the very question I wish to answer. The very matter at the heart of me. The cure for what ails me."

Asphodel's heartbeat picked up. Had she, then? She nodded. The reading was often thus; she knew not why or how. Took a sip of whisky to give him time to answer. The Islay whisky tasted dark and honey-peaty, redolent with mist, poetry, and ancient stories.

"There was a time as you describe in my life." His deep voice pitched low, rasping with long-suppressed emotion suddenly given unexpected life. "I am lucky to have that time, that memory, at all. And while my life has been something else these many years, those golden days are what gave it shape and meaning. And I am here to right a very great wrong." He drank his whisky.

Something unwound and relaxed in Asphodel. It

was working. The reading was unravelling itself. She often just had to set the course, be the star in the dark night, and the person talking saw their past, present, and future stretched out before them as a map.

"My childhood memories? Those lawless days of sunshine and rainbows?" He stared into his glass, swirling the whisky, and watched the liquor spark amber in a beam of sunlight. He met her gaze, his dark gray eyes wide and cloudy with memory and old pain.

"I was a carefree urchin on the goldfields of Ballarat, careering around with my grandfather Forley Blackitter. He was zesty and crazy-mad, filled with jokes and loud laughter, a mischievous child himself. He had the greatest collection of eccentric friends, who all talked to me as though I was a man, not a child, and they told me ridiculous yarns and taught me unsuitable and surprising things."

Farlan laughed, his face soft and amused and his gaze abstracted with memories.

"He always said he was an English black sheep, sent out to the goldfields. He never told me much about my family or background...until the end." Farlan's smoky eyes locked on hers.

She took a jerky breath.

"He never did talk about his origins except to make jokes. And after he made a string of bitter jokes about his family, he often drank himself into oblivion. From love or hatred, or a painful mixture of both, I knew not."

He regarded her. "Now I know it was a fierce, burning desire for justice."

Farlan swirled his glass but put it down. He drank a draught of the cool water instead.

"Then, when I was a lad of thirteen, a true goldfields limb, a veritable terror, we were recruited by the English army and sent to the New Zealand land wars as scouts and hard men. We were expected to be creative, resilient, and plain crazy. I showed an aptitude…"

His black brow lifted. "In the service of English intelligence, I raided coaches, stealing documents and dispatches."

His throat pulsed. Eyes flashed molten mercury. "I became their possession, their weapon. They layered training in skill and physical development on me, until I was a machine. A sniper, a hunting and killing machine. A thief in the night. Even a social man, a gentleman, who winkled out secrets and stole them later."

He was looking at her but not seeing her any longer. As he spoke, back in that former self, his cheeks flattened and hollowed, his jaw tightened, his body pulled itself in, straight and whiplash flexible. His fingers curled around his glass, fingernails pressing pink and white.

His eyes met hers then, in a silver blaze. "We did that for two years. But I wearied of it all. I could not see the right in dispossessing other peoples of their lands and countries. And so when I was fifteen, we shrugged off the demands and entreaties of the English army and returned to Ballarat, to the Victorian goldfields. We found gold, plenty of gold, and my grandfather insisted I have the training of a gentleman."

He laughed. "How hard all that came, at first! I was a headstrong youth, and the manners required even in goldrush Melbourne, where most of the world had come to visit, abraded like the veriest restraints!"

Asphodel said, "I can imagine! I am a child of brisk winds and high crests and rail against restrictions myself."

"Luckily Gentleman Jack is a persistent sort of fellow. He managed to charm, persuade, and amuse me into some semblance of manners. The university wrought more changes. My mind was starved for learning. My passionate desire to master the knowledge of medical training settled me further."

Expressions played over Farlan's face, normally so shuttered and controlled. Amusement, wonder, fierce determination. And then his iron eyes darkened and his cheeks lengthened in grief.

"Your grandfather?" she asked quietly.

"That mad, beloved old man, my grandfather…" A very long pause. He stared at the wooden tabletop. At her hand still holding his.

"Speak, Farlan."

"On that big old bed in his mansion. Dying. That's when he told me. The truth? Or entertaining lies? About our family, the Blackitters and the curse. He suspected my father's death was not an accident. *Murder.* That's why he took me so far away, to another life altogether."

"The Blackitter bane! And you were the heir after your father died in the carriage accident. So he believed if you stayed, you were next! And perhaps from a human hand plying the curse."

"Yes." He drank whisky, rolled it on his tongue, eyes unfocused and gazing where Asphodel could hardly follow. "The story may just be a lovely romance emanating from his wicked brain."

She prompted, "And the old Blackitter place? Blackleech Castle?"

Another very long silence. He looked up at her. The gray of his eyes was a gathering storm, reflecting pain and terrors. When he spoke, his voice was a whisper, hardly louder than the deep vibration of a fiddle string being struck with a tentative finger.

"My grandfather told me as he lay dying that my actual legal name is Farlan Blackitter, Baron Blackleech, Lord of Blackleech Castle. My grandfather himself was the third baron, Forley Goforth Blackitter. He said somebody shortened my father's life and stole the proofs of my inheritance, except for a few items which Forley gave to the safekeeping of various friends."

Asphodel's eyes were stretched wide. "Isabella!" she breathed.

Farlan gave a quick answering nod. "They loved each other for years."

Asphodel let out a breath on a long, long sigh. "And so you became the document highwayman, searching everywhere for your inheritance papers."

She searched for words. His pain clanged within her. At last the great crack deep in his heart and character opened to her. Honor and strength vibrated in all his cells. She could feel how much this moment meant to him. She must shape her words just right. She parted her lips.

He meant too much to her. She was overthinking her response, instead of letting it flow naturally. She was caught up in his war-induced mental wounds, scarred more deeply than the silvery-white scars crisscrossing his beautiful hands. The searing, burning sense of injustice burned her too. She was too empathic. She could not deliver her normal relief.

She cared too much that they would be the right words.

"You are an honorable man." The deep sense of truth and rightness of these words propelled her on. "You are strong—so strong!—that you cannot accept the grief that lies within you. The grief of what you to do to others in war. The grief of your father's untimely death. Your rage at injustice."

She swallowed. This was not the right track at all. This was not healing for him. He knew all this.

Was Farlan too powerful for her? Was his pain so deep, and derived from such terrible experiences that she could not imagine, and was that why she faltered?

No. Human pain, human desire for vengeance, to keep what was yours, they were all the same. She tried to summon her words again. But her reading wasn't working.

Asphodel chose truth. "Farlan Blackitter, this is not how it normally works. Now, in a reading, I tell you back to yourself. But instead of being the detached but empathic healer, I find I am a participant. I am unable to do the normal healing! Forgive me!"

Farlan squeezed her hand and smiled kindly and…She spoke quickly before he uttered a platitude. "Farlan! I find I am not an observer of your drama. I too must hold what is mine. Neither of us appear to have the law on our side. We must fight tooth and claw for our rights and our legacy." She leaned in. "We are the same."

And soon, she promised herself, *I will somehow, with truth and courage, find words to tell Farlan Blackitter back to himself, revealing his glorious character.*

She knew he was a hero, driven by honor and valor.

She would find a way to make him believe it.

****

All that long sunny day, the clients' and patrons' moods had matched the fine spring weather, full of bonhomie and good cheer, fine manners and laughter. Asphodel climbed the tower stairs as the long clement day drew into night, weary yet calm and content.

Shock slammed her like a rush of freezing water. There, in the turn of the stairs. *She* was there. A shimmer. A figure made of shadows and moonlight and the dark, secret places in Asphodel's mind.

Her grandmother walked.

Asphodel started back, took a long moment to collect herself. The figure remained, rippling but as solid as fear and imagination could make it. A portent.

"Ahh! You always said I was fey, did you not, Nana? A dizzy, delirious happiness in the morning presages disaster in the night!"

The image rippled, fading in and out of the shadows. *She does not want to hurt me. She would not harm me!* Asphodel urged herself. *So what does this apparition mean?*

"Nana!" Asphodel said softly. "Isabella! Why do you not sleep peacefully in your grave? What troubles you? What binds you here?"

The eyes and mouth in the apparition opened wide, wide, wider, until they were dark holes in the shimmering fabric of the thing, expanding and black. For a moment, the specter resembled a screaming woman, her face a rictus of horror. A long silvery arm clad in cobwebby drooping drapery stretched out a hand to Asphodel…no! It pointed at Asphodel and then west through the tower, the face still a mask of dread; and then the eye and mouth holes widened and blackened until they tore the shimmering substance around them into shreds which flew around and then faded into the shadows of the tower stair.

Terror glued Asphodel's feet to the stairs. Metal bands constricted her chest. Shock and fear froze her eyeballs wide open.

Then like sensation returning to cold limbs, her blood thundered in her ears and sparked in surging currents in her veins. She heaved in huge gasps of air, trying to calm her shaking limbs.

Bonelessly, she slid down the wall to sit doll-like on the stairs.

Alarm pinged through her and jangled in her ears.

Isabella loved the hotel, and she loved Asphodel. Yet her grandmother's specter walked—a warning from the grave.

That ghostly face shredding into screaming tatters!

Dread coursed through her.

The hidden papers! She must read them, and read them now, no matter about fear of discovery.

Asphodel crept up the tower stairs, peering around every turn and jumping at her own shadow. *I must get to the room. Isabella's and now mine.*

She will not hurt me, she will not hurt me, she chanted under her breath in time with her steps.

Asphodel reached the tower room. She closed the door, locked the bolt, and carefully pulled heavy furniture to reinforce the heavy door. She lit two candelabra and placed them on the little inlaid bureau. She stared around the room in the flickering candlelight, her throat squeezing tight. The windows shone clear. The shadows were just shadows.

She moved to the cavity in the bed head—would the papers still be there? Her heart gave a frightened pound as she pressed the scratched asphodel symbol.

She carefully took the roll of yellowed documents from their hiding place and sat at Isabella's neat writing bureau.

There were Isabella's marriage lines and her mother's birth certificate.

And what? It looked like…Farlan Blackitter's birth certificate! Born on this Twenty-Second Day of November in the Year of Our Lord 1852 to Fairley Edmund Blackitter and Lavinia Blackitter. He was twenty-eight years old to her nineteen years.

And a will. Signed by Forley Goforth Blackitter, the Third Baron Blackleech, in the presence of witnesses—Isabella Flora McDonnell and Donal Angus McDonnell.

She scrunched her eyes. Leaving all lands, properties, and possessions, entailed and unentailed, to his grandson Farlan Goforth Blackitter: Blackleech Castle and all its contents, farms, industries, and accoutrements. A controlling share in a Pickering tweed factory.

Asphodel blinked and stared into space. Dougie's tweed factory! *What?*

Her heart smashed in her chest. So the old man on the goldfields spoke truth! Farlan was Baron Blackitter. Her hand shook as she squeezed the paper in her fist.

There was more. She carefully unrolled another fragile paper. Her own name leaped out at her… All to come to Asphodel Isabella Quick, my granddaughter, on her twenty-first birthday, Sixth Day of June in the Year of Our Lord 1882. The Black Hart Hotel.

The room spun. Asphodel's eyes blurred. She scrabbled through the rest. Where was the deed naming her guardian?

Missing.

Asphodel carefully gathered up the papers and made to return them to their hiding place but then hesitated. Should she copy the Blackitter will? Keep it to give to Farlan?

Better not. This secret place had kept them safe for many years. As she replaced the papers and did her best to obscure all trace of the hidden bedhead compartment, she mused, what was Dougie's game? Did he hold certificates declaring him her guardian? Or did they name someone else? And if so, how did he get hold of them?

There were strange threads in all these stories, that seemed to be coming together in a most unhappy way. The tweed factory was *Farlan's*? Farlan hiding from the law. Looking for documents. These documents? It would seem so.

And Dougie? She had never, not once, asked to see the writ that made him her guardian. Asphodel struck her own forehead. *Foolish girl!* Isabella had schooled her better than that! Always read the whole document. Read the fine print. And don't believe anything—no promises, no threats—until you see the paperwork. Acquire a copy of your own. Creditors have not paid unless the gold gleams in your palm.

****

Asphodel slept restlessly. Her grandmother had walked this night, why? What danger loomed? What action should she take? Police? Magistrate? At the very least, she must find Farlan and show him the documents—the ones that related to his inheritance. Were these the ones he had been seeking? Most likely.

But! The missing guardianship papers. She sat bolt upright in her bed. She didn't need any guardian. Surely she could somehow be declared competent and able to manage her own affairs, despite lacking the requisite twenty-one years. Her breathing slowed as the ripe fullness of that grand notion stole over her.

Repressing the terror engendered by her grandmother's manifestation, and her fear and curiosity regarding Farlan's inheritance and what it could all mean, she at last slept in a twisted tangle of sheets and blankets, their turmoil a mirror for her emotions and thoughts.

****

Angry hammering banged into her dreams. She jerked awake, bleary eyed and muddle-minded. Someone pounded on her door, shaking the heavy wood until it threatened to burst from its sturdy hinges.

A voice shouted, stentorian, officious, with the slam of authority. "Open! Open this door!"

Asphodel sat up and clutched her blankets. Pale gray shadows streaked in through the windows, though stars were still visible in the paler sky. Before dawn.

"What is the meaning of this?" she shrieked in her best outraged voice.

A cacophony of rumbles and squeaks, voices raised in argument, anger, and distress, added to the hubbub. Possibly her entire hotel staff must be wedged in the tower stairs, protecting her.

The loud voice commanded, "This is the

magistrate! Open this door now!" More thundering and banging underscored his words.

"Or we will break it down."

Chapter Ten

March 1881—Black Hart Hotel

Her heavy door vibrated. The trunk wedged against it slowly began to shift. Ignoring the yelling and banging, Asphodel quickly washed her face and dressed in a practical day dress. She checked the papers' hiding place. Smeared dust from the floor over the join.

Not a moment too soon. The banging changed to a loud cracking thud as the magistrate employed a different door smasher. A bang like a gunshot split the air, and the bolt on her door pinged across the room, shattering her wash jug in an explosion of china shards. The door quivered; the trunk screamed as it was forced forward, and simultaneously a whole collection of people fell into the room.

Two heavy uniformed thugs stepped across the doorway after the first men entered, holding back the tide of her angry staff. A fat jowly man and a tall thin man with eyes cold as a frog's marched into the center of the room and halted. Dougie squeezed through the guards and stepped into the room, his face red as a beet, and now smiling evilly and rubbing his hands.

"What," said Asphodel in the coldest, haughtiest voice she could muster, "can be the meaning of this intrusion, and indeed heavy damage to the premises of *my* hotel?"

"Miss Asphodel Quick?"

"Who wants to know?"

The tall man's nose wrinkled slightly, and his mouth pursed in suppressed temper. Oh dear. One of those.

The jowly man said, "I am Magistrate Wilbur Westgarth. You are accused of theft, Miss Quick."

"Theft? Nonsense! Who accused me? That great fool behind you, who merely wants revenge for a broken engagement? How can you be so obtuse?"

Asphodel watched with satisfaction as the fat man and Dougie both went bright red and opened and shut their mouths in stupefaction.

The tall thin man paled and blinked his eyes, slow as a lizard. "Your guardian has declared you mad and prone to fits. You must come with us, Miss Quick."

"He is not my guardian."

"You see?" Dougie sputtered. "Her grip on reality falters more every day. For her own safety…"

The tall man jerked his head, and the two thick-armed thugs advanced into the room, replaced by another couple at the door. They each took hold of one of Asphodel's arms. She kicked one and elbowed the other. The tall man approached and struck her hard on the side of the head. She stared at him in startled horror, her left ear ringing.

"I see your guardian is correct," he said to her. "Take her," he said to the thugs.

The two uniformed men at the door cleared her staff before them, not hesitating to push and whack with short truncheons. The two holding her bustled her through the room and sandwiched her between them as they proceeded single file down the tower stairs.

Asphodel walked down the stairs pressed between the two men, her flesh creeping away from the hot breath of the one behind on her neck and ear, his fat finger prodding her painfully in the kidneys.

Terror clawed her ribs. Fury heated her blood—until the icy realization that she was totally alone froze the breath in her lungs.

Her mind stuttered and whirled. Who could save her now? The papers—nobody knew where they were. How long until they forced her to disclose their whereabouts? They were her only security. Her only leverage. Dougie must possess the guardian deed.

A tiny flame of hope blossomed. If Farlan could know she faced trouble…

The hope in her heart went black and flat. He was a wanted man. He could not declare himself to the magistrate, or he would be identified as the infamous document highwayman, put to trial, and sent to Wakefield Gaol. Pushed into a small dark cell to battle his devils, to reopen those mental scars. Hanged by the neck until dead.

Oh, by all the old moors gods and goddesses.

She was lost, drowning in a mire.

They reached the bottom of the tower stairs. Could she run, if she was quick? *Too late.* The uniforms bundled her between them again, hard fingers clenched on and bruising her upper arms.

"I must write a note!" Asphodel cried. "I must let—" There was nobody. All her people were here at the Black Hart, or hidden in Blackleech Castle, or dead. "I must leave instructions for my staff!"

"No need for that, dear girl," Dougie said, pacing forward, strutting like a little rooster. How she had ever let him touch her! Kiss her! Agree to marry him?

"Naturally, I will assume management of this place, as your grandmother, my dear sister, wanted." He sighed theatrically.

"Hardly!" said Asphodel. "She was not your relative at all!" She attempted a struggle against those that held her. Futilely. "You are a younger *half brother* of her *husband.*"

She stared directly at the thin man with his pursed pale lips. "He wants my hotel."

The man just stared back, his face expressionless, except for an ugly light in the back of those cold eyes. His lips quivered slightly, as though he withheld a sneer or sarcastic smile.

She looked around to Iain and Malcolm, their strong, honest faces as outraged and fearful as she had ever seen them. Maeve was there too, her work-reddened hand over her mouth, eyes wide and afraid. "Get help. Legal help."

"Hysterical!" said Dougie, striding to position himself in front of Asphodel's direct line of sight, so she could not make eye contact with Iain and Malcolm.

Iain moved so she could see him.

"Even in *far lands* this treatment is wrong," she said, desperately. "Such bullying is like a *black leech* to my bones." She stared at him, trying to communicate the import of her hints, trying to get him to understand she was giving him a message.

But it was Maeve, bless her humble woman's heart, who quickly understood.

White with fear, she stepped smartly up to the men holding Asphodel. Her voice quivering, visibly swallowing, her little chin high and proud, Maeve said to the men holding Asphodel, "Have some decency, men. She will need to visit the necessary house before you take her. You can wait outside its very door. I will attend her in case she has need of owt."

"That will not be necessary. Dignity is not part of where she is going. Out of the way," said the cold man.

Maeve stood firm. She hissed, "Miss Asphodel has plenty of jammy friends, and her grandmother had more. Have a care." The cold man and the barmaid stared each other down, and to Asphodel's great surprise, the man suddenly nodded. "Be quick," he said.

Maeve took Asphodel's arm and jiggled her away from her guards, hurrying her along the corridor to one of Isabella's new indoor bathroom lavatories. The guards were one step behind, practically breathing on their necks.

"I am so grateful," Asphodel whispered. "You have saved my dignity, at least for this hour."

"Is there any message to owt…?"

Asphodel bent her head closer. Should she tell the maid to hurry to Farlan?

"No talking!" barked the burliest guard.

Asphodel twitched. She smiled silent thanks to Maeve, astonished at her bravery and loyalty. There was no doubt, one got tough tending bar in a great hotel.

What an unusual and unwelcome feeling—to be at the mercy of her friends' valor, brains, and social connections.

All her drive and courage came from Isabella. Her nana taught her to keep her own counsel, make her own decisions. To not need anyone's help except what she paid them for.

Well, she must rely on her staff now. And she was very touched by their friendship and fealty.

Her last thought as she was bundled out to the dark carriage led by four restless black horses was for the papers hidden in the bedpost. Would they be safe? Her entire sanity and future depended upon it.

****

Late March blazed unseasonably bright, the warm air more summer than gentle spring. She could taste on her tongue the close air in the shuttered, confined carriage, heavy and viscous with the stink of her guards' body odor and rotten-toothed breath. Did she imagine the smell of old fear from women who had been transported before her? Faint vomit and urine, and stronger, the malodorous leather squabs and seats of the carriage, slimy with use, assailed her nostrils and added to her discomfort.

She gently eased a thigh away from the guard on her right, whose beefy leg pressed into hers, his legs propped wide apart as though to reflect the size of all his appendages and relative importance.

The thin man traveled in another carriage. Her flesh crept in revulsion as she recalled his pale, dead eyes boring into hers, floating in her vision like an unclean specter, feasting on her distress. At least she was relieved from that cold, cruel scrutiny.

Not for long. The carriages stopped in the hot sun, and she was made to stay inside, sweltering in the heat. She had just resolved to brave whatever punishment they would bestow and step out of the carriage for a breath of air, even a last sight of the landscape, when the door opened, letting in a blessed gust of fresh air, and the thin man stepped in and took the seat facing her.

With a jerk, the carriages took off once more. The thin man stared at her with his pale, unemotional eyes.

"Where are you taking me?"

"You will address me as 'sir,' or Master Shuttlestick."

"And I am Miss Quick."

They glared at each other.

"Miss Quick," the thin man said silkily, "we do not tolerate rudeness, insubordination, or willfulness. You will not be released until we can be sure that you are a docile and obedient member of your sex."

"Released."

"You are going to the exclusive Harrowlick Lunatic Asylum, Miss Quick. And there, I hope, you will learn the error of your ways and find relief from unfeminine anger and displays of willfulness."

"I'll kill him!"

"And you will have learned to overcome and expel these urges to violence."

Asphodel regarded her enemy in front of her. She had the strong sense he knew she was perfectly sane but did not happen to agree with female "willfulness," as he termed it.

The thin man, Master Shuttlestick, had drawn up the terms of engagement then. It would be a battle of wills. He with all the power of the law and the threat of incarceration and loss of freedom hanging over her head. The power to release her.

She with nothing but her wits.

****

An indication of her life to come came as they drew into the outskirts of the small town of Harrowlick.

He had not stopped her from drawing back the window curtain slightly and opening the window a mere inch. The moors marched away in gloomy rusty brown desolation, fading into dull gray in the distance. A lone hawk hovered over the landscape, then dived for the kill.

Shuttlestick leaned forward and nodded to the guards. They took hold of her arms. Asphodel's head turned from one to the other. What now?

Chills ran all over her body as the master drew out a flat leather case, which when opened, showed a brutal-looking syringe and a number of pharmacist bottles.

"No!" she said. "There is no need to sedate me, if that is your current scheme." All the men ignored her, except for a flare of the thin man's nostrils.

"You are strange and cruel," Asphodel said. "Surely you cannot just cart away an innocent woman, inject her with pharmaceutical products of dubious nature, and lock her away?" Fear shivered in her voice. A glint flashed from Shuttlestick. Yes. Her terror and discomfort pleased him. Dread clawed in her belly.

"Your guardian has had you committed, until you have your devils cast out and you learn docility."

"Did you ask him for proof of guardianship?" she hissed. The thin man looked disconcerted for a brief moment. "You didn't, did you?" She bit her tongue. She had almost mentioned the papers, which might free her—or they might be destroyed if discovered, and then she would have nothing.

It was a gamble she couldn't take until she knew more about these people, Harrowlick Asylum, her entire situation.

The thin man filled a syringe. Panic possessed her. Her arms, torso, and thighs wrenched in futile strain against the guards' physical strength. Sickening fear fogged her mind. And then his bullies held her down, and the master injected some vile chemical into her veins.

She felt violated. More furious and angry than she had ever been. Even as she internally vowed revenge, escape, resolution, a strange peace stole through her veins.

"They are going to think I am drunk!" she said.

The thin man grinned at her. It was the first time she had seen him express any overt emotion. "I think I prefer you emotionless," she slurred.

The last thing she saw with her usual bright mind was the large scrollworked metal sign over their heads as they trotted through the grand entryway:

Harrowlick Lunatic Asylum.

Welcome to the Harrowlick Hospital for the Insane.

Chapter Eleven

March 1881—Harrowlick Hospital for the Insane, Harrowlick

Asphodel woke in a small room. At least it had a window, high up and barred. She strained toward the tiny space, which framed a few wisps of cloud floating in a patch of blue sky. Daytime, then. The same day she had arrived, she hoped. *How much time had she lost?*

She sat up and quickly put her head in her hands. The room spun, her throat was scratchy-dry, nausea thrummed in her guts, and her head pounded like the wild hunt.

She looked down. Where was her day dress? She seemed to be clad in a grayish nightgown, washed and institutionalized into a nondescript garment. Cold air bit her bare toes, and her hair hung about her in long, messy hanks.

"Oh no. Oh no no no no." The memories were coming now, distorted and black, swimming out of a dream—arriving in an office, falling over herself, indeed as if she were drunk. Or drugged. Which she had been, just not by her own hand.

A large office. Big, wooden desk. The thin man, guards, and a…whip? On a stand by the wall. Someone behind the desk. Big, bristly beard. Black eyes. Menace.

She shook her head. Struggled for recall. There had been conversation. She had tried—over the thin man's tale—to protect herself. Dougie not her guardian. She was quite sane, a businesswoman. Satirical laughter. And then…falling, falling over herself, crashing on the hard floor. Her head. And being carried on a trolley. *Strapped* to a trolley. Fighting and cursing.

And now here she was.

She staggered up. Spied a flap on the door. She pushed it and peered out. "Hey!" Asphodel yelled. "Somebody!" She rattled the flap.

A large muscular woman thudded up the corridor, stopped at Asphodel's door, took a large ring of keys from her belt, and unlocked the door.

"What's the matter? Don't like the service at this hotel?" She said it with the weary air of someone who had said the same joke many times, until even she didn't find it funny. *Must be part of the initiation.*

She smiled at the woman, who just stared blandly back. "I'd like some water," Asphodel said. "If you would. The thin man—Master Shuttlestick—injected me with something on the way here, and now I have a terrible thirst."

"They all say that." Now she did crack a smile, as though the earth itself furrowed in an arid drought.

"Maybe because it's true," Asphodel snapped back. Instantly the warder's face hardened. Her hand hovered near the truncheon on her belt. Asphodel blanched. Stared straight back into the woman's pasty face. Unexpectedly, the woman nodded. "I'll get you some water."

While Asphodel waited for her water, she pondered. Would the woman spit in it? Fetch it from somewhere filthy? *Listen to me. I really will go mad in here. Just take things as they come. You have to worry about tomorrow—make plans—otherwise you will never get out of here.* Even if the woman did spit in it, she would still survive.

She would survive.

Farlan Blackitter's strong face swam into her mind and gave her strength.

****

Some hours later, Asphodel was wondering if she would, in fact, survive this. Or ever get out.

She was eating dinner—at least that was the name given to the activity, but it did not resemble any repast with which she was accustomed. It was given in the middle of the day, so she must have been asleep for only a few hours.

Her usual robust health sang once more in her veins, but her spirits had plummeted.

Asphodel looked around her. She was in the women's section of the asylum. Most were dressed in similar grayish rags like hers, but she could still intuit something about each person there.

Some were clearly institutionalized, going about their business as though bred to it. Some poor souls appeared genuinely mad, shuffling around in swollen and cracked shoes and ill-fitting garments turned the wrong way, muttering and moaning to themselves, scratching themselves in odd places, and peering suddenly at one of the other women and making startling or confusing pronouncements. Others sat at their tables eating quietly, with the isolated air of total despair.

Some were very, painfully thin, with huge dark

circles under their eyes. Others had deep healing scratches on faces, arms, and wrists. Asphodel didn't want to think too much about the causes.

She was very, very out of her depth. The rules, especially the unwritten ones, would be brutal.

Asphodel spooned some of the mush and muck into her metal bowl and looked around for a place to sit. As she walked over to a vacant spot on a bench next to a young man, the dining room erupted into whispers and giggles. She glanced around. Most of the room stared at her, eyes avid, or curious, or full of suppressed mirth. Oh-oh. Was this young man dangerous? At least he looked safe. Not actively cursing or waving his knife around.

As she sat, their eyes met. Not a man. A woman dressed in men's clothing. Shirt. Jacket. Trousers. Trousers! Short hair. Asphodel forgot the room and hissed conversations larding the air like steam.

Without breaking the woman's gaze, she put down her meal. "What an absolutely brilliant idea!" she said. She was half aware of the room going dead silent behind her.

"Oh?" the woman said. She had a friendly, funny, dough-like face with twinkling hazel eyes under arched brows.

"What I would give to be able to dress like that! Do you find it immensely freeing?"

The woman curled a lip. "Not especially, given that these clothes are what landed me in here. Apparently, it is a hanging offense to wear the clothes in which you feel most comfortable. They allow me to wear them— in theory, I must *choose* the prison of female clothing for release."

Asphodel almost forgot to eat, hungry as she was. "And do you not?"

"No!" The woman frowned, gazing down at her meal. "Who am I harming by dressing myself so?"

"Indeed. Perhaps, given I am stuck in here anyway, I shall adopt so-called male clothing, and they can all go hang."

The woman stared at her. "Are you mocking me? Making light of my choices?"

"No! Nononono! Oh, I'm so sorry. It's just I feel quite inspired. Why should we wear that horrible constricting stuff because we are female? I *hate* corsets with a passion. In fact, now that I consider it, can it be possible we are made to wear such stuff to keep us in a kind of *bondage* of clothing? Unable to move freely, unable to run, unable to *breathe*, even?"

Almost reluctantly, the woman smiled. Her bright eyes sparkled, her rosy cheeks puffed, and her white teeth shone in a grin. She stuck out her hand. "You keep talking like that, little sister, you'll be stuck in here for a while. A good long while. So we may as well get acquainted. I'm Rose Robin."

Asphodel shook her hand and smiled as she introduced herself. Was this a friend? What were the whispers about? She didn't feel in danger. In fact, she liked this forthright, intelligent person.

Asphodel picked up her spoon and tasted the mush.

"Best just shovel it in," Rose advised.

She grimaced and complied.

While she was eating, Rose said, "I have been in here for a week now. They throw me in, every now and again, until I pay a huge ransom, and then they release me."

Ransom? Hope blossomed for a sweet second. She shook her head. Dougie's fat fingers gripped her gold. His malign influence chained her in here.

Her skin prickled. A client-needing-a-reading kind of twinge. She put down her spoon and focused fully on Rose. "Annoying, but at least you do not need to feel completely trapped. If they will release you soon." Was this a pitch for money? A test? She added delicately, "Or are you not currently in funds?"

Her new friend smiled satirically, clearly reading Asphodel's face. "I am not hitting you up for cash. I am worried about my wife. She is only young, and a Romani girl."

Asphodel choked on a spoonful of mushy gray-green peas. She squinted at Rose. "I did not know...wife?"

Rose smirked. "Yes. I am not made to love men."

Asphodel's brows shot high into her forehead, although she desperately wished to appear smooth and sophisticated. A faint memory tickled in the back of her mind. Oscar Wilde and whispers. The convict colonies and the Hobart female factory and lovers and fancy-women. Perhaps all that hotel talk hadn't completely washed over her. She stared at Rose with unabashed curiosity. "But...?"

Rose raised her brows enquiringly. "Yes, my dear?"

"You know, I don't even know what I was going to ask. What to ask you. Oh, I feel a fool. Isn't that illegal?"

"Not if you are a woman, Asphodel. The men who love other men can be executed for the crime. This is the one case where men making the laws works to our advantage."

Asphodel stared and laughed. "I am pleased to hear it! In one law women are better off! Astonishing indeed."

"Shh," responded Rose, with a wicked wink. "Not too loud, or they will realize, and I will be sentenced to hang, instead of committed in the asylum for wearing male garb and identity."

Asphodel laughed merrily. She had never thought to laugh in this place, and gratitude swelled. She reached out a hand and squeezed Rose's fist.

"Tell me about your wife, if it will relieve your anxiety."

Rose said, "Most women of your class scream and avoid me in case they catch it."

Asphodel cut a proud stare around the room. Many observers looked transfixed, eyes wide in their faces. Others had decided there was no entertainment to be had and went back to bullying those weaker than themselves, or endlessly, monotonously chanting their own strange songs, or staring hopelessly into their dinner.

Asphodel said, "Perhaps these unusual surroundings create honesty. We are so desperate we must help each other or be damned in this place, by those horrible men."

Rose fetched two cups of weak tea and set them on their table. "My wife...she is vulnerable when I am not there to protect her. She can easily disappear into the landscape, it is true, but I fear she may be hanging around here, waiting for a chance to see me, or to slip me some decent food. Bad things happen to young Romani women alone and unprotected."

Asphodel drank some of her horrible tea. "This would taste worse if I did not have you to converse with," she said. "Please, tell me more."

"I am not sure how much you are aware of Romani people. Nan was stolen from her Romani family as a small girl and sold to do domestic work. She became pregnant to her employer, at the age of fourteen—very much against her will. I rescued her and the child three years later. Nan and I fell in love and have been together ever since." Rose gulped her tea. "The Romani welcomed me because I brought Nan and her child back to them."

Asphodel's tea was pale and swirling. She stared into its depths as she could hardly face Rose's anger, to see her own reflected back. "Your poor wife! What a terrible story."

Rose nodded. "I am hoping she left with her people at the turn of the seasons. They live in different places at different times of the year, much like you rich folk with your summer estates, town houses, and hunting lodges for the autumn. But I think she may be hiding, waiting for me. I must escape. She has been badly treated by men before and must not endure that again."

"And I must help you!"

A woman slid onto their table, smiling saucily at them both. Her cheeks glowed pink with carmine, and boot-blacking darkened her brows and eyelashes, rendering her features very defined and quite beautiful. Her gray asylum sack-dress had been artfully torn and knotted until it mocked a town dress, low-cut to the extreme, revealing expanses of plush, snowy bosom, and hitched in tightly to a narrow waist. Her plump lips shone rosy red with rouge. And she had that particular look in her eye.

Asphodel blinked. A bobtail, here?

The woman grinned charmingly. "No, darling, not a slapper, strumpet, or whore. I am a *courtesan*."

Asphodel opened her mouth, disconcerted. Finally she responded, "Courtesan! I like it."

The woman smiled her lush smile again and said, "People will do all sorts for a peek into my glory box. I want to help. And I've got more tools for combat than either of you two innocents."

Rose laughed. Asphodel found her jaw had sagged downward and snapped her lips together.

The woman stretched out a hand. "I'm Evie Lovelace."

"Why would you help?" Rose asked. To Asphodel she said, "They have all sorts of snitches and narks in here. Get better treatment by dobbing in their sisters' plans for freedom."

The woman stopped smiling. "I've seen how those Romani girls are treated. And the starving Scots and Irish. No one to help them. At an age when most of us are yet happy girls. Makes my blood boil. But you are respectable." She bowed her head to Asphodel. "No doubt you will want no truck with the likes of me."

Asphodel was entirely and completely out of her depth, but she could read character. She made a snap decision, hoping it was not too informed by sentiment or desperation rather than sense. If she was to survive this place, she needed friends.

She said, "No doubt I will soon find out if I am wrong." She stared hard at the courtesan. "You are so cheerfully indestructible, with, as you say, such an array of weapons and tools at your disposal that you can only be an immensely strong ally. It would be churlish to refuse. Your compassion does you justice."

"Speak English, lovey, and we will con each other all the better."

Asphodel laughed, and her cheeks heated. "My pardon. I'd love to be your friend."

Rose narrowed her eyes and sniffed but did not object further.

Asphodel said to Rose, "I had no idea. We tend to leave Romani people living in their camps quite to themselves. I am sorry. I did not know they needed my help. The girls."

Rose nodded. All three of them touched clenched fists together in the center of the table.

Apparently even that gave rise to accusations of misbehavior.

****

The first Asphodel knew that someone had indeed "snitched" was the heavy stamp of boots across the hard floors, and the clamp of thick fingers around her upper arms once more.

Two male warders hauled the courtesan to her feet, their motions rough and intrusive to her person.

Asphodel watched in horror. Nothing was safe here. There was no respect. She shrugged the wardresses' hands from her own body and rose. "Must you demonstrate such disrespect to the people in your purported care?" she demanded, as haughty and cold as she knew how. "Are the authorities aware of how your inmates are treated?"

Evie shook her head at her. Rose picked up her metal bowl, her whole body tense with purpose, ready to spring into action.

One male warder released Evie and sauntered around to breathe into Asphodel's face. His voice was an evil, low-pitched hiss, redolent with venom. "What have we here, Miss High and Mighty?" His face twisted in a malevolent sneer. His arm snaked out, and he gripped Asphodel's chin in iron fingers. Pain shot through her jaw; a great throb of fear pulsed through her innards.

Evie said in a coaxing, teasing, flirty tone, "Come on now, boys, leave the girl alone. Come have your sport with me instead. The lass doesn't know the rules yet." Evie deliberately smiled at the man holding her. The one gripping Asphodel's chin intercepted the look. A flash of jealousy crossed his brutish features, and he released Asphodel, turning to the courtesan.

While his gaze was averted, Rose aimed her metal bowl and threw it unerringly across the dining room to hit the head of the largest, fiercest woman, who immediately screamed, swore, and hurled her own bowl as a missile straight back into Rose, Evie, and the warders. The whole room erupted into a riot.

The air vibrated with colorful invective, screaming and yelling and fighting, wrestling women. The warders released Evie and went to break up the fights.

Asphodel was frozen with shock and horror, rooted to the spot with her mouth open. Never had she seen such scenes.

Evie was right. She didn't know the rules, at all.

****

Asphodel had been dragged off to a tiny, dark room. An isolation cell. They had manhandled her into an offensive garment in which her arms had been inserted and then tied around her body—a straitjacket.

The worse kind of corset to which she had *ever* been subjected.

As for the room itself, there was literally nothing in it. She had nothing to stare at except strange rusty marks on the wall. Bloodstains?

She was in deep, desperate trouble.

She racked her brains, conducting a frantic audit of her talents.

None of her hard-learned skills were of any use here: who cared if she was a wizard at calculating sums and budgets, or managing staff, or coordinating all the concerns of a large and successful enterprise?

She had grown up expecting respect as her due, because of her station in life and her role as Isabella's granddaughter and heir. Without all that, what was she? Who was she?

Footfalls shook the corridor outside, a steady, heavy stamp. A rattle of something hitting doors and walls.

Her door opened, and the warder who had pinched her chin stood in the doorway, smirking all over his thick face. He shut the heavy door behind him and locked it.

The warder said, "Your guardian warned us you were willful and obdurate." He extended his truncheon, slapping it lightly in his hand. Asphodel listened to the regular thwack, thwack, thwack, like a bell of ill-omen, a foretaste of suffering.

She wriggled in her straitjacket. Her eyes fixed on his. Lust gleamed there and something darker which she could not name. She wriggled again. Her throat constricted, and her breath came faster. Her blood thudded in her temples. Nausea swirled in her stomach.

A ray of anger gave her some spirit. She would *not* let this man abuse his power over her.

Then the thought struck her like a lightning bolt: she had refused to allow her guardian power over her—and now she was here in this hell. Indeed far worse than being compelled to marry Dougie.

The warder smirked, drawing closer, still beating that tattoo with his truncheon. He came close and circled her slowly. Sickness rose in her gullet. Was he *smelling* her?

"We get all sorts in here, my dove," he murmured, so close she could smell the sausage and onions he had consumed at luncheon. "Scullery maids, sexless wives, disobedient daughters. Heiresses like yourself, refusing to do what their guardians say is best. You never get out, you know. Best to learn to do as you are told from the beginning. No harm done, that way."

He paused in front of her and began to undo his flies.

"If you do get out, it won't be until you are glad to be obedient. But your menfolk don't want you, once you've been in here. Hysterical. Diseased. Insane. Who wants that in their family? But the few ladies who get out, we make sure they will scurry to do their masters' wishes. Finishing school for rebellious…little… whores!" He finished on a shout, bringing the truncheon down where a moment ago, Asphodel's shoulder had been.

She was a publican, after all. Gently bred, educated, but able to put up a fight if it was warranted. Her grandmother had made sure of that.

Asphodel twisted under the truncheon. There wasn't much she could do with her arms in restraints, but as she twisted and dived, she kicked him as hard as she could behind his knee, and as he wobbled and lost balance, cannoned into him, and then, with a deep breath, kicked him in his most vulnerable parts. She stood, shaking, listening to him gag and curse. She had never done that before. She had only heard the principles of it.

Her mind was a panicked whirl. What to do? How could she get out of here? Out of this cell, where currently there was just her and the warder? Nobody came if one screamed here—screaming and ranting were merely business as usual.

She had to give it a shot. She bent to the flap in the door. "Help! Rape! Violence! Somebody, please come! *Help me!*"

Out of the corner of her eye, she saw the warder stirring and beginning to regain his feet. How long did she have? She banged her whole body against the door, yelling, "Help! Help!" at the top of her voice. She was making noise—thank goodness it hadn't been a padded cell. She had heard whispers of those.

She ran toward the warder and kicked the truncheon to the corner of the room. His hand snaked out and grabbed her ankle. She lost balance and landed, half-winded, on top of him. He reached out to grapple her to the ground, his face a red mask of fury and vengeance.

"No no no no no noooooo!" She rolled and, with all her strength, kneed him in the groin, stood, and kicked him in the temple.

She was going into shock. Terrified tears sprouted from her eyes; she took a shaking step away, aghast at her own violence.

Keys rattled suddenly in the door. Her limbs froze.

The warder shouted from the floor, "This bitch attacked me."

Two female warders stripped the straitjacket from her body and hustled her out between them. They ignored the guard still writhing on the floor, one woman merely shooting him a contemptuous glance.

As she stumbled along, hauled between the two silent, grim women, thoughts hammered chaotically in her mind. Where were they taking her now? Somewhere worse? What would they do to her? She felt so powerless, so stripped of humanity.

There were so many things she had never fully been thankful for. Even cold air and freezing winds—at least she had been free to feel them. Daffodils heralding the end of the long North York winter, their happy yellow faces turned to the sun, splashes of bright lemon and yellow in generous profusion.

Gentle people. The time before she had heard these inmates' horrible personal stories. Could she ever regain equilibrium again?

Doors clanged open. She was pushed into what appeared to be a large washroom, lined with baths and basins.

"The master says for you to tidy yourself up. He wants you in his study."

"W-who?" Asphodel stuttered, her bones juddering with shock and the freezing air in the bathroom.

"Master Shuttlestick."

What new torture or humiliation was in store for her now? That cold-eyed man wanted her in his rooms? And cleaned up? Asphodel wrenched her petrified thoughts away from the terrifying prospects parading themselves in her mind.

All these women here who had been incarcerated here for weeks or months, or…years…if they were not insane when committed, surely they must be mad by the time they were released.

If ever.

The warders briskly stripped Asphodel's asylum uniform from her body and pushed her into a large tin bath filled with greasy water which was tepid at best. Asphodel had one horrific thought about how many bodies had shared this water before her, and then resolutely blanked the images from her mind.

Survive.

As one of the warders scrubbed her roughly with a harsh-bristled brush and the other doused her hair in the murky water until she was sputtering for air, Evie sauntered into her field of vision.

"What are you doing here?" Asphodel demanded and then quickly shut her mouth against another bucket of water pouring over her head.

The courtesan laughed. "I have my methods. This place is not for such as you. Or for women who love their own kind. The male warders are beginning to threaten Rose with sex 'to teach her how to be a real woman.' "

The warders stopped washing her. One hauled her out of the tub, and the other flung a thin scratchy towel at her. Asphodel clutched it around herself. No one had seen her body naked since she was young. Her entire body flamed red.

None of the others were at all concerned. Asphodel pressed her towel to her body in her best insouciant manner.

Evie said to Asphodel, "And I heard them saying they were going to do one of the new treatments on you. Put a brain clamp on you to calm your violent tendencies."

"*What?*" All modesty fled before the great tide of combined outrage and fear which soared through her brain. Her mind? They were going to damage her *mind*?

Everything spun into red and gray. Asphodel couldn't suck in any air. She gasped and flailed, and the room whirled dizzily around her.

Cold floor tiles smacked hard against her right cheek, and her mind slammed into blackness.

Chapter Twelve

March 1881—Blackleech Castle

Farlan's whole body was stiff with cold, despite the woolen blankets and feather comforters on the bed. Cold bit his nose and exposed left cheek and froze his fingers as he wrenched back the bedclothes.

Someone was hollering at the main gates, shouting, "*Blackitter, Blackitter!*" in a strong Scots accent. Something to do with the Black Hart Hotel then.

Farlan leaped from the high bed, instantly awake, and dragged on pants, shirt, vest, and coat, wrapping a cravat around his neck as he hastened down the corridor. He paused at the top of the grand staircase and stared for a while from the high window. It was difficult to see the man's identity from this distance, but the shape and demeanor did not resemble that shabbaroon Douglas McDonnell. Farlan doubted that barnacle would bestir himself so much in any case.

"Blackitter!" The Scots voice grew harsher and thicker with shouting, laced with urgent despair. As he gained ground, Farlan identified Iain, the doorman from the Black Hart, along with the wizened helper Wragg, the one who was as brown, wrinkled, and peaty as if he had sprung from a bog.

"Come around the side, men, and stop letting the entire neighborhood know what's afoot!"

Farlan unlocked the side gate.

"It's too late now for gammon and stow-manging," Wragg said. "The game is sprung. You'll need to become Baron Blackitter."

"That puffguts Dougie has had the young mistress taken," Iain clarified.

Shock and panic hit Farlan like a punch in the stomach. For a moment he couldn't breathe. "Taken? Where? By whom?" He stopped. Iain and Wragg were blue-tinged with the cold. Anxiety crawled over their normally wooden features. "Come in, men, come and warm yourselves and tell me."

Farlan escorted them to the kitchen, made tea and porridge, and doled it all out.

"How did you know who I was?" Farlan asked Wragg.

Wragg grunted and wheezed in what Farlan surmised was a laugh. "They's allus a Blackitter at Blackleech Castle," he said in tones of great satisfaction. "You'm the Blackitter iron stare."

Farlan raised his brows, used his iron stare on Wragg, who issued another grunting laugh, and stowed the thought away to examine later. "Get some of this food into you and explain what has happened."

Iain and Wragg described the magistrate, the master of the asylum, and the thugs taking Asphodel. "That cold-eyed fish Master Shuttlestick ain't one to cross. We mun get her away from that one," Wragg said. "But how to rig the game is a tricksy puzzle."

The cold of the morning was nothing to the ice slicing through Farlan's veins. His whole body chilled—stark fear, familiar as his own haunted dreams. His mind, however, overheated, boiling and maddened with images of Asphodel and the choices to be made.

As Iain and Wragg talked, McEvoy appeared, washed and dressed, fresh from the stables, shortly followed by Gentleman Jack. Farlan made the introductions and then told them all he was stepping out for a moment.

Farlan paced through the overgrown, tangled grounds, littered with fallen rubble and masonry, toppled statues, and bizarre household items long abandoned.

He pulled at his hair and pushed his forehead into his hands.

There was a clear choice before him.

Save Asphodel. It could be done—easily—without too much fuss. No need for the elaborate, dramatic rescue which the men in the kitchen were no doubt planning while he walked.

He could save her, but by so doing, he would destroy everything he had been working for, fighting for. He would have to declare himself. If he claimed his identity and his birthright—before he had the proof in his hands—it could all go to dust.

Whoever had wanted the Blackitter heir dead could still be in the locality. His father—slated to become the fourth baron if old Forley spoke truth—had been killed fewer than twenty years ago.

And the worst risk. If he declared himself, came out into the open, someone might look more closely at him, might recognize him as the document highwayman.

He would free Asphodel—and the cost?

His own neck in a noose.

Or worse, trapped for years in a gloomy prison cell,

the walls and the darkness closing in, until his very sanity departed him.

Farlan laughed, and the sound was bitter in his own ears. All these years he had survived dangers and hazards and enemies; his finely honed instincts for dangerous people and situations had saved his skin again and again.

Everything within him tolled *danger*!

He sat on a decaying bench within the overgrown yew walk. Its gloomy greenness suited his mood. He rasped his palms across his forehead and then rubbed his thighs.

There was no choice.

There had never been any choice.

As soon as Asphodel faced peril and grief, all the cells of his body clamored to rescue that fine damsel. To employ every weapon in his arsenal, every trick and trap he'd learned over the reckless years.

He had survived so he could be here to save her when she needed him most.

And if his useless neck broke on the end of a gallows, so be it.

There in the dim green tunnel of the overgrown yew walk, there on his own ancestral lands, his heritage and his birthright, Farlan Blackitter, Baron of Blackleech Castle, was blindsided by a lightning revelation.

He loved Asphodel Quick with every fiber of his being.

Farlan strolled back to the castle kitchen, looking around him. He breathed in the Blackitter air, lost to him for so long when he was boy and man in the colonies. He looked with bitter love on his ruined castle and every stem of his wild garden.

It might be the last he ever saw of it.

Farlan stooped in the doorway of the kitchen and waited for silence.

"I'm riding Black Branwell now," Farlan told them. "I won't need you at the asylum. Be waiting here with horses ready in case I do not return by close of day." He ignored the shouted questions and remarks and stalked off upstairs to his room. He donned his highwayman garb, pocketed two pistols, opened the chest, and grabbed what he needed. McEvoy followed him upstairs and watched.

Farlan walked downstairs and through the kitchen and tipped his hat to his men in case it was goodbye. Without another word, he strode off to the stables.

Gentleman Jack and McEvoy would know the risk he took. He didn't want to hear their reasons for delay or caution. He didn't want to hear their farewells.

Farlan saddled Black Bran and rode away like a storm.

****

When the brutish male warders pushed Asphodel through the door of Master Shuttlestick's office, she balked in the doorway. The strangest scene met her terrified gaze.

Master Shuttlestick was standing, not sitting, behind his desk, his thin features suffused with a poisonous rage. Dougie sat in a chair to one side, his mouth open. His words ceased abruptly as she and her warders crossed the threshold. A few phrases trailed off in what appeared to be an enraged speech "…imposition…will not tolerate…"

Two thugs lounged either side of Master

Shuttlestick.

And a tall, broad-shouldered man, clad in a many-caped riding cloak, spattered with mud to the thigh, turned as the door opened.

His silver gaze burned into her own. Farlan Blackitter had come for her.

Her first emotion was relief: she was saved! That emotion was short-lived, and panic consumed her. Farlan must not be here! What if they realized he was the document highwayman? Dougie would bundle him off to his friend the magistrate before anyone had caught a breath. What was he *doing*?

A startled sound had escaped her when she first met that mercurial stare, but she had control of herself now. *Careful lass!* said her grandmother's voice in her mind. *Mind how you go now.*

Asphodel drew herself up and assumed her haughtiest stare. No matter she was clad in shapeless gray asylum clothes, she was the proprietor of the prestigious Black Hart Hotel, and she would command their respect as such.

The highwayman's famous iron stare ignited into molten mercury. He stepped toward her and gestured at the swelling bruise on the right side of her face.

"What is this?" he demanded in terrifying tones. "Who has dared to strike *my ward*?"

The room erupted.

"About time someone disciplined the little bitch," snarled her putative guardian Dougie, rising from his chair and pointing at her.

"She is under the constraints of this hospital," interjected Master Shuttlestick. "Therefore subject to whatever disciplines are deemed necessary to subdue willful behavior." His eyes were cold and dead.

One of the warders gripped Asphodel's upper arm, and Farlan turned, saw the hand, and hit the warder flush on the chin. The warder crumpled to the floor with a load moan. The two thugs next to the master lunged forward as though to trap Farlan between them. Asphodel stepped in the path of one, who pushed her; Farlan leaped over the fallen warder, elbowed one thug in the ribs, and slammed the other in the windpipe with the side of his hand. Both staggered and tripped, scrabbling against the desk and bookcases, causing Master Shuttlestick's office paraphernalia to slip and slide underfoot and spray across the room.

Dougie fell backward in terror as Farlan advanced and overbalanced a bookcase, the books cascading everywhere, on the fallen warder and tripping the thugs.

Master Shuttlestick stood still as a statue behind his desk, his thin features a mask of fury.

Farlan pulled out a pistol and fired it in the roof.

Everyone and everything stilled in the echoing silence.

"*Your ward?*" said Asphodel.

The highwayman spoke. "Come, Miss Asphodel Quick. I am relieved to see you somewhat sound of limb and body. We are leaving this establishment." He leaned forward and tore a document from under Shuttlestick's hand, folding it and placing it in an inner pocket.

The flood of relief buckled her knees. Asphodel wanted to cry. She wanted to hug Farlan. The jaws of the trap had been sprung. She stepped closer to Farlan, allowing him to escort her from the room, still frozen in a chaotic tableau.

As they left, Dougie's voice barked, "That man—I have seen his face before…"

When would he realize? How long did they have? Dougie had seen Farlan holding the business end of a gun as the document highwayman.

The baron took her hand, and they began hurrying down the wide white corridor.

She halted. He swung around to face her. His eyes crinkled at the edges, and his lips pressed in, half amused and half exasperated. He pulled her hand a little toward him. "Why are we stopping, Miss Quick?" His voice was low but held a dangerous note.

"I cannot leave—not yet."

"What?" Farlan let the roar out.

Asphodel gripped his upper arms and looked into his lovely, dear, rescuing face and tried to make him understand. "There are two women here—probably many more—who should not be incarcerated here. We must rescue them."

"I see." To Asphodel's surprise, he sounded as though he did.

"I cannot leave without them."

Farlan's hands clenched and unclenched. His lips parted, and his black brows lowered in a glower. "My men will come for them. Right now, we must away. Before the warders come to their senses. Before your great-uncle remembers. It is only the context has him confused."

"Promise me! I cannot leave them to…to rot in this abysmal, wretched horror of a place!"

"Yes, yes." Impatient. Mercury met sapphire, bright and stubborn.

"I promise." The words were wrung from him. He

was crowding her, protecting her with his size while he sent urgent darting glances along each way of the corridor.

"Thank you," she breathed, and her voice wavered. She swallowed and summoned up a watery grin as the sound of raised voices floated once more from Master Shuttlestick's office.

An imp of mischief twitched her lips into a half smile. "Why are we dallying here, sir? Do we not have better claims on our time?"

Farlan barked a short laugh, gripped Asphodel's hand once more, and led the way at a run down the corridor. As they fled, her hand clasped firmly in Farlan's strong capable fingers, a kind of euphoria possessed her. It was almost worth getting locked up for Farlan to come and claim her so ruthlessly, so completely. They turned a sharp bend, and there ahead! A square of sky and garden beckoned through an open door. She sprang forward with a cry. Freedom! Sunshine on her face! How utterly sweet and lovely. She stilled for a moment and allowed the weak April sun to pour over her.

She turned and clasped Farlan's hands. "You don't know what this means to me. That you came!" Her words stifled in a sob. "That you risked all…" She sobered. All the risk he had taken coming here! He could be recognized and taken himself. She doubted she had the means to free him.

"Asphodel!" He leaned in, intent, burning her with his gaze. "I told you. I will *always* come. You will not suffer harm or misadventure so long as I can protect you." His lips were close, almost grazing hers. Her face tilted up of its own accord. The size and heat of his body enclosed her like a castle. He tore his face away.

"We must go." His voice gritted like gravel in the air.

He assisted her onto his huge black steed, settling her behind him, pulling her arms around him. His thighs shifted against hers as he pressed on the horse's flanks, and with a soft word in Black Bran's ear, they raced away.

Man, woman, and horse took a lower side gate at a gallop; Asphodel's heart was in her mouth, and she shut her eyes as the great horse bunched its muscles and then soared over the barrier. She laughed with dizzy glee. Even with the additional weight of Asphodel, the proud black beast leaped to a gallop and raced away down the road to freedom.

****

The red hammering need to get Miss Asphodel Quick away from that place was beginning to calm in Farlan's fevered brain. As he put miles between the Harrowlick Asylum and themselves, with as yet no sound of the chase, Farlan slowed the horse to a canter and bethought himself of his next moves.

Asphodel's body pressed against his back, reassuringly warm and pliant. Her lovely arms held tight around his waist, and her forehead rested from time to time on the middle of his back. She alternately shook and trembled, then squeezed him closer until she soothed. His own heart still bolted and hammered in his chest with reaction. Thank all the gods he had got there in time!

She needed a respite, a calm moment. To hell with his own clamoring need to see her safe, his frantic urge to gallop until sweat flew from horse and man and they were home safe.

He cast around for a resting place, somewhere away from the road and possible pursuit. There! Farlan walked the horse into a gentle clearing protected by a small grove of alder trees and enlivened by a tinkling brook.

He supported her with two hands on her slender waist as she dismounted. She treated him to a tremulous smile. Asphodel staggered on unsteady legs to the stream, bent to wash her hands and face, and then cupped her hands and took a long drink. She glanced up at him, her face gleaming with pink from the cold water, her lips shining. He swallowed and forced a smile.

"*Ward!*" said Asphodel.

A fist of anxiety squeezed Farlan's heart. Not yet. He wasn't ready for… His brain careened around seeking to manufacture explanations which had the ring of sincerity.

"What a genius conceit!" Asphodel added. Her smile was a beautiful vivid thing, like a magical caress on his hardened senses, calling him from his wanders in a harsh and lonely land, Sleeping Beauty waking the frog prince…

"I cannot help but wonder what you actually said to make Master Shuttlestick succumb to that outrageous piece of gammon, as Wragg would term it. The master is not easily swayed, I am persuaded."

Farlan's thoughts leaped and dived. *Trouble on the horizon. Danger! Tread warily.* His lips parted and then closed over one rejected response after another.

Asphodel's eyes narrowed as she examined him. "Did you show him a paper? I cannot imagine Master

Shuttlestick would call me to his office otherwise. Did you forge something? Adding forgery and trickery to your growing list of outlaw behaviors? What are the penalties for those crimes?"

She was stern now, the smile gone, changing from the girl smiling at the stream to an avenging angel calling him to account.

"I…am…" He choked on a cough, and then he chose the coward's way out. "Are you rested? We must hurry away. I will explain everything when we are returned to Blackleech Castle. Or perhaps the Black Hart Hotel. I need to decide where you will be safest. If that bladderwrack your great-uncle can remove you so easily from the Black Hart, perhaps you will be better protected remaining with me and my men—at least until we put protections in place for you."

Farlan had managed to distract her from her first dangerous topic, but he still had to bear the brunt of her ire.

Her eyes flashed like blue lightning. She fisted her hands on her hips. "I am the proprietor of the Black Hart Hotel, now and once I have my majority. If I give it up so easily now, do you not think some *man* will decide I am not fit to govern the hotel?" When she said *man*, her tone could have withered that fine ash tree overhanging the stream. "I will be harder to dislodge actually in command of the place. Do you not agree?"

"Yes, tactically that is a fine decision. But I fear for your safety. Your great-uncle is bent on taking ownership however he may. As you have seen, he will stoop to any means he can. I remind you he has powerful friends."

"Pooh! That dumpling will not take what is mine,

especially now I am alert to his knavery. At the hotel, I am protected by being on my own ground, with the shade and spirit of my grandmother to strengthen me when I need it. You must know yourself the strength of being in your own place, where your generational roots go deep."

"I hope to have that luxury—one day soon." He hesitated. "Your uncle stole you away from the Black Hart once already."

Sapphire fire blazed at him. He inhaled. *Magnificent.* Lust pulsed hard in his groin.

Her plush lips trembled. "He will not do so again. I will employ more sturdy moors men; the hotel will be barred to Dougie and his friends…I will prepare hiding places, escape routes…" The words tumbled out, faster and fiercer as terror thickened in her tones.

Farlan stroked her hair until she soothed. "Come now. Are you rested? We must depart from here and make for Blackleech Castle, at least to begin."

"I will not spend a night there, however."

"As you wish, my lady." Farlan gazed at Asphodel, and his heart flip-flopped in his chest. His famous control of himself was slipping. Desire melted him, but also a kind of gallantry drove him hard. He would lay himself at her feet.

He lingered, studying her vivid blue eyes, her sweet round rosy cheeks, her plump lips, her fine flexible form, and the strength in her womanly limbs. He drank her in, her strength, her humor, her zest for life and fierce determination to hold what was hers. And then, because she needed him strong and tough, she needed the warrior and survivor that made the greater part of him, he pulled himself together and

177

pushed all that softness deep within.

"Come," he said. He assisted her back onto Black Bran, settled her rounded arms around him once again, and they trotted to a small track he knew led from the clearing over wild country.

Before he urged Bran to a canter—a pace the great black horse could maintain for miles—Farlan said to her, "I will keep you safe, whether you will or no."

He shifted his weight, murmured to Bran, and the horse leaped forward and away.

Chapter Thirteen

March 1881—Blackleech Castle

Farlan lit a fire and heated water for Asphodel to bathe. He tugged the large copper bath close to the fire in the big old morning parlor, filled the tub, proffered plain soap and clean towels, and left her.

He paced the kitchen; he could not settle. What to tell her? She would be furious with him. A part of him recoiled, but another less-reputable part—the larger part of him, he thought ruefully—wanted to see her fired up, red-cheeked and full of spirit, red-gold hair cascading around her like a golden dawn, arms out and words pouring from her in a torrent that lashed his unworthy hide.

His imaginings made it difficult to sit. Indeed, he must stop, or he would not be fit company for a gently bred woman, should she cast her eyes to the front of his trousers, becoming more pronounced with each vision.

Food. Cook something for her to eat. Warming drink of tea. Farlan busied himself with these small tasks. Jack and McEvoy appeared in the doorway and made their rude presences felt. Jack lounged in a chair and put his feet on the table.

"Get your clodhoppers off! I've just cleaned that!"

McEvoy grabbed a cloth and tidied up after Jack. "Why so grand, Baron Blackitter?"

"We have company," Farlan gritted. "Mind your manners and your language, if you please."

"Oh ho! There's a grab! The baron vanishes and returns a flash man. Gentle company of the female persuasion, if I'm not mistook!"

"How delightful," drawled Gentleman Jack. "It is past time that you practiced polite manners, Baron."

"What's got into you two?" Farlan asked, laughing. "You are very pompous of a sudden?"

"Might be the sudden uptake of lordly airs," McEvoy retorted. "You are in a scrape, and you charge away, full throttle, without letting your team know anything aboot it."

At that moment, a vision hesitated in the hall doorway: a dewy, rosy, and smiling Asphodel, with clouds of garnet hair escaping in curling tendrils from a loose, braided crown on top of her head. Her clean garments adhered to her damp body in the most alluring way.

Men's garments. The military tailoring suited her. And her freshly defined form summoned reprehensible, wicked imaginings from Farlan's stunned brain.

McEvoy gaped. Gentleman Jack leaped to his feet and performed a graceful bow that would not disgrace a prince. Farlan swallowed. Gestured to a comfortable couch pulled up to the fire.

"My men were just leaving," he said in a firm voice.

"Actually I thought I might pertake of a lovely cup of tea," responded McEvoy in a mincing tone. Farlan glared at him.

"It is delightful to be able to entertain feminine company," purred Jack. "I yearn for a civilizing influence on these two, but I am afraid they are both a lost cause. I will do my humble best to entertain a lady."

"Miss Quick does not want to see that simpering smirk plastered all over your ugly face, Jack Darnley," said Farlan. "In case you falsely believe that that horrible grimace is an endearing expression."

"Miss Quick is quite able to speak for herself," retorted Asphodel with some spirit. "And I am most charmed. How do you do, sir?"

Farlan simmered.

Jack lifted her hand and bent over it. Asphodel blushed and looked up at Jack, then over to Farlan with raised brows, her vivid sapphire eyes sparkling with questions.

McEvoy spat on his hand, rubbed it on his less than salubrious breeches, and made to offer it to Asphodel. To Farlan's surprise—and secret approval—Asphodel took McEvoy's hand gravely and said, "How do you do?"

Asphodel sat in the chair near the fire and smiled, filling the room with her particular sunshine. "Lord Blackitter was just about to describe how he managed to remove me from a…dreadful place."

His men both wore extremely foolish expressions; he suddenly wondered if that was how he appeared whenever he was in Asphodel's presence. He schooled his features to the steely expression of a man who had survived wars and the wild colonial goldfields. The kind of man she needed.

Asphodel's laugh rippled through the room. "Your lord frowns like the very image of a black-hearted evil baron."

"Aye, that he is, ma'am," McEvoy at once responded. "We live in terror of the man."

Farlan snorted. Jack grinned.

"Perhaps he suffers from indigestion?" Asphodel enquired, with a quirk of that delicious rosy mouth. Farlan let out a breath. "Or perhaps…" She looked at each of his men, a merry twinkle making her eyes sparkle. "…he is in pain. He punched a large thug equipped with a truncheon and chopped another in the neck. To rescue me."

She looked at him, glowing, and he went weak at the knees. "He did this to save me," she said, and her voice gentled, a sweet caress, so redolent with strong emotion that for a moment Farlan was stricken speechless.

And then, when he was soft, and defenseless, and unprepared, she struck her blow.

"*Ward*," she said. "Why on earth did the master believe I am your ward?"

The room rang with silence. His men looked between them. They knew nothing of this, but all their well-honed instincts for survival fully activated. McEvoy and Jack melted toward the exit door and the freedom of the yard.

Cowards.

"Wait!" she cried. McEvoy and Jack jammed in the doorway in a comedy of tangled legs, arms, and muscled torsos. "Come back, please!"

Farlan's instincts gave a sudden pulse of danger. The no-nonsense tone in her sweet voice augured a coming trial, with him the hapless victim.

Jack and McEvoy lurked just within the shadow of the doorway. Gentleman Jack's wicked eyes gleamed with mirth. Farlan could see he was considering how to make it all worse, whatever she was planning.

Asphodel regarded Farlan through long dusky lashes. "Your promise," she said silkily. The damn promise. How could he have forgotten?

Gentleman Jack took a pace into the room. "My Lord Blackitter here is a man of his word. He has made you a promise, has he?"

"Jack…" Farlan warned. "Now is not the time to make mischief. Miss Quick's safety may depend on it."

Asphodel said, "Lord Blackitter somehow sprang me from a most uncomfortable trap, and I am deeply thankful. However, much as I desperately desired to tear myself from that hellish, nightmarish…" She halted. Farlan watched her inhale a sharp breath, manifestly trying to still the shaking that possessed her limbs. All his protective instincts rose.

"No!" he growled. He strode forward and put a hand, as gently as he could, on her still-damp hair, on the back of her neck. Did he mistake, or did she press her neck back into his hand?

"McEvoy! Bring the lady a cup of tea. The best china!" McEvoy sprang to do his bidding, his willingness more of a sign of allegiance to Asphodel than any habit of obedience, which was generally sadly lacking.

Gentleman Jack sauntered fully into the room and sat at the wooden kitchen table. "I do not wish to create more distress. However, I would hear more of this promise," he said.

Farlan made daggers of his glare, but Jack only laughed.

Asphodel took a sip of the tea McEvoy handed her,

and it did seem to calm and center her—perhaps as had his hand on her neck. He watched in fascination as her plump lips wrapped the edge of the delicate cup. A lightning shudder jolted through him.

She said, "There are many women in…that place…who do not deserve to be there."

"Forgive me," said Farlan. "But surely your acquaintance was of the briefest? I understand lunatics may sometime seem as sane as you or I."

"Lunatics!" exclaimed Gentleman Jack. "The baron sprang you from *an asylum*?"

He looked questioningly at Farlan, who spared him a short nod. "Incarcerated by her putative guardian who desires her considerable property. He is in some haste—he wishes to anticipate the imminent Married Women's Property Act by forcing Miss Quick to a marriage."

"Jacketing a mollisher. That's scurvy lay," contributed McEvoy sagely.

Jack said to the air, "A veritable miracle to secure her release. How on earth did you—?"

Asphodel put down her cup and rose. She was clearly too excited to remain sitting. "The inmates—my point exactly! If the Wicked Baron here"—her smile danced with mischief—"had not broken me free in the most exciting and dramatic manner!" Now she did smile widely, her sunny expression lighting up her face, the entire room, his own shriveled, broken, black heart…

She sobered. "Then I too would be still one of those unfortunate women, damned as 'hysterical' or other malignant term. Do you see?"

"How would one tell the difference?" Jack asked

cautiously.

"Well, I do not know. But two women—friends—in there, who supported me in that nightmare, do not deserve to be there. I wanted to take them when we left. Instead, Lord Blackitter has promised to go back and rescue them."

McEvoy broke into Gaelic cursing, fluent and expressive and full of guttural "rrr"s which effectively conveyed his opinion on the matter.

Gentleman Jack burst out with one sharp bark of laughter, which ceased abruptly when Asphodel said, "I will come with you."

"No," said Farlan. He was indeed a man of his word, and certainly he would rescue those women if she asked him to, but she was not going anywhere near the place, or any other danger he could keep her from. What use was his tarnished past if he could not use it in her service?

Asphodel described her friends.

"A spangle-rumpus and a bobtail!" interjected McEvoy.

Asphodel blinked at him.

"Which means," said Farlan, walking to the table and taking a seat, which gave him a better view of the luscious Asphodel, still rosy and damp and casting such a spell over his senses that he struggled to formulate a coherent plan, "that Jack and I—or perhaps Jack and yourself, McEvoy—may be able to bowl right up to the Harrowlick Asylum and demand their release into our keeping. Perhaps they are there for vagrancy, especially the woman Evie Lovelace. The bobtail."

McEvoy grinned. "They'll bang you in irons for pimping, if you say she is yours."

"The solution is clear," Asphodel announced crisply.

All the men turned to her and waited. It was clear she was accustomed to command; it came so naturally, Farlan thought. Mistress of herself too.

"Lord Blackitter shall explain how he was able to convince them to release me. We will employ the same ruse to release them too, but into my care at the Black Hart. I will give them work there."

His face likely mirrored his men's appalled grimaces. Both McEvoy's and Jack's eyebrows shot into their hairlines, and their mouths clamped shut as they manifestly struggled to decide which objection to raise first.

"Ye canna have a blowsy bobtail at your hotel," McEvoy explained. "No canny mollisher would come, and she'd put the clamp on her man, neither. Your business will be nibb'd."

Asphodel sorted her way through this mysterious speech. "No respectable woman would come, or permit her husband to attend my hotel? That is my concern. Now, Lord Blackitter? If you would be so kind?"

Farlan studied her. He had to explain. He dreaded those sparkling eyes turning flinty furious. He dreaded her marching out in a temper. There would be little he could do.

"Haven't you men got work outside somewhere?" he gritted, never taking his gaze from Asphodel.

McEvoy muttered an oath. Jack sniggered. The doorway darkened.

And then he and Asphodel faced each other across the hearth.

****

Asphodel waited. A dark suspicion curled in her mind. Farlan avoided her gaze and drew his brows together as he prepared his disclosure. Clearly, everything in him rebelled at the notion. What could this great secret be?

Farlan paced around the room. He disappeared through a doorway which led to a stairway. Asphodel's curiosity—and temper—mounted.

Farlan returned with a soft blanket, which he carefully placed around her. He made more tea and, this time, produced a bottle of whisky from inside a vase on the mantelpiece and poured a slug into her tea. She took a sip and enjoyed the burn of the whisky sliding down her throat.

"I suspect your grandmother, Isabella McDonnell, and my grandfather, the third Baron Blackitter, were lovers. Does that shock you?"

Asphodel jumped. She should have expected plain speaking, once he had made the decision to speak. It was true to his character.

"Oh! I…er…I had not…" She performed some rapid mental calculations. "She loved my grandfather dearly, but he did die many years before her." Her cheeks heated. Farlan stared at her, so intently, his iron gaze burning her, asking, demanding…what? She swallowed.

"Go on," she whispered. She needed time to gain some control over spiraling thoughts, emotions escaping and running loose like a flock of black-faced sheep.

"Either she took a great gamble or somehow she heard I had returned, I know not how. Her information sources must have been impeccable!" He took a chair and pulled it up in front of her. Their knees were almost—not quite—touching. He leaned forward and poured another slug of whisky into her cup.

"Don't try to distract me with another story, fascinating and intriguing as it may be!" She smiled, unable to resist him. He loomed so large, *so safe*, so wild and beautiful in the flickering firelight in the half-dark kitchen. The severe planes of his face and his slashing brows shouted *male*!

A coil of sensation stirred within her. A tendril of desire flamed into hunger. With his proximity, his scent enclosed her. Heather and lemon, clean man, a tang of fresh sweat from their daring ride.

His hands, crisscrossed with old white scars, rested on his knees. He flexed his fingers. Reached out and touched the back of her hand. His were so large, so capable, calm and strong. Just looking at them made her feel safer, feel as though she wasn't quite alone in the world. When he touched her, a pulse of energy somersaulted inside her.

He said, low voiced, the deep resonance thrilling her skin and tickling at the apex of her thighs, "I believe, as she grew ill, your grandmother needed someone to trust, apart from yourself. To hold secrets for her. To hold secure the two things she treasured most in the whole world—her granddaughter and her hotel."

"What are you saying?" Asphodel whispered. The whisky had smoothed the pricks of anxiety and recent terror. His deep voice, his masculine presence, the unfolding tale held her spellbound.

"You saw me that night, Asphodel Quick."

"The night Isabella lay dying. The dark-garbed

stranger. *You*?" Of course it was him. That silver gleam of eyes in candlelight. That tall presence, filling the tower room. "What did she say to you?"

"She made me promise, for the love she bore my grandfather, that I would protect you. With my life, if necessary."

Asphodel managed a shaky laugh. "And here I thought it was for my strawberry-gold hair."

Farlan made a growling sound in his throat.

She waited, but he didn't elaborate. "You made a promise to a dying old woman you didn't know, about a young woman you had never met? Madness!"

"My grandfather loved your grandmother," he said. "I believe there was some ancient tragedy and misunderstanding, with each of them marrying the wrong person. Yes, I know your grandmother loved your grandfather Donal McDonnell, in her way. But her lifelong passion burned for my grandfather. It was only in their later years they could…"

Asphodel blinked, her eyes almost starting from her head. This was a whole new Isabella indeed! "How do you know this?" she asked sharply. "Are these the fancies and wanderings of your grandfather in his dotage? Your own giddy imaginings?"

Farlan took her hand. "She told me that night," he said simply.

Asphodel reeled with shock. Her world shifted. She hardly heard what Farlan said next through the clamor in her mind.

Then his words penetrated her mental storm. "I must be grateful that they did not manage to marry."

"Why?" asked Asphodel dazedly.

"Because then you would be my close relative

instead of a beautiful stranger."

A moment's thought had Asphodel orienting herself again. "Are you telling me this simply to distract me again?" she demanded.

Farlan laughed, the bitter note evident once more. "I am explaining why she gave me such trust. Why she chose me. She was an extremely clever woman, your grandmother."

"And? I await your revelation. Except I have a dark suspicion…"

Farlan stood and rested his forehead on the mantel. He kicked a log on the edge of the fire with his boot. "I am your legal guardian," he said.

Chapter Fourteen

March 1881—Blackleech Castle

The expected stormfront hit.

Farlan turned to face Asphodel as she threw off the blanket he had so carefully tucked in around her and leaped to her feet, facing him down. Her eyes sparked jagged blue lightning. Her cheeks glowed; even her plush lips blushed. She fisted her hands on her hips. Even her marvelous chrysoberyl hair—which he did love, desperately, despite his inability to say so a few minutes earlier—seemed to crackle with furious golden energy.

"*Another* guardian!" she spat. "Truly, I have a surfeit of guardians when I need none. And you..." She visibly struggled for the right epithet. "Craven, disingenuous, *lying* to me!"

"There is no possible excuse," he responded. "I know it. Perhaps I wanted you to know me for myself, first." He stood straight, staring down at her while she lashed him with her scorn.

"Pathetic!" she ripped back. "You proclaim all these things, you care for me, you protect me with your life, and yet you allowed that parasite Dougie to paw me and slobber over me with his objectionable slimy lips..."

Fury and jealously ignited in Farlan's chest, in his

brain, *in his loins*.

"You did not tell me this!" he hissed.

"Why should I, pray? Tell my troubles to a random highwayman whose only action to protect me from a monster was to steal the symbol of that bargain, my engagement ring?"

He paced for a few moments, but the restless movement did not relieve his urge to action. *Any* action.

"And besides, you saw. You saw him in my room. You must have known what he was capable of."

Farlan sat down and plunged his head in his hands. It was truth. He had failed her.

"But I am not concerned about that. I can look after myself."

Farlan jerked up and stared at her in disbelief. How could she think that, after all her recent experiences?

Asphodel hissed, "You lied to me, by omission at least. I—stupidly—believed we were friends. I was—" She cut herself off. Her eyes glistened with unshed tears. Her chin came up, proud and fierce.

What Farlan would have given to hear her complete the sentence!

Asphodel drew up herself up and cloaked herself with what dignity she could muster. Pain lanced through her; her mind sang with turmoil, a buzzing sound rang in her ears, her stomach rose and crashed as though she was falling from the cliffs at Ravenscar Beach.

All she wanted was to flee, to escape this man, this friend, whom she had begun to harbor such warm feelings for…

Men! They were all deceivers. She could not trust anyone, could not rely on anyone. She only had herself.

And she was strong! She would survive.

She should return to her hotel, in any case. What was she thinking, dallying here? Allowing herself to feel those softer emotions…to imagine…

"I thank you for your timely rescue," she said stiffly, grinding the words out as though they were sharp-edged chunks of rock.

Farlan still had his head in his hands. He said nothing. His whole body, held stiff, leaning against the mantel, emanated a wall of defense.

She waited.

And then she left.

Asphodel set a fast pace, striding back to her hotel, her thoughts and emotions as frenetic and changeable as the mad dance of spring lapwings. She could not settle. There were so many different ways she could think of what Farlan had told her.

Her steps slowed. Halted. The man had saved her. Protected her. Risked his own neck to release her from that hell. A guardian indeed, like a strong protector from her grandmother's old mythic tales.

Asphodel took three steps back toward Blackleech Castle. Hesitated. Turned.

Four steps toward the Black Hart Hotel. Stopped.

Swiveled and faced back toward Blackleech Castle. Were there three horsemen springing away to the west? She scrunched up her eyes as she squinted into the distance.

This was ridiculous. "Pull yourself together, lass," she said in her grandmother's voice, managed to laugh at herself, and set out with a brisk pace to discover what had gone on in her absence in her business. *Her* hotel.

Why was she so furious with Baron Blackitter?

Because he didn't tell her he was her legal guardian, when he had known all this time?

Because he hadn't saved her from Dougie earlier, when he could have?

Because by coming into the light and claiming her, he risked his own safety, liberty, and inheritance? And what was the mystery there?

Because she had feelings for him, growing rampant within her?

Asphodel picked up the pace, hoping to press down anything to do with Farlan. Back to business.

****

Iain greeted her at the door with imperturbable Scots calm. His eyes betrayed no more than a flicker at her men's garb. "Welcome back, Miss Asphodel," he said in his best welcoming burr. "Not before time too," he added in gritty tones.

"Oh?"

"Himself is lording it over the place," he said. "I better come with ye beyond."

"No, I will be fine, thank you. I may need you in a little while—I'll call."

Asphodel headed to the tower staircase. The old hotel enfolded her in its beloved embrace; after the terrors of the asylum, joy danced in her skin as she paced through the fine outer hall, with its paintings and flowers, and tripped lightly up the tower stairs. *Mine. This is my life, my destiny, my work, my legacy. Dougie shall not have it.*

She trailed a finger along the stone walls of the tower stair, loving its familiar cold stone. How many times had she done just this, child to woman? This was her place.

When she reached her grandmother's room at the top, the shock nearly sent her toppling back down the stairs.

The door was propped ajar.

The room had been destroyed.

Furniture lay around the room like flotsam after a storm. Her washstand was tipped over, a pool of soap-scummy water flooding out from the broken china jug. Books spilled everywhere, spines open, pages torn. Her clothes lay in untidy mounds across the floor, a coat lying dismally in the pool of water. The blankets and pillows from her bed were scattered over the heaps of clothes and books. Pictures had been flung off the walls, one pastoral scene slashed with a knife, the handle still protruding from the painting.

The bed, her grandmother's bed.

The entire top had been sawn away and smashed with the hammer which lay on the floor before the splinters and pieces of bedhead.

The secret hiding place, which had kept the papers and documents hidden for untold years, was exposed.

The papers were gone.

How had they known? *How?*

Asphodel stood, swaying, hand on her erratically beating heart, gasping for air. The shock and despair might kill her this time.

Her fingers, splayed on her chest, clutched a military button. Farlan! No one must know. She seized a gown, miraculously undamaged, from the gaping cupboard. With swift hands, she stripped off her men's clothes, donned fresh underthings pulled from a tangled heap, and tugged on the gown. She shoved the borrowed uniform behind the cupboard.

"I told him."

Asphodel swiveled abruptly. "Maeve! I'm so glad to see you! What on earth happened here?"

"I told Dougie McDonnell what I saw that night."

Asphodel reached for a support. She picked up the fallen desk chair and folded into it, her body heavy and her muscles refusing to work properly. "What, Maeve?" she whispered.

"The papers. I told him about the papers." The girl preened. She twisted her face into a horrible simper and flashed one of Isabella's bracelets. "Dougie fancies me. Says I deserve to have fine things and be raised above my station. We are to be wed."

Her words hit Asphodel like blows. They made shapes in her mind but yielded no sense at all.

Asphodel gasped, her throat thick and scratchy, "You saw me with the papers that night? *And you told Dougie McDonnell*? Oh, Maeve, what you done? He won't marry you, you know."

The barmaid's expression turned mulish. "He says I have the face of a fine woman and should have the chance to wear fine clothes, and dainty shoes, and have me own little cottage…"

"Dougie will never be happy in 'a little cottage.' How could you, Maeve?" A horrifying image flashed in her mind. "How can you stand him pawing you? You haven't permitted him to…touch you?" Asphodel stared as the maid blushed and tossed her head. "You are under my protection while you work here. I cannot allow Dougie to take such advantage of you!"

"We are to be wed," she repeated stubbornly.

"I very much doubt it," Asphodel retorted. "Go on then. Get out of my sight." She looked up. A pang smote her. In a way, she couldn't blame Maeve, although she was utterly furious with her. That perfidious creature Dougie was at the root of this problem. "I do not mean that you must leave my employ immediately. Just go somewhere I can't see you. I'm that angry with you."

Maeve smirked. "It doesn't matter what you think, *Asphodel*. You'll be calling me Aunt McDonnell soon enough. And you'll show me respect for a change." The girl sneered and flounced away.

Asphodel was left to survey the visible wrecking of her hopes, her secrets, and possibly any hope of Farlan being able to claim his freedom and his rights.

Why hadn't she told Farlan about the papers she had seen? Was she keeping it as a special surprise? Why hadn't she told him about the papers she had glimpsed when he confessed to being her guardian?

He had every right to be angry with her, as she had been with him. Angrier. They were no doubt the papers he so assiduously sought.

And she had stupidly let them be stolen and probably even destroyed by that monster, Dougie.

What a fool she was.

Why did she ever think she could manage all this alone?

And soon, it all became even worse.

A familiar, dreadful shape filled the doorway. Her great-uncle Douglas McDonnell—Dougie—watched her, his face twisted in a terrible sneer, his baby mouth screwed up in a pout.

"Ruthlessness runs in our veins," he said. "Your grandmother was entirely composed of steel. You have it in unequal share for such a young woman. But you forget—McDonnell blood has its share of ruthlessness too." He heaved himself from the doorway and stepped into her bedroom.

Asphodel stood straight and proud amidst the overturned furniture, the spilt water, the torn and tangled clothes, the wooden splinters and shards from the smashed bedhead all around her like tears. Ice clawed at her throat. All her senses snapped, tense and alert.

He said, voice as poisonous and sibilant as a snake, "You bested me at the asylum. I give you that. This works better for me in any case."

Asphodel stayed ramrod straight as Dougie put a fat finger under her chin and flicked the skin so it stung like a little bee sting. She flinched and glared at him.

He said, hissing his words, "I recognized that hero who barged in so noisily and took you. A certain highwayman has been haunting these parts. My friend the magistrate has offered a large reward for information pertaining to his capture."

Dougie let his hand travel down to her collarbone. Asphodel shifted her stance, ready to do damage. She wanted to hear what he had to say first, though, if possible. She needed to know the worst.

And she was sure, his worst would be very, very bad indeed.

"I hold interesting papers regarding Farlan Blackitter, the man who took you from where I put you, *for your own safety*!" Dougie shouted this last and raised his fist, but Asphodel nimbly sidestepped the heavy blow and watched in some satisfaction as he almost overbalanced amongst the rubble and ruin of her room.

Dougie screamed, "I hold Blackitter's life in the palm of my hand!"

Asphodel gritted her teeth. "And so?"

Dougie came close and leered at her. He tried again to touch her, but Asphodel smacked his hand away. "Say what you have come to say and stop malingering and maundering like a winnow in a wind. Speak, man!"

"You have a choice before you, Asphodel Quick," Dougie said triumphantly. "Marry me, and I will not bring down the magistrate on the highwayman!"

Asphodel pressed her lips together lest what she wanted to say somehow squeezed itself out. She stared at him, and an imp of rebellion took her. "Where is your darling intended wife?" she asked sweetly. "The lovely Maeve?"

Dougie snorted. "That little trollop. Why would I want her when I can have quality?"

"You have given her the strong impression that you have asked her to marry you. She regards herself as affianced to you."

"As we know, duckling, these matters of fiancées shift around from day to day."

Asphodel's cheekbones heated. "It's not the same."

Suddenly, to Asphodel's great mortification, Dougie creaked down onto one knee. "*You* are my little moors flower," he said.

"Dougie! Get up!" Asphodel said urgently from between clenched teeth.

"I have always loved you. Always wanted you. I know this is the only way I can have you. I don't care." Dougie's pale watery eyes pleaded.

A pang shot through her, a kind of frisson of sympathy. She thought of Maeve, and the asylum, and a cold hand replaced the little warmth his speech had created.

"You tried to take my liberty—my very sanity!" she retorted. "How you could ever, *ever* think I would consent to marry you after that!"

Dougie grunted as he heaved himself to standing once more, pulling himself up on the legs of a collapsed chair. Asphodel prayed that the chair would tumble again and take Dougie with it, but it did not oblige her.

She strode to the door and held it farther open. "I will never marry you."

Dougie's lips thinned, and his eyes went squinty and mean. His fat lips turned down at the edges, and his jowls wobbled. A rush of color purpled his face. "If you refuse marriage, then you will deed this hotel over to me in exchange for your paramour's freedom." His voice was thunder, or maybe that was just the noise hammering in Asphodel's temples, in her ears.

"You utter villain!"

Dougie's mouth twisted again. "Just a reasonable man, asking you to be sensible. You have forty-eight hours to give me your answer."

Asphodel's hands clenched and squeezed as she watched his departure, listened to his stamp and heavy breathing as he negotiated the steep stone stairs.

She raised her fists to her face.

What could she do? Never had she floundered in such despair, perhaps not even at the asylum, when all hope and liberty had seemed lost.

A terrible choice loomed before her.

She could marry Dougie—that way she would keep the hotel, in a way. She would be here. Under the law, it would be his. She shuddered in strong revulsion.

Everything in her revolted. No.

An idea: Could she marry Dougie and refuse to consummate the marriage? Get it annulled later? This would provide time to find the papers.

Or she must sign over the hotel in exchange for Farlan's freedom. Her heart squeezed. She could barely conceive of the idea, let alone countenance it. Her grandmother's legacy, her life's work. Asphodel's own passion for the business. Never!

But could she trust Dougie to keep his word not to have the highwayman arrested? No, and *no*.

There *must* be another way.

She must somehow steal the documents back—if Dougie hadn't already destroyed them.

And then a most unlikely ally put her miserable, tear-stained face in the doorway.

"Maeve!"

Maeve's face was streaked with grimy tears running tracks unheeded down her cheeks. The girl burst into violent sobbing. "I heard what Dougie said. I hid around the stairs, and I listened."

In amongst screams and wails and loud sobs, Asphodel distinguished broken words and phrases including, "But what if I am with child?" and "The great lummox," and "I'm a fool!"

Maeve eventually quietened. Her face hardened. "I'll get them back for you, miss. The papers."

"You have given me little reason to trust you."

"You've never made a fool of me, miss. Not like that great mimsy nob-pitcher, your great-uncle Dougie McDonnell."

Asphodel hesitated. "He is a vengeful, dangerous man as well as a lustful one. Do not imperil yourself.

He has risked more than I thought he could recover from, and yet retains his status as a gentleman. I wish you would leave things well alone, Maeve. I will come about."

"I'm best placed to get the papers for you, miss. He won't suspect a thing. You'll see, miss. I'll have my revenge on that great lobcock."

Asphodel watched her go, a curl of worried premonition threading through her own panic. "Be careful, Maeve," she whispered. "Do not underrate his cunning. Nor his ruthlessness in getting what he wants."

But she spoke to the empty air.

I should have just asked her to clean my room. That would have been adequate recompense. After all, it was likely Maeve who caused a generous amount of the damage.

Then she forgot the barmaid and turned her mind to pondering her predicament, her thoughts twisting and turning like a trapped eel, not able to secure a purchase on any plan.

This was her room, her sanctuary. They could try to destroy it, but she would restore it, every time. They would have to burn the whole place to the ground—and even then, she would find a way to rebuild, stone by stone.

Such determination firing in her core cheered her. She summoned Maggie and Malcolm to assist her and began the weary work of putting the room to rights.

Chapter Fifteen

April 1881—Blackleech Castle, two days later

Rose Robin lurked in the stables with McEvoy.
The glorious, brilliantly colored, full-bodied spectacle
that was Evie Lovelace amused herself by entrancing
Gentleman Jack, tangling up his wit and his tongue as
they flirted and bantered by the fire.

Now that Farlan had kept his solemn promise to
Asphodel Quick to rescue her chance-met friends—
employing large bribes and hard fists—what on earth
was he to do with the women? They were not good for
his men.

Evie Lovelace sensed his stare. She tore her
melting brown eyes from Gentleman's Jack's adoring
and sheep-like face and raked Farlan from head to toe
with her wicked gaze.

"Come and join us, Baron Blackitter. The fire is
warm, and the witticisms are warmer!"

He shook his head. "I am content to see you free,
safe, and enjoying yourself, honing your impressive
talents on my poor companion Jack Darnley."

The courtesan shrugged one shoulder high, blinked
her thick black eyelashes at Farlan as she smiled
alluringly, and shook her curves into place, a maneuver
which made Jack's eyes widen and intensified his
lovestruck expression.

Evie hitched a hip, paused theatrically, and undulated toward Farlan, the half smile on her face flirting in and out.

"Why so solemn, my baron?" she crooned, the husk in her voice giving a delightful rasp to her honeyed tones.

Farlan looked at Evie and then Jack. "By my calculations, we are almost out of time."

She gave him a slow, seductive blink, but Farlan saw the gleam of intelligence in her soft brown eyes. It accorded with his ideas of Asphodel that she chose friends by their intelligence and character, their courage and heart, rather than their station in life.

Farlan elaborated. "I have a notion—indeed I am quite sure—that Asphodel's great-uncle will waste no time holding my nefarious ways over her head, in order to extort some untenable promise from Asphodel."

"Like what?" The hard edge in Evie's tone could have winded a mountebank.

"He tried to trick her into marrying him after her grandmother died, then attempted to force her into wedlock, to secure ownership of the Black Hart Hotel."

"Disgraceful!" pronounced Evie, with an ironic smirk. "I enjoyed saying that. I rarely get to say that about anyone else."

Farlan added, "Dougie wants Asphodel, into the bargain. He is obsessed with possessing her." He regarded Evie. She didn't need weasel words. "Sexually. He wants her body."

"Does he now?" Evie drawled, assessing Farlan under her lashes. "So why are you idling here, my lord?" Her tone had turned dangerous. Good. He liked to think Asphodel had hazardous friends.

He ignored her question—it was one he had been asking himself for the last hour, tossing up what was best, what would render Asphodel the most assistance. "I think that if Dougie extorts a pledge from Miss Quick—Asphodel—he will immediately break his part of the bargain and bring the magistrate and a posse of men here, to arrest me and my men."

Evie cocked her head and made her mouth into a luscious *O*. Jack drifted to Evie and Farlan, as though on a string. His eyes hungered, fastened on her lips.

Farlan continued, "I have been debating what to do with you women, so that my men and I can fade into the hills while I arrange my circumstances."

"Ooh, why did you not say so? That is simply too easy." Evie laughed, a delightful trill, which conjured images of fingers lightly scaling along a flute—or something. Farlan raised his brows and set his lips. He was in no mood for games.

"It's so simple! Rose Robin shall take you three men to stay with her Romani wife and her companions. You will effectively disappear."

"And you?"

"I, my darlings"—in this sweeping endearment, she generously included the seriously addled Jack, who promptly fell to his knees and kissed her fingers—"I shall proceed to the famous Black Hart Hotel, and I shall seduce this monster of depravity, this great-uncle, and bend him to my will."

Farlan choked.

"You do not think my plan will work?" she enquired, fake-artlessly, eyes bright and naive.

"It's brilliant!" a voice interjected from the doorway—and there stood Asphodel, well and hale, laughing and applauding. "Except I will not permit you to do such a thing. You must not sacrifice yourself so, my dear Evie." Asphodel bounced into the room. Evie ran toward her, and the two women embraced heartily.

"And you," said Asphodel to Farlan. "How very pleased I am. How utterly heroic of you to return to that den of misery and rescue my friends!" The glow in her face, the shine in her eyes—he could feast on it, wallow in it. It was the kind of glow which transformed a man, made him veer onto a different path, a better path, just to engender that fulsome expression once more.

"I only did it so you would look at me precisely with that admiring gleam in your beautiful eyes," he admitted. He held her gaze, pinned it. "I grow mawkish!" he growled.

"Oooooh!" said Evie. "A pretty compliment from so manly a baron. Did that hurt, my sweeting, to utter such a mild compliment? You must practice, dear one, and then such phrases will roll more readily from your heroic tongue. A man of action, rather than soft words... Although that fierce blaze igniting now in your infamous iron stare... Oh, Asphodel, I do envy you!"

Asphodel was laughing, damn her. "I love your schemes," she said to Evie. "But nobody will be hiding away with the Romani, unless of course, that is their preference. It does sound both very enticing and adventurous, but also perhaps uncomfortable?" She shot a mischievous look at Farlan. "Although I believe you would have myriad opportunities to study and perfect a lovely dark glower. Perhaps you should go, Baron?"

Farlan struggled to smooth his expression, not

frowning nor glowering, to soften his lips instead of pressing them together. By the women's laughter, he had signally failed.

He was not used to being teased so cleverly by two charming women. He was more accustomed to simpers and flattery, even in what passed as high society on the goldfields. He stuttered, tongue-tied and helpless; more fool him.

He resorted to masculine pride. "Shall I arrange the disappearance of your great-uncle?" he offered, once he had regained a semblance of self-possession.

Evie visibly thrilled with exaggerated delight. Asphodel regarded him steadily with a cold blue stare. "N-no," she answered. "Dougie says he loves me. Says he has always loved me. That he can't help wanting me. There may be the tiniest grain of truth in that."

"Oh, my darling, you are too susceptible to believing the best in worthless people! I must inspect this dreadful beast for myself, and I promise, I will tell you what sort of man he is."

Farlan answered shortly, "A liar and a man who happily takes advantage of a grieving girl. A greedy man. A man who has committed more crimes than I, far worse crimes—I only take the odd document—and yet because his crimes are sanctioned by the law, he walks free."

Evie stretched out a graceful hand and splayed it across Farlan's chest. "Quite a speech, my sweet."

"I would prefer you to return to tormenting Jack here, if you please."

"Are you sure? I offer a nice line in torment."

Surprisingly, Asphodel supported him. "Yes, Evie, do stop teasing poor Farlan. You are scrambling his brains, and I need him thinking with his head."

Farlan shot her a look, which she met with a limpid, blue-eyed stare.

Jack said, "Yes, Miss Lovelace, please do resume your most exquisite torture. I happily volunteer my services as victim."

"Volunteer! That's what you said on the Victorian Goldfields, and we ended up fighting for the English in New Zealand for three years," Farlan responded, glad he was no longer the target of their mirth.

"Ah! A brave soldier. Tell me more," Evie murmured and, crooking a beckoning finger, drifted back to the fire, Jack following meekly after her like a man bespelled.

Farlan regarded Asphodel's round rosy cheeks, flushed with mirth and the pleasure of discovering her friends were rescued. Her sapphire eyes danced and sparkled like sun on water. Her curves were more subdued than Evie's, more laced in, more covered and compressed, but what he wouldn't give to see her shake them into place as her friend had just done.

His groin shifted at the thought. He cleared his throat and forced his dazzled brain to think of plans, rather than Asphodel's glowing beauty.

"Are you safe, at the hotel?" he asked her. He placed a curved hand on her soft cheek. Allowed a stray finger to curl itself in her magnificent garnet hair. His hand slid down. His fingers caressed her neck and ran down to her collarbone. Her skin was tender and so sweet. She smelled of flowers and healthy woman, of brisk heathery breezes and a slight tang of woodsmoke.

He wanted to take her in his arms.

What was he thinking?

"We will all be safe at the hotel. Rose Robin may wish to join her wife, but I suggest you all come as my guests. It would be so easy for the magistrate to capture you here, but at the hotel? There are many eyes to see and tongues to wag."

"It didn't stop them taking you this past week."

"Ah, but you see, I am a mere woman, a young one, younger than her majority, who dares to claim the right of property and of business. While most who knew and admired my grandmother clamor for me to govern and manage the hotel in her stead, in the way she trained me, there are those—Dougie's horrible friends, powerful men—who detest seeing a woman behave so."

"It is wrong of them."

"You see, if they allow me to go about my business, especially as I am a known success, their wives and, worse, their daughters may demand they be let out from under the fist."

"They may yet take further action."

"Yes, they may. So if you will not come for your own sake, come for mine."

"Has your great-uncle returned to the Black Hart?"

"Not for some hours after his last devastating visit, in which he seduced an innocent maid, wrecked my tower room, and threatened me again. I expect such blessed calm cannot continue for too much longer."

Quick anger fired in Farlan. He must not leave her unprotected.

He imagined being close to her, more often, over many days. *Many nights.* His brows came down in another glower. How could he keep his hands... He could not ask her to marry him, not while his claim to

209

the title and property was unproven. He had riches, yes, but she had a right to all he could offer her.

Arm in arm, Evie and Jack ventured out the door into the day.

An unwilling smile twitched at his lips. "Surely you cannot allow Evie to come to your hotel? You will have to keep her hidden. I don't like your chances—she is as bright and noisy as an antipodean parrot."

"Pooh! Of course I will not keep her hidden. Evie will be my guest, and she shall behave just as she chooses."

"I fear the opinions of the York country goodwives will not accord with your own remarkable tolerance."

"We will contrive. I think Evie will be a record success, and customers will flock from miles to exchange conversation with her."

"Asphodel…"

"Yes?"

"I love your loyalty to your unusual friends. I love your sunny confidence and your hope. You somehow make me feel life doesn't have to be so serious."

"And I, Farlan Blackitter, even love your glower." Asphodel's smile melted his insides to mush, even though she teased him. All the humor suddenly fled her face. She paled. "Farlan. Baron Blackitter," she said. His name was thick and rich as honey in her mouth. "I must tell you something."

He gathered her in his arms, held her for a moment, enjoying, *reveling* in warm, soft woman, his vibrant, lovely Asphodel.

She pulled herself away. "I am afraid you will hate me when I tell you, so…so please kiss me first. In case…you never want to kiss me again after."

Farlan laughed, startled. He looked to the fire. They were alone. "I could never hate you, Asphodel Quick. Quite the reverse. As for kisses—" He made a low, predatory growl, which wasn't entirely humorous.

"Stop talking and kiss me," she snapped, eyes sparking, cheeks flushed adorably.

Farlan ran his fingers down behind her ears, along her jaw. She gasped a little. Her plush lips parted. He smoothed a curl dangling to her shoulder, followed it down. He put both his hands, heavy and warm, on her shoulders. He wanted to make her feel anchored, feel safe. And then he lowered his lips onto hers, barely a touch, a graze of their lips. A sharp breath hissed in her mouth.

He nudged her plump bottom lip with his, testing its bounce and softness. And then—and then he fastened his mouth on hers, gently, teasing, withdrawing before she had time for more than a taste. He did it again, with a little more pressure, more demand, dancing with her desire, stoking it with the touch of his mouth. She took a step forward and tangled her fingers in his hair and slammed her lips on his, urgent, demanding, and passionate.

"Asphodel," he groaned into her mouth, and then he flung his arms around her, anchoring her, holding her firmly to him as he tasted and plundered her mouth. She shifted and softened as though her legs weakened and could not support her; he guided her over to the fire and sat on the large upholstered couch, bringing her with him onto his lap.

She was melting, she was urgent, her breath came fast. And then she wrenched herself away from him. Her voice was a breathy gasp laced with wonder and a note of such joy that he thought of fresh air and the wild ridges. "I will never be able to tell you if you persist in that most…seductive behavior!"

"Seductive in a good way, you mean?"

"In the best way."

He was interested to note how her chest heaved with each emotion-laden breath, how the laces on her bodice strained and tightened with each rise and fall. His fingers itched to unlace those laces, rip them out, and free those white jiggling breasts to his caress, his kiss.

"Farlan, pay attention!"

"I am, Asphodel Quick. Currently, your sweet wiggling breasts, your plump rosy lips have all my attention."

Asphodel looked down at her breasts with a comical expression. Then her blue eyes darkened to twilight. She put one hand to the laces at the top of her bodice, and pulled out the bow, and loosened the top laces. She leaned forward, keeping her dark blue intent gaze on his.

He might explode at any moment. His groin ached like the devil. He bore a cockstand that could frighten a soldier.

"Farlan," she said, in a soft witchy voice, "I saw your papers."

"Papers?" Those soft white breasts strained over the bodice laces. *More*, his body clamored. "Undo another section. Please." He heard his own voice, as hoarse and rasping as the old gate in the wind.

He watched, fascinated, his entire body one spear shaft of aching need, as she slowly undid another two eyelets. Now those plump, firm mounds threatened to fully escape their moorings. A line of lace just covered…was that a rosy nipple, protruding through soft white lace? A strip of fabric bound the lower curve of her breasts…a miracle of gravity. Two more eyelets undone and all that lushness would bounce forth. His hands ached to hold them, to kiss them.

"Farlan, are you listening?"

"Yes. Of course. Continue. With the story…and the unlacing." God, he was huge and stiff as a mountain. His cock gave an almighty throb. He kept his hands on his knees, white knuckled now.

She undid one more eyelet. A section of pink nipple peeked over the lace. Almost…almost the tip. Teasing him, pointed and erect, pushing out the lace, much as he was protruding from within his trousers. He was almost cross-eyed with desire.

She put her fingers under her breasts and, still watching him, her eyes dark as midnight, gave them a jiggle. Mounds of soft white flesh. Her erect pink nipples popped free. Farlan emitted a helpless moan.

"I will finish what I have to say," Asphodel whispered, and then her words tumbled out in a rush. Her agitation made her breasts bob and joggle. Farlan was transfixed, his mouth dry, his need mounting like a storm.

"I saw your papers. Your birthright. They were hidden in my grandmother's room. While I was in that place, someone smashed up my room, and now they are gone. I'm so sorry, Farlan Blackitter. I have failed you terribly."

"Hang the blasted papers!" roared Farlan, Baron Blackitter, and reached starving hands for the lush promise of her exposed breasts.

Chapter Sixteen

April 1881—Blackleech Castle

Asphodel leaned forward, allowing him to feel and knead and caress her breasts. She hardly knew where the impulse had come from. Each touch, each tweak of a nipple, each warm soft wet kiss of his hot mouth sent spirals of desire, spikes of sizzling heat arrowing straight into her center. She moaned aloud. She was beyond sense.

The sound of laughter drifted in from outside.

Farlan stilled. He pressed her to him. "Your pardon, Asphodel." He expertly reassembled her disordered clothing and smoothed her hair. His heat, his hands and fingers moving over her body so skillfully, the hard planes of his face so close to her breasts— doing up her clothing felt as intense as the reverse process.

With a delicate fingertip, she traced his firm crimson mouth that had just been kissing her with such passion, the small curls of black hair at his hairline, the faint black bristles studding his jaw.

He stole her breath away.

"Asphodel…" His voice cracked. "Miss Quick. I want you more than man has ever wanted a woman. My desire for you is burning through me, scrambling my brain. And yet—" His lips closed and parted. His face tensed.

"Farlan," she said, stroking his cheek, enjoying the rasp of bristles. "Farlan Blackitter."

"That's just it," he responded. "How can I ask you to marry me, when I still must prove I am any such thing? Currently I am a wanted highwayman, a remnant from the Victorian goldfields, a hard-bitten soldier, and a physician. But no baron. Not to the world."

Asphodel sat back and gave him her best haughty stare. "Perhaps you could begin by actually making such proposal, and then, once you have secured my answer, you can do your agonizing—that is, indeed, if my response is the favorable answer you have assumed it will be?"

Farlan took a moment to unpick this speech, and then he gave a bark of laughter.

He took her hands. "Asphodel Quick, should I return to my birthright as Baron Blackitter, would you make me the happiest man on earth and become my baroness?"

Asphodel regarded him. She slashed down her brows and made her lips a tight bud. "This proposal of marriage is conditional? A strange proposal in that case, sir. Either you love me, or you do not." She pulled her hands away. "What makes me so unfit for any wife except that of a baron?"

"Asphodel…"

She rose. "I had dreamed of a most romantic marriage proposal to a man with whom I was shatteringly in love. This smacks more of business, calculating the weight and cost and value on each side. I will marry someone who wants me in any guise, with no what-ifs or wherefores, *for better or for worse*."

The weight of disappointment crushed her. This man, larger than life, a romantic, swashbuckling, heroic rescuer, was counting coin like a merchant when all she wanted was for him to claim her as his alone and carry her away, dizzy with desire and happiness. She had enough of commerce at the hotel.

Voices at the doorway heralded the return of Evie and Jack, glowing, laughing, filled with sunshine. Asphodel scowled. She put a hand to a stray curl and tucked it back into place. Then she smoothed a social smile onto her face.

She didn't, couldn't, look at Farlan Blackitter.

"There's people coming, my lad," Gentleman Jack said to Farlan. "Uniformed people. We'd better take the ladies—and Rose—and away to the coast."

"Get Rose Robin and McEvoy from the stables," Farlan answered curtly. Jack's eyebrows rose, then his face blanked. Evie looked with lively curiosity from Farlan to Asphodel.

Shouting echoed from the gates as McEvoy and Rose Robin darted into the kitchens. "The beaks are here," said McEvoy. "That useless gundungus Dougie McDonnell is with them, shouting and cursing with the rest."

Evie, McEvoy, and Rose began packing food and blankets into saddle bags. Jack pulled firearms from under couches and up in the rafters. Asphodel and Farlan glowered silently at each other.

After a few further seconds of glowering, Farlan sprinted into the hall, and his boots clattered on the stairs. She followed swiftly and stood next to him where he had halted at the oriel window, regarding with some dismay the spread of mounted uniforms rattling and shouting at the front gate.

Farlan stalked to a bedroom. Asphodel stood stiffly in the doorway, clenching her skirt, as he distributed papers in inner pockets and bags of gold and coin about his person, surely enough for a king's ransom. He jammed two pistols into holsters and belted them around his lean hips.

"Here," he barked and threw her a small heavy bag. It clinked and shifted as she caught it. More gold.

In moments, all six of them were mounted and racing away from the stables at the rear of the ruined castle, well away from the line of sight of the those at the front gates. They picked their way through brick-walled lush gardens, threaded through a mile of overgrown paths, and drew up to a tumbled part of a back wall.

Jack held his hand for silence, slid from his horse, and warily ventured through the opening, checking each way for watchers. Nobody. In seconds he remounted, and they were out on the wild moors and racing with the wind, east toward the coast and Ravenscar.

The Blackitter stables had boasted five horses: three great beasts and two local-bred ponies. The three men rode their own magnificent steeds; Rose Robin and Asphodel had a sturdy pony each, both riding astride, and Evie shared Jack's large mount. She had said squeakily, "I can't ride!" Jack had scooped her up and placed her behind him. A thread of worry undercut Asphodel's exhilaration; would Jack and Evie's mount tire sooner than the horses with single riders?

They rode through grasslands and along the edge of the escarpments until they reached the main carriage road, where they were able to set a good pace. McEvoy peeled off and cantered back the way they had come.

Soon, McEvoy galloped back toward them in a thunder of hooves and a plume of dust. He reached Farlan where he cantered alongside Asphodel. "The law, and her uncle yon, hot on our heels, Baron! We won't be outrunning them; they sure have fine nags." He cricked his head toward Jack and Evie and raised his brows.

"Better put speed on, lads," called Farlan.

"Stop!" cried Asphodel. "Do you know the secret ways across the moors to the coast?"

They all shook their heads. McEvoy shot a wary glance back along the carriage road. Disturbance rumbled in the air, a vibration in the distance that presaged horsemen riding at pace, although they remained out of sight.

The escapees had a bare minute to change course.

She said, "There are paths through the hills and dales which are dangerous unless you know the way. Any slip can be death. There are bogs and quicksands and sudden hidden crevasses. Shaky overhangs obscure underground caves. Sinkholes appear like magic. The safe ways are secret and known only to locals."

All the horses halted and milled around prancing and restless as Asphodel and Farlan clashed stares.

"I am unused to handing over command," he said. "I am accustomed to shouldering risk, and blame, should a venture not come off."

"Be damned to your pride!" said Asphodel, and she laughed, as free in spirit as the soaring lapwings. "I am a child of these moors. This is my home and my place. I know the old ways to safety, and I will lead you now, Farlan Blackitter."

Everyone waited as Farlan battled himself. "Would not your uncle know them too?"

"That blancmange! He never troubled himself to spend time in the knolls and hollows, while I ran free there my entire childhood."

"The horses might break a fetlock in those quagmires."

"Nonsense! These two are local-bred ponies, sturdy and valiant; once in the wild, they will beat your large beasts for speed and stamina both. Our ponies will lead your mounts in safety. I know not where you bought them, but someone has a good eye for the right horse."

McEvoy gave her a glimmering grin and strained a watching gaze back along the carriage road.

Farlan said, "Very well, Asphodel Quick. Take us on the secret ways. Take us somewhere safe on the coast, perhaps where my men and I can get a boat if we find ourselves in extremity."

"I have better than that," she said. "We can stay in comfort at the Smugglers Arms. The proprietor is a lifetime friend to Isabella. Nobody there will reveal your whereabouts. It will give us time to plan our next moves." She paused and looked southwest to the horizon. "After I see you safe, I will return to the Black Hart Hotel. Who knows what harm Great-Uncle Dougie is wreaking in my absence? And which of my faithful staff he is now suborning and ruining?"

As they streaked in single file from the carriageway into the first overhang, distant shouting and cursing hung on the air; she did not look back but leaned low over her pony and gave it its head.

She would never forget that dashing ride across the moors. The day had turned to evening, and the sky was streaked with the beginnings of sunset, pink and apricot and the exact crimson-red of Farlan's mouth. Lapwings danced and soared, an eagle hovered just over the hill, and the high country spread before her, beckoning like the promise of a new life.

The chill wind whipped their heated cheeks, slapping their faces and ears and fingers. Asphodel's heart soared and thrilled within her as they raced, despite the danger. She was free; this was her precious home, her place, where her spirit ran wild. She and the moors were together in this; her strength in this landscape would save them yet.

They sprinted down into green dales, lush with grass, and leaped the horses over low stone walls marking out the farms. Early spring wildflowers peeped everywhere, glad yellows and startling periwinkle blues and sweet pinks.

They climbed stiff short hills until they reached tall summits, vistas stretching out green and brown and yellow in every direction, the setting sun rimming the heather and grasses with golden fire. The fine clean air scoured their faces and lungs with cold, energizing them. The birds shrilled encouragement, their arrow-flights a dare to dream. The sea speckled and sparkled in the far distance, as bright as hope.

The sound of pursuit had faded, and there was only the soft clopping of the rugged ponies, the other horses, and Farlan's great black steed. Asphodel's pony whickered when the salt tang of a stray sea breeze tickled their noses, and she leaned forward and patted his valiant neck.

At last, they reached the edge of the clifftop. *What a view!* Astonishment exploded in her mind. Although she had known this scene her whole life, she paused to drink in its magic, like a healing elixir, reminding her who she was and what she loved.

The edge of the great plateau tumbled down sharply into the jagged coastline. The sea sparkled with dancing pink and yellow diamonds. Gulls hovered and swooped in the air, and a curlew screamed. Mounds of glistening bladderwrack lined rocky pools formed by the receding tide.

Farlan kicked his horse next to hers. "Well done, Asphodel Quick and your valiant pony! You have led us truly along your hidden, twisty tracks, as deceptively welcoming as winter sun. But I doubt how we will descend this sharp cliff?"

Asphodel laughed at him. "You, sir, are welcome to throw yourself to the sharp white edge there and see how long you last on that crumbling shale. I will take Evie and Rose Robin down—"

"A secret way, I know." Farlan grinned. "I'll make a highwaywoman of you yet." He looked around him, the sea wind whipping his dark curls around his face, the sharp wind striking color into his lean cheeks. "Where is this hostelry?"

"Aha! Do you not trust me to produce one in a timely fashion?"

"I bow to your superior knowledge of hotels, ma'am. But I can see only the wild coast?"

"Do not only believe what your eyes can see, Baron Blackitter, especially on these moors."

His gaze darkened. He bent close and murmured, "My sight and belief are one. My eyes gaze upon the most beautiful woman on ridge or fen, regal and lush, her fire-opal hair streaming in the wind. My heart knows its one true desire: that same lovely woman, her courage and stalwart heart offering strength for my strength, and softness for the cracks deep within my battered heart and mind."

Asphodel's heart somersaulted in her chest as his gaze trapped hers. Her mouth parted as he bent his hungry gaze on her lips. Could he mean such words? Nobody had ever spoken thus to her! Despite this danger and urgency, his nearness wrought a bolt of fizzing heat to where she sat astride on the saddle. Her breasts tingled.

He said, his voice a low growl which curled her toes in her boots, "And her delicate white skin and lush curves drive me mad with desire."

Asphodel licked her lips, which only made his eyes darken, and summoned a bold haughty stare from she knew not where. "We had best get on, Baron Flirty."

He responded, "Watching you all this while moving up and down on your horse—it has completely undone me, Asphodel."

"Then keep your eyes on the view," she retorted, ignoring the stirring where she sat. "It is reputedly one of the best in all England."

"The view has been the best in all England, I can assure you. And in all Victoria."

Asphodel laughed and turned her pony toward a steep and impenetrable-seeming thicket near a sharp overhang.

Farlan followed her, leading the others. Sure enough, somehow she picked her way down an invisible and precarious path, which only became apparent as they inched their way along it. As the horses zigzagged down the cliff path, Farlan attempted to obey her strictures and keep his mind on the extraordinary view assaulting his senses. He partly succeeded, merely stealing looks at the fine figure Asphodel made on her pony, as natural and proud as the country from which they both had sprung.

The sea blazed red and gold. Birds soared, silhouetted black against the brilliant rose sky. Salt wind blew like an invitation on his face, overlying the fresh clean peaty smell of the moorlands. The cliffs rose from the sea on either end of the curving bay. The gulls screamed a welcome.

As they rounded the last bend in the path, they encountered a majestic hostelry nestling into the curve of the overhanging cliff. A small seawall held back the sea a hundred yards out from the pub, and a long pier had several small fishing crafts and tinnies bobbing along it.

Their cliff path led to the side and rear of the hotel, into a fine large yard with extensive stables adjoining the hotel, where the cliff flattened back. McEvoy gave a shout. An ostler ran to greet them and assisted McEvoy and Rose Robin to take the horses for a well-earned grooming, oats, and water.

The pub itself was old, built solidly of stone, and partly meshed with the rock of the cliff, as if it had grown out from the cliff itself. A cobblestone path led around to the front of the hotel, where thick diamond-paned windows held out winter storms, and gabled turrets and high balconies offered sea views for prospective guests.

The door stood open. Warm fires flickered within, and the homely smell of country cooking assailed their nostrils. Several men's voices were raised in song, a song of the sea, lost love, and fish.

Asphodel stepped through the low entranceway; Farlan and Jack had to duck their heads significantly. She led the way to a small inner taproom and called, "Ahoy, publican!"

Farlan looked around. A series of small bars opened from the taproom, up and down one or two stone steps, each with a blazing fire to warm the air. This snug ale room sported wooden benches and tables squeezed into booths. Haphazard corridors crammed with tiny tables led off into dimness. Paintings of the sea, sea birds, ships, and the jagged coastline adorned the walls. A large anchor hung in one corner, and a cabinet full of curious shells stood next to the bar.

"Asphodel, my love!" A short, comfortably proportioned woman emerged from a corridor, bringing with her a cloud of yeasty bread-smell. Her curling silver hair contrasted with strong black eyebrows, which gave her a fierce, almost piratical appearance. She put doughy fists on her apron-clad hips and narrowed her sharp gray eyes at Asphodel, then calmly assessed her companions. Her shrewd gaze lingered for a while on Farlan's features; something lit in her expression, quickly shielded.

"Biddy Birkenshaw, we find ourselves in extremis and bid you shelter us and for goodness' sake feed us, while we decipher a way out of our coils."

"Well, for certain, my dear, troubles seem a great deal less when you've eaten. Here, come through to the private parlor, and nobody will be troubling you there. If you like, once you have dined and refreshed yourselves, you may tell me all about it. I would help you any way I could, Asphodel Quick, for your beloved grandmother's sake, and for your own."

"Thank you, Biddy, you are a darling!" Asphodel declared and followed Biddy through a corridor, up a small stairway to a charming small bar with a view over the beach and the approach to the pub.

"You will see anyone coming from here," Biddy pronounced. "And if you wish, you may step through to this hidden room here, if you find yourselves further tangled in your pickle. Now, you must try my jugged hare and Yorkshire pudding, and you need your greens too, of course. Curd tart to follow."

"And some of your famous bitter ale, for everyone, I think." Farlan's hearty nod joined the rest.

"And Biddy? I particularly ask that you do not allow my great-uncle Dougie McDonnell to know we are here, should he venture by. I will explain all later."

"Certainly, my love," responded Biddy comfortably, as though she were used to hiding vagrants, escapees, and runaways every day of the week. Which, reflected Farlan, perhaps she was.

Before exiting the room, Biddy cast another thoughtful glance over Farlan, her clear gray eyes registering something; but he found her very hard to read.

"Asphodel," he said once she had gone, "are you sure you can trust Biddy Birkenshaw? She gave me a very knowing look."

"With my life," Asphodel retorted, and Farlan had to be content with that.

McEvoy and Rose Robin burst in with a blast of cool, stables-scented sea air, and all fell with gusto onto the York puddings and dark bitter ale.

Chapter Seventeen

April 1881—Smugglers Arms, Ravenscar, the next morning

Asphodel had caught her breath, eaten, washed gratefully in a sumptuous room with a view of the roiling seas, and had at last slept like the dead, awakening to the glittering promise of a new day. She lay contemplating the mystery that was Farlan Blackitter when a sharp knock on her door heralded a much-agitated Biddy.

"Asphodel, sweet, there is trouble abroad at the Black Hart. Now I don't want to tell my tale over and over, so I want all of you there in the parlor where you ate your dinners last night."

Asphodel clutched her arm. "Biddy, wait! What kind of trouble? You do not expect me to wait until all the others are assembled? Please, for pity's sake!"

Biddy turned her penetrating gaze on Asphodel. "Your great-uncle Dougie McDonnell kind of trouble. A vain man, and a greedy and reckless one. I'm surprised Isabella didn't set a better guard over you."

"Oh, but she did, Biddy Birkenshaw." The gravel voice came from the doorway. Farlan! "She chose a wild man and a wanted highwayman—but one who knows how to protect those dear to him."

He sauntered in, freshly washed, smelling of clean

vital man, his dark hair damp and curling across his brow. "She chose someone who can fend off the meanest of the goldfields scum and survive working as a frontier spy in a foreign land." His voice softened. "She chose someone who knows gold quality, who will fight to their last ounce of power to protect her."

Asphodel's heart skipped and thundered under her ribs. Such words! Such a picture he painted, of a brave man who had known little softness in his life.

"I will take you now, Asphodel. We will go and see what evils that reprobate has committed."

"It is too dangerous for you!" she said.

"I am not one to hide and cower away. It goes against my grain." His fierce, charming grin tilted the corners of his mouth. "I welcome the fight, to incite climax and resolution. Not for me wise and cautious moldering while we ponder the safest move!"

"But your claim—your legacy…"

"Oh?" said Biddy, her brows rising.

"Baron Blackitter, at your service." Farlan swept a magnificent bow. "I grow tired of waiting for proof. Bored with planning a claim through the courts. Weary of seeking and never finding the papers that prove my claim. Be damned to all this running and hiding!" He laughed, and yes, a revitalized carmine flushed his lean face. *So heartbreakingly handsome.* His eyes gleamed bright silver, his grin challenged, and his cheeks stung red with passion. Invisible sparks crackled along his tanned skin.

Who could deny him?

Farlan said, "Let us go then. We shall sort out your uncle and claim my birthright—and let them try to take it all away again!"

"Impressive!" Biddy breathed, lifting a teasing eyebrow at Asphodel, which she pretended not to read.

She tossed her head. "We will listen to Biddy's information before we gallop off to wreak havoc on our enemies." Asphodel pushed a curl behind her ear with ruthless fingers. "I will win this battle. It is not my aim merely to make a grand gesture. So we will collect information, plan, and respond accordingly."

She and Farlan matched blazing stares and flaring nostrils. He had aroused her with his words—aroused her in more ways than one. How she yearned to gallop alongside him, kicking flints and pebbles flying as they pounded across the heather!

But she would not lose her hotel with ill-considered valor.

Her lips pressed tight, and her crinkling brow no doubt mirrored his darkening visage. She widened her eyes and treated him to her best lethal stare. A smile flirted on his lips. His mercury eyes softened and creased at the corners.

Biddy's chuckle wound between them. "What a fine pair! You'll be the terror of the district." Mischief danced in her expression. "Your children will—"

Asphodel looked daggers. Biddy grinned.

Farlan gestured to two upholstered chairs in the bay window. "Oblige me by describing your news, Biddy Birkenshaw, if you will."

Asphodel hesitated but took one of the chairs indicated. If Biddy's news was dire, she might need the support. Biddy took the other chair. Farlan remained standing, one boot propped on the hearth fender.

Biddy made a production of rustling and settling her clothes. "Your great-uncle has assumed possession of the Black Hart Hotel." Biddy was never one to prevaricate or gild the bald truth. "He contends that despite your removal from an asylum…?" Biddy's eyebrows rose into her hairline. "He says you must be found and reinstalled in that institution, as you *suffer from hysteria.*"

Neither Asphodel nor Farlan said anything but waited for her to continue.

"A less hysterical lass I've never seen in my born days, and so I shall say in a court of law, if needed."

"Thank you, Biddy." Asphodel heard her own voice low and grave. She appreciated her friend's support, but with all those powerful men ranged against them? Hope for a just decision seemed as remote as daffodils in winter.

"He is ordering the Black Hart staff around. That maid Maeve is hanging on his arm and his every word, telling all who will harken to her that she is promised to him in marriage."

Maeve! As changeable as spring sunshine, it seemed.

"There is worse," Biddy said, turning to regard Farlan. "You have a price on your head. If you march into the Black Hart Hotel with Asphodel, the magistrates will throw you in prison. It is near impossible to prove one's innocence from deep within the dread dungeons of Wakefield Gaol."

"I'm not innocent," he replied shortly. His gray eyes glimmered with mischief. "I stole Miss Quick's engagement ring."

"Which you still have not returned!" she retorted tartly.

"I shall give you a better one." Now his eyes

scorched her with blazing desire. Asphodel could not tear her gaze from his. Her cheeks heated; a bolt of fire lanced the pit of her belly.

Farlan said, "To hell with their scheming and stealing. The greater crime is their effort to dispossess my legal ward, Asphodel Quick. They will have me to deal with in this matter."

"Can you be my legal guardian when you are a wanted man?"

"It is time to thunder in as Baron Blackitter. They will have a much harder time trying to indict a peer of the realm."

A pulse of fear mixed with her thrill of admiration. *Magnificent!* "You have already risked all to come to my aid in the terrible Harrowlick Asylum. You came into the open and revealed yourself before your plans had matured, to save me. And I am so grateful! But the fact remains I am the legal owner of the Black Hart Hotel."

"It is in trust for you until you reach your majority—or your marriage. In which case it will become your husband's property." His answer snapped. Temper on a short rein. He said, under his breath, not looking at her, "It is not your *gratitude* I want."

Asphodel turned to Biddy. "By what right does my uncle claim the hotel?"

"As your nearest relative, my dear. As Isabella's husband's closest living relative. He has a strong case, it must be admitted."

"Nonsense! He is patently trying to steal my legacy from right under me!"

"I am your legal guardian and a peer of the realm. We will go and simply take it back." Farlan's tone brooked no argument. He was smiling at her again, charming, enticing, teasing. Tempting her to abandon all her caution, and ride with him and the wind, to rescue her life's work, her vocation, her great passion.

She swallowed, battling everything in her that wanted to do as he said. She fought for *his* safety, as he apparently would not. "And the magistrate? You would hate to be imprisoned, deprived of your liberty, of the free air!" She pressed her hands flat on the table.

"They will not lay hands on Baron Blackitter."

"But how will you prove that you are? Dougie will maintain that you are a chancer, a gambler, a fraudster who heard about the missing heir on the goldfields and came to claim the barony."

"Why, that is all true! I will not deny it."

"Farlan…" She made her tone fierce, threatening damage to his person.

He laughed. "I did hear it on the goldfields—from my grandfather, the third Baron Blackitter."

The baron received an unexpected ally in Biddy. "He will have no trouble claiming his birthright."

"What? What are you talking about, dear Biddy?" Asphodel cried.

"Farlan Blackitter has the famous iron stare and the hawk nose. He is a Blackitter, of that there can be no doubt. Anyone who knew his grandfather may testify to that."

"Really!" Hope soared in Asphodel.

And then Biddy crushed it again. "Proving he was born on the right side of the blanket will be the gnarl."

"Arrgh!" Asphodel groaned. "Then despite his infamous iron stare and hereditary hawk nose, we are no further forward."

"I do not wish to disagree with a lady," responded Farlan, "but you will be amazed what I can do with an iron stare."

Asphodel sniffed. "You have no problem disagreeing with me in the usual course. Has Biddy made you find your manners?"

Farlan strode forward and, despite Biddy's avid stare, put his hand on Asphodel's shoulder. His weight and steadiness lent her much-needed strength.

He said, caressingly, "You must forgive me if my manners come and go. I rely on you to correct me. Remember I am a savage, come late to civilized society. I was taught manners by tutors such as Gentleman Jack when I was already a young man—and even Jack's cultivated civilities come and go!"

Biddy wore the most foolish expression on her face and her hands clasped in front of her. "Oh!" she breathed. "I believe a wild man lately tamed will suit you best, my fierce moors-bred Asphodel."

"Biddy! Who would have thought such a romantic heart thrummed in that practical chest!"

The publican's cheeks colored, but she narrowed her eyes. "I want you both to bide there a moment while I fetch something. But methinks a chaperon is needed here!"

Farlan made his face solemn, but the smile kept breaking out. "You think I will ravish my ward in your parlor?"

Stars sparkled within her, matching the silver-bright glow in his eyes. How she loved this Farlan, relieved for a short moment of responsibility, teasing Biddy and enjoying himself. "Ravish my ward" echoed in her brain, robbing her of breath, let alone a suitable retort. *Ravish.*

"Ye are a Blackitter, aren't ye?" said Biddy, her local accent thickening. "The Blackitters take what they want, when they want it, and everyone else can sing to the devil."

"We will sit courteously for five minutes only," said Farlan, the laugh plain in his voice. "After that, I will not be responsible for the consequences."

Biddy blushed like a maiden and actually simpered. This situation was rapidly growing out of control.

"I note my guardian speaks for me, in his great wisdom," Asphodel said in as acid a tone as she could manage.

Not surprisingly, Biddy took Farlan's part. "You do as the man says, lass, and I will be back." She faced Farlan, plump hands on broad hips. Her voice firmed. "*Within five minutes.*"

Biddy left, and in the sudden silence, shyness consumed Asphodel. She couldn't look at him, for fear of what she would see.

Or not see.

She pushed her chair and stood, jutting her chin, sucking in a breath, facing him.

Farlan held his hands in the air in a very comedic manner and stepped backward two paces. He assumed a most sinister leer, wiggling his hands, and said, "In five minutes, my little chicken."

Asphodel could not repress a snort-laugh sound and then blushed at her lack of ladylike behavior. "You assume a great deal, sir."

"You heard Biddy. I assume nothing. Blackitters take." This time he leaned in toward her and gave her a smoldering look which had her toes curling in her boots.

She said haltingly, her breathing erratic and making her words come out breathy and with more invitation than she had intended, "What would you take, once the five minutes is elapsed?"

Farlan's eyes had locked on her chest, which heaved with emotion which she struggled to control. His gaze shot to her face. He parted his lips, looked at hers. She held her ground. Waited.

And then...

Biddy burst into the room. Her head swiveled from one to the other. Asphodel swallowed against a dry throat and gasped a breath.

" 'Tis lucky I was only four minutes by the atmosphere here," she rebuked.

"I kept my word," protested Farlan in injured tones. "I was merely about to tell Miss Quick what I would take after the allotted five minutes."

Biddy made a movement like a shimmy and sighed quite audibly.

Asphodel laughed and rolled her eyes. "So was that an excuse to leave us for four minutes, Biddy, or did you really have an errand?"

"Come." Biddy beckoned them back to the table. "Sit." She put a tight fist on the table. "Your grandfather was a canny man," she said to Farlan. She looked at Asphodel. "And your grandmother a canny woman."

She uncurled her fist and there, on her palm, lay a heavy gold signet ring, engraved with a bird and a coronet. "Isabella gave me this to hold for the missing Blackitter heir, should he ever come home. When she lay dying, she called me to the Black Hart."

"I remember!" said Asphodel, in some surprise. She had thought at the time it was a kind gesture from an old friend to visit her grandmother.

"In the name of our friendship, she bid me hold this trust for her." Biddy slid the gold signet onto the last finger of Farlan's left hand. "Your grandfather gave it to Isabella before he took you away off adventuring," she said as he stared at the ring. "Gave it in her safekeeping. Isabella told me he left many a token distributed around the countryside, for you to claim when you returned."

Asphodel saw Farlan's face then, radiant with a kind of hope, almost trembling beneath the surface.

"Did you—" He cleared his throat. "Did you know the old villain then? I have not met people who knew him before, when he was the third Baron Blackitter of Blackleech Castle. I only knew him as a rough goldminer and a clever soldier."

"Only in passing, lad. Such as he did not mix with the likes of me, cook in a pub, I was—I married the owner, and here I am. Not that the baron put on airs, mind, but he was so much above me, it wasn't expected."

She studied his face, crestfallen now, and took pity on him. "He was a fine figure of a man, your grandfather. He would be so proud to see you now, so tall and straight, with the iron stare and hawk nose. The blood runs true in you, lad."

She laughed a little. "Forgive me, Baron, calling you lad like that. But you seem but a lad to me, for all that you are the Baron Blackitter of these parts."

"Do you know why he left? Did Isabella say?" The

yearning was plain in his voice, which cracked on the last word.

"The curse, lad. He left because of the curse. His own son, your father, and his lovely wife, died in that terrible accident, neck or nothing driver though he was. Nobody could credit it. We all said it must be the Blackitter bane. The first-born heir of every generation disappears or dies soon after he begets an heir. Or before he can. The succession meanders through the generations."

The day darkened with her words. Through the window, thick purple clouds roiled in over the sea and made fantastical shapes in the sky.

Biddy added, "He left to protect you, lad. He thought that relentless Australian sun would scour away any ancient devilry. And look at you, sitting here in my hotel, fine and strong. He was right, the baron."

Farlan sat stiff and still, absorbing every word like a man starved.

Finally, after a long, echoing silence, he said, "Thank you, Biddy. For everything. I long to hear more of my grandfather, but I must first reunite Asphodel with her own birthright."

Farlan stood, took Biddy's plump, work-worn hand in his, and bowed over it as though she were a princess. Then he bent and kissed her cheek. "Thank you," he said simply.

Biddy smiled her comfortable smile. "There will always be safety and comfort here for the Blackitters. Make sure you send word, lad, if you need help. Because it's here."

She hugged Asphodel. "And you, take care, for your grandmother's sake. Don't let that great slug

Dougie take your hotel. 'Tis hard for a woman in this business, but you've been bred to it. Don't let them give you any nonsense." She kissed Asphodel. "Be gone with you then. I'll keep your friends entertained, to let you get a start. Leave by way of the kitchens; I've ordered food and drink for your journey. Eat some breakfast before you go. And you are always welcome here, both of you. Now, get you gone."

Asphodel noticed Biddy's eyes were very shiny, but she merely hugged her again and went out into the corridor with Farlan.

"Come, then, Baron Blackitter. The secret paths await."

Farlan bowed. As he rose, his eyes blazed with intent. "We will explore them together."

"I'm just glad Biddy isn't here to sigh at such manliness."

"Manliness, hmm?" Farlan grinned and gestured for her to precede him down the twisty stairs to the kitchens and thence out to the stable yard.

Asphodel halted on the stairs. "I'm surprised your grandfather didn't snap her up. What a tough and interesting woman! Now I'm grown, I see people differently."

She could see Farlan battling with a variety of answers. He settled for two: "How do you know he didn't?" and "Grown, are you?"

Asphodel tossed her hair and led the way down.

Chapter Eighteen

April 1881—The Secret Paths

They took Black Bran, Farlan's steed, and Asphodel's trusty pony. The day gleamed bright once more, golden sun pouring down in abundance, gilding everything with luster.

Farlan admired how Asphodel's red-gold hair caught fire in the golden morning; she flamed like an avenging angel, sitting ramrod straight astride her horse.

"You only need a spear!" he said. "You look like Jeanne d'Arc about to cut a swathe through injustice."

"I wish I had a spear—or a Viking axe—and we lived in such times that I could cut off that viper Dougie's head with no qualm."

"I see the vision matches the inner woman—bloodthirsty, vengeful, and angry." He drew his horse up to hers. "Glorious!"

She only laughed and clicked her tongue to her horse.

As they rode in the fresh, delightful morning, part of Farlan wished they could ride thus forever. The air was brisk; early birds swooped and called; small furred creatures darted away into the heather. The fresh salt and seaweed air was underlaid with that particular moors smell: centuries of peat, heather, flowers, and the many birds and animals which dwelt there.

This was a different aroma for Farlan, one that triggered sensations that belonged only to childhood. The soft morning light, rippling birdsong, the scents which assailed his nostrils—all alien to those he had experienced in the Victorian goldfields; yet they were the sights, sounds, and smells of his earliest memories. Gratitude unfurled in his chest. A silent voice shouted and clamored within him. *Here is my home! This is where I belong.*

He tried to concentrate on the scenery, because the view right before him—Asphodel's rounded bottom, moving gently in her saddle, her narrow waist and strong shoulders and that vibrant hair, curls escaping to dance with the wind—all this played havoc with his mind and senses.

Asphodel led them to a small grassy dell sprinkled with tiny blue wildflowers and enclosed with heather and small stunted trees. They were sheltered by an overhanging surge of the high moor, and a stunning view stretched west over the wild country.

"Tea and scones," she said, smiling at him. Her eyes were bright and her cheeks rosy with the exercise.

Farlan leaped to assist her to unpack one of the generous saddle bags. He spread a tartan blanket on the grass and poured Asphodel a cup of tea from the flask. She stood sipping the tea, exulting in the harsh country surrounding them, her bright hair gleaming. *Spellbinding.*

"You are part of this land," he said. "Sprung like a goddess from the heather." *Lovestruck loon!*

"Have a buttered scone," she answered, handing him a small plate. He took the plate but couldn't eat.

He was transfixed by Asphodel. Tiny curls escaped her braids and quivered in the slight zephyr tickling their skin. His awareness of her body was extreme, her slender yet plush shape outlined against the horizon. She smelled like flowers and peat, and fresh warm woman enlivened by exercise.

She ate her scone. Her lips, so lush and rose-red, closed over the scone, the butter adding gloss. Her throat moved as she swallowed her tea.

He delayed until she had finished her repast. "Asphodel," he said, and took the cup from her hand. "I can no longer constrain myself." He put his hands on her shoulders and paused. She smiled at him and his heart leaped.

He stroked the soft skin under her left ear and tucked a strawberry curl back behind her lobe. "Asphodel," he growled into her ear, stealing a shiver in response.

Slowly, he brought his lips down onto hers, so soft and warm. He grazed her lips with his own until she gasped and they parted for him. He gently outlined her lips with the tip of tongue, tasting sweet butter and glorious Asphodel, and then he plundered her mouth.

Farlan brought Asphodel down onto the picnic blanket with him. He sat with her cradled in his lap and continued to kiss her with all the passion he had withheld for so long. He was fired by the unbroken country, by the goddess in his arms, by his own blood thundering in his head and veins and muscles.

He murmured into her ear, "I have been tormented with images of your mouth, your body. Once before I stroked your breasts, so soft and generous…"

Asphodel moaned a little into his kiss.

His fingers slid into her dress behind her neck, tracing the shape of her shoulders, teasing forward along the delicate ridge of collarbone. All thought, all calculation fled. Desire possessed him, utterly inflaming him. There! Satiny soft flesh bouncing back under his fingertips.

One by one, he released the fastenings on the front of her bodice and bared her bosom to the golden light, the twin globes bobbing into the air under his hungry gaze. Pink nipples tightened into buds under his stroking fingertips. His hands traveled her body, exploring the curve of her waist, the swell of hips, the delicate strength of her back.

His pulsing erection threatened the seams of his trousers. He laid her down on the blanket and reclined next to her, kissing and stroking and murmuring to her.

When she put her hands on him, blood rushed through his body like a song. She rubbed her hands over his shoulders, his arms, his back, feeling him, knowing him, learning him. She stroked his hair and his jaw, and everything in him shouted, *Mine! This woman is mine!*

Asphodel put her hand on his thighs, ribbed with muscle and tense with desire. Every cell in him held its breath as she tentatively, carefully, moved her hand to his inner thigh, up, slowly, to his groin.

"Ohhhh." Farlan groaned as she touched his cockstand. He lay back, helplessly, on the blanket and let her feel him through the straining fabric of his trousers. "Asphodel." His voice came hoarse, a mere croak. "Asphodel, stop. We cannot…"

"I say we can, and we will."

Farlan sat up. He stared at her, a fierce joy rippling

through him like a shockwave. "You would give yourself to me, here amongst the wildflowers?" He shook his head. "No, no!"

"Yes. We do not know what awaits us back in Fangmoor Beck, back at Blackleech Castle. Everything may change. One or both of us may be imprisoned. We may be lost to each other."

Farlan swallowed, speechless.

Asphodel, his goddess of nature, said, "Teach me love, Farlan Blackitter, here on the moor where both our hearts belong."

Farlan struggled with himself. He should not. Must not.

Asphodel kissed him.

He was undone. He could refuse her nothing.

They lay facing each other on the rug.

Farlan's gravel tones racked her to her core. "Sweet, lovely Asphodel. Such delectable skin. Extraordinary hair. Your eyes." His large hands cupped her shoulders, and he rasped, "I love your womanly strength here."

He trailed fingers down her arm and danced them around under her breasts and back up and over them just where her skin swelled. Asphodel pressed herself forward, but the man merely teased and maddened her, tracing her silky skin, circling closer and closer to the sensitive nub crying out for his touch.

She decided to reply in kind and ran her hand up and down his thick, tense thighs, up to his stomach and down the other thigh. A thrill of feminine power pulsed through her when he stiffened and moaned in her ear, muttering impassioned syllables that were not quite words.

He put a warm, strong hand full on her round hip jutting in the air. She reveled in the weight of him, his strength, his size. He squeezed her round plumpness there, and rubbed the full heavy width of his hand across and down, and gripped and squeezed her rump. He groaned aloud. "Asphodel…watching you ride your horse, your delightful round rear bouncing up and down, has been more than a man can bear. Your rich curves tilting at me…"

Asphodel laughed. "I'm glad the sight of my bottom has given you pleasure, my lord."

His voice went husky. "And these. Your luscious, delectable, bouncing, jiggling tits." He finally brought his hand around and placed it full on her right breast and moaned as he squeezed her. His eyes were molten silver, dark with desire and need.

She sat up a little and, half undone as she was, wiggled and shook her *jiggling tits* full in his face. He raised himself, put a large hand on each satin globe, and then sank his face in her chest. When he took a nipple between finger and thumb and gave it a tug, she emitted a small, surprised shriek as a stab of heat jolted her right in her sex. She felt herself heat and flower open. Before she knew what he was about, he sank a hot wet mouth on her nipple and sucked. Asphodel sang a high note and thrust her breasts harder into his eager hands and mouth.

He laid her on her back, the better to plunder and caress her body with his clever sensitive fingers and slippery hot tongue. She moaned aloud.

Farlan reached down and pulled up her skirts. The fresh breeze slid cool fingers along her bare calves, her knees, her thighs.

Then the breeze became Farlan's touch, stroking her legs, teasing the sensitive soft skin of her inner thighs. Asphodel quivered and arched her body toward him.

She gasped and sighed when he touched her swollen, slippery, secret self. She grabbed his fingers when he withdrew them and put him back where she needed him. She reclined, completely at his mercy, on a rollercoaster of emotion and passion, as he touched and teased her in her most sensitive, private part.

And then…and then, glory be! He slid a finger into her heat and said her name. He stroked his finger into her, and she squeezed her body around him, writhing and panting. By all the old moors gods and goddesses, how extraordinary! He pressed close to her, his size and body heat, his fascinated stare *there* as she bucked against his hand and fingers, his own breath coming hard and fast sending her more thrilled and wanton.

Suddenly she reached the cliff edge…

And she called out, shattered, and flew out across the peaks.

He held her, grounding her, saying her name—and wiping tears from under her eyes, from her cheeks.

"I'm in love with you, Asphodel," he said, his voice a hoarse croak. "I love you. You are mine."

She looked at him, shy now, and amazed, and jubilant. "I want to pleasure you like you just did for me." She stretched a shy hand to his trousers. She couldn't stop smiling at him, laughing like a dizzy girl, as she unbuttoned his flies, giggling as she could barely pull them over his huge erection.

Asphodel stopped what she was doing and blinked. She was a country girl, she knew what male animals bore for procreation, but this! A fine, upstanding, gleaming, velvet-sheathed…

She traced his length with a soft finger and watched in female satisfaction as he bucked under her touch. He moaned and clutched her hand to him, stilling her movements. "You don't need to—"

"Please, you will have to show me what to do, my lord," she said, soft and seductive as she knew how. She made her voice low and thick like liquid honey, full of promise, redolent with desire. He shivered with want as she spoke the words.

He studied her, the expression of his gray eyes completely open to her, not veiled now with humor, or decision, or plans, open and almost wounded, shy, full of need. "Like this…" He took her hand and put her fingers on him and moved her in time with his desire.

She was fascinated, watching the change as his eyes darkened more, saw the need and lust take him. She pushed his hand away and took over, watching his reactions, what was pleasure to him. She bent forward and sighed a breath over his member, and he made a strangled noise in his throat.

Thus encouraged, she licked him, and he bucked and groaned. Taking that for affirmation, she bent and enclosed his thick hard length in her mouth, tasting him, caressing him with her lips and tongue, moving up and down his great cockstand. He tensed, then gently pushed her head away and enclosed himself in his own fist. She stared, fascinated. Then she stayed his hand.

"Love me, Farlan Blackitter. I would have you this day, while we are together and free. Who knows what the future holds?"

He stroked her face with trembling fingers. Tried to

speak. Choked. "Are you sure, Asphodel?"

She could only nod, desire licking and flaming on her skin and heating her softening lady parts.

He pulled her over him, holding her body poised just above his enormous cockstand. "You decide," he said, voice hoarse. "Ride me as you will."

Their gazes locked. Asphodel's blood hurtled and sang. He was all molten silver, lush lips, glorious muscle, and hard, strong man. Her body twanged, hot and slick and wanting. She guided herself onto him. "Oh! So... Oh!"

And then passion took them both into the wildest ride of Asphodel's life.

"Holy hell, Asphodel!" He flopped back on his back and gathered her to him, clutching her tight. Her head rested against his sturdy chest, his heart smashing and pounding in his ribs like a storm-racked sea off Ravenscar. His body shook and shivered like a man who had run a hill race.

When he had his breath again, he sat them both up. He stroked the sides of her face, her hair, her shoulders.

"Marry me, Asphodel Quick. I must have you to wife. I want you; I need you. I love you."

"I want you too, Farlan Blackitter, utterly and completely."

Farlan breathed out and pulled her to him, but she dragged herself away so she could look at him.

She said, her heart breaking a little, but she must stay strong, "I have an offer for you. You may have my body, wholly and completely. Marriage? I am but nineteen and with a hotel to hold fast. I cannot marry anyone until this matter is resolved."

"As your husband, I could drive matters to your

satisfaction, ma'am. It would be my pleasure."

"Yes, that is true. But also you could be put to a prison cell or a hangman's noose, and declaring yourself my husband would likely trigger that fell ending. We will wait."

Farlan gritted his teeth, ran agitated hands through his black hair, already curling in wild disorder. He dragged off his signet ring. "With this ring I claim you. Keep it safe for me. I will come for you and take you as my bride, come hell or high water. Or both."

Asphodel permitted him to slide the heavy gold ring onto the ring finger on her left hand. "I will keep it safe, as I keep your heart safe, Farlan Blackitter. And when the time is right, you may claim both from me."

With that Farlan had to be content. He took to kissing her deeply once more, until laughing and teasing, Asphodel drew herself away and began preparations to continue their ride across the untamed moors.

Chapter Nineteen

April 1881—The Black Hart Hotel

As Asphodel approached the familiar hotel, her
beloved landscape, her business, her grandmother's
living heart and soul, she checked her horse and held a
hand in the air to halt Farlan riding behind her.

A false note hummed in the atmosphere.

All appeared calm: the great stone building nestled
as ever in the hand of the moor. Bees buzzed around the
spring flowers in the courtyard. Birds flipped and flitted
overhead in a cerulean blue sky.

Black Hart patrons were taking advantage of the
fine spring weather, and many sat around the outdoor
tables in the narrow front courtyard. Doubtless many
more customers—farmers, goodwives, people from the
towns, visitors walking the ridges and dales—enjoyed
their noonday dinners in the large rear garden terrace,
which boasted fine views down the dale to the beck
beyond.

Asphodel watched her staff—Maggie, Malcolm,
even Wragg, and once the cook, Mrs. Kell—whisking
in and out of the front doors with large flagons of ale
and plates of nuncheon.

None of them smiled.

A premonitory shiver coursed up her spine.

She chose a quiet way across the field, picking a

path around to the rear of the hotel and the stables.

"What's amiss, Tebbs?" she said without preamble to her gnarly old stableman.

"Himself prancing around ye gramma's pub like a knacker who thinks he's a thoroughbred. Sprung in the withers, that one."

"You mean my great-uncle."

"Aye, young Asa. That great half-nib lushy-cove has brung the quod-cove." He jerked a thumb at Farlan. "The lagging dues for yem."

Farlan said to Asphodel, his voice brusque, "I speak convict and underworld cant like a native." He turned to the stablemaster and asked sharply, "Dougie has brought the gaol-keeper from York?" He paused. "No lagging dues for me, Tebbs. I won't be transported."

"That's as mebbe."

Farlan gave him a short bow. "I leave you the last word, man, as you are warning your mistress in timely fashion."

Asphodel swelled with anger. "Thank you, Tebbs," she said crisply.

His face seamed in a gap-toothed grin. "I have prime prads to saddle up in a trice, young Asa. I kep' them all ready for you. You can ride thence to York and away."

She looked to Farlan in agonized indecision. What to do? This might be the only chance the baron had to escape, to see him safe. "You go," she said to him. "I will take care of my uncle. I have Iain here, and Malcolm, Tebbs, and Wragg. I cannot leave the Black Hart to his filthy, grasping, greedy clutches." She shook now with fear—for Farlan, for herself. And with anger, uncoiling in her, a great female fury, born of male injustice, male grabs for power, for ownership, for possession. "He shall not take what is mine!" she hissed.

Admiration flared in Farlan's gray eyes. His lips quirked up. "A fine husband I would be to leave you to fight alone!"

"And yet, you must! No prison for you. I want you beside me…" She sought for the words to convince him. "In my bed!" she added with ferocity.

Farlan shot a look at Tebbs, who merely spat out the straw he was chewing and remarked, as though on the fine spring weather, "We breed 'em feisty on these here moors. Make sure you'm up to her weight, my lord."

Farlan barked a laugh. He grinned at her, making her heart turn over. So debonair, even in peril. *Especially* in peril. "There you have it," he said. "If I take my leave and abandon you in your trouble, all your faithful staff will decide I do not measure up and will plague me with obstacles and barriers. I have no choice but to stand beside you in whatever transpires within."

A tumult of emotions smote Asphodel. Fear for him. Worry about the "quod-cove," the prison governor. Gratitude that he refused to leave her. That they would face Dougie together.

"Very well," she breathed. "You lend me hope and courage, Farlan Blackitter."

"At your service, now and always," he said, and treated her to a full gentlemanly bow, all raised arm and smirk.

Tebbs grunted his approval and reached for their tired mounts.

Asphodel took a deep, fighting breath, twisted his ring on her finger for courage, met his eye, and nodded.

****

There was Maeve, behind the bar, arching her back and pouting at Dougie and a tall, cold-faced man in uniform so crisp it might snap. A huddle of soldiers threw dice around on a table. Maeve poured ale, smiling and flirting, but Asphodel saw no coin being exchanged. Well!

Asphodel sailed in and said in a clear, carrying tone, "What on earth is the meaning of this outrage? Maeve, I trust you are running a tab for these gentlemen, as I have not seen any coin changing hands."

The entire room sprang to its feet. Silence twanged like the instant after a thunderclap.

Dougie's face transformed into a horrid simper. "Asphodel. Here you are." Then his eyes went cold and blank, and his lips twisted. He clicked his fingers at the soldiers. "Take her." The soldiers moved as one and then almost skidded to a halt.

Dougie's mean little eyes widened as Farlan stepped into the room, a pistol in each hand. He smiled and there was no warmth in it at all. "All of you will pay your dues owing, including you, Douglas McDonnell, and then you will leave forthwith."

The cold-faced man barely changed expression. "Farlan Blackitter?" His voice was as chill as his face, turning the marrow in Asphodel's bones to ice.

"I am Baron Farlan Blackitter, the missing heir to Blackleech Castle and landowner of these parts. As such, I am the law here. You are not welcome in this establishment, and you and your men will pay what is owed and go quietly."

Dougie's face purpled. "Arrest him! He is a fraud! He cannot prove it. We all know the heir is dead and this man is a goldfields adventurer."

A single pulse of alarm smote her, and then Wragg said in his thick York accent, "That man standing there is lost heir to Blackleech Castle. He'm the hawk nose and iron stare."

"Nonsense!" Dougie sputtered.

Wragg spat in the hearth. "*I knew that lordling there when he was a wee lad in petticoats*. He'm the lost heir. The very spit of the old lord."

Dougie shouted, "Arrest him, and he can prove it at trial! If you don't take him now, he will disappear back to his fens and dales and take to robbing stagecoaches once more."

The cold-faced man jerked his head at his soldiers. "This needs more investigation." He regarded Dougie, and his expression was redolent with icy contempt. "You invited us here, so you can pay the bill for my men."

"Take the woman!" Spittle sprayed from Dougie's mouth, and he was shaking as though about to have an apoplexy. "She is incapable."

Something ugly lit the prison warder's eyes. They travelled up and down Asphodel's person. Farlan stepped in front of her. "Get your filthy eyes off my ward, who is saner than any of you in this room. I am her legal guardian and have the papers to prove it. This hotel is hers. You will remove yourselves from her presence and choose to partake of refreshment in some other establishment, from this day forth."

Asphodel had never heard these chilly tones from

Farlan before. Tall and commanding, his presence filled the bar. He loomed over them all, the threat of violence a palpable force emanating from him like a stormfront barely held back. He would protect her. He would put his body before hers, risk his freedom for hers, risk his inheritance for her.

She sighed to her toes, and something relaxed in her that had been tight-held inside since Isabella died. *She was safe.*

Silently, Iain, Malcolm, and even laconic Wragg ranged themselves alongside and behind Asphodel and Farlan. They stood firm as their staunch hearts and faced down the enemy to their hotel and their mistress.

The prison warder reached into his pocket and flung a gold sovereign on the table. "I would be quit of this scene, which appears much other than I was told. Here. Never say I do not pay my dues."

He nodded at Asphodel and led his men from the door.

Farlan, Iain, and Malcolm marched on Dougie, who shook his head and edged away. He glanced over at Maeve and jerked out, "Come on, then, you little whore." Snapped his fingers.

Maeve lifted the jug she was filling and marched over to Dougie, her face twisted. "Do you think I have not more pride than that? Do you think I can forgive your manky words I heard you say to Miss Asphodel? All I've wanted since then is to make amends to Miss Asphodel for being so foolish as to believe your lies, Dougie McDonnell!" Her voice rose, enraged. "I would have made you a good wife, you slimy, lying, deceiving cretin, but you took my honest admiration and made a joke of it, threw it in my face because I am poor, an honest hard-working barmaid. I deserve respect too."

Dougie backed to the bar. Maeve lifted the jug and poured the contents over his head and splashed the last amount on his groin.

She hissed, ignoring his writhing and cries of protest, "So I preened and simpered and flattered you, pretending I was still believing that you would marry me after taking my favors. And now, you complete bastard, you understand that you underrated me. Never, never, underrate a woman of the York moors. For I pretended thus until I found the documents. I have taken the precious papers back again for Miss Asphodel and the baron, for I must make right with her. She never crossed me, not once, not even after I so sadly betrayed her."

By the appalled look on Dougie's face, Maeve had got her revenge, far more bitter than the dark ale dripping even now down his face.

Hope flared in Asphodel's chest. "You have the papers? The documents Dougie stole from Isabella's room?"

"I have," said Maeve, and laughed like a banshee. Then she burst into tears. "I'm so sorry, Miss Asphodel. Please, please, keep me here. This is my home. This is where I belong. Dougie turned my head, and I have suffered for it."

Asphodel took the few steps to the girl and wrapped her in her arms. "Shh, shh. You have made all right. You have done brilliantly, Maeve, my friend. Come. Come now."

Iain took Maeve from Asphodel's arms. Malcolm and Farlan picked up the damp Dougie and marched him to the open front door, from whence Asphodel guiltily enjoyed watching him being thrown bodily from her premises. He landed with a cry in the dirt and dust.

"You have brought it on yourself," she said, and she found that a burning need for revenge and retribution which had been simmering inside her since the asylum—nay, before that—since he had taken calculated advantage of her grief and despair and laid grubby hands on her person—was satisfied.

The papers. The very first thing they must do was to retrieve the papers.

****

Asphodel was delayed.

Her staff wanted to talk to her, to complain about Dougie's vile treatment of them, to reassure themselves that they could overturn his capricious and clutch-fisted orders. The cook, Mrs. Kell, gave forth at vocal and injured length about the changes Dougie had forced upon the kitchen. "Poor quality mutton and rancid fat has never been served in this fine establishment, under my aegis!" Mrs. Kell's considerable chins wobbled in fury and distress.

Her bar staff, doormen, maids, cellarmen, stable hands, and grooms all emerged from their various places in the pub to "Thank all the old gods ye are back with us, Miss Asphodel!" and "A crying shame I missed the blessed sight of that rogue eating dirt!"

She wasn't sure where Farlan had gone; perhaps once she was back in the protection and care of her staff, he had ridden hell for leather back to Blackleech Castle. She couldn't blame him; it just seemed strange he would vanish without a word. It gave her a pulse of unease. But that was ever Farlan, the Man of Mystery, she reminded herself, and attended to all the myriad concerns of her business.

How she loved her beautiful hotel! How precious to be back within these walls that had harbored her and seen her grown to her womanhood. She escaped her staff for a blissful moment, climbing the stone stairs to the tower room, trailing her fingers along the cool stone curving walls, reclaiming her hotel and her center.

She hesitated on the threshold, but the room was mercifully unsullied by Dougie or any other person he could recruit to his fell purpose. Her room sparkled as clean and fresh as she had left it. Someone had not given up on her return: a fire crackled cheerfully in the grate and a wash jug of warm water stood on the washstand. A small posy of early spring flowers opened their pretty faces to the room. Asphodel breathed in the room and stood for a moment with her eyes closed.

Nobody would wrest this from her. The Black Hart Hotel was hers. This was her legacy and birthright, and bedamned to those who thought that because she was young and a woman, she could not run it or should not own it.

The papers. She must find Maeve.

Asphodel sought the barmaid in the likely places. It was strange Maeve had not immediately sought out Asphodel to give her the promised documents.

"No," said Maggie in her high voice with its strong local accent, "I've not seen her, ma'am. Likely gone after that Dougie McDonnell."

"No," said Mrs. Kell. "Maeve kens she is no longer welcome in my kitchen."

"No, Miss Asphodel," said Iain. "She'm not left by the front door."

Wragg poked the fire in the small front bar and eventually remarked, "Trouble goes with that un. Take care, Miss Asphodel."

Well! Where was the infuriating girl? She tapped her fingers against the mantelpiece as unease gripped her. Was this why Farlan had so precipitously vanished?

Her stomach flipped. Something was badly amiss.

This long, eventful day was darkening to evening. The Black Hart Hotel sang and glowed with the evening rush. She must tend to her business.

****

The next day, Asphodel resumed her search. She enquired of staff and visited the maid's rooms and staff accommodations. No Maeve.

In the golden morning, Asphodel wandered out to the rear terrace, greeting customers and stopping to exchange pleasantries with neighbors and regulars. Her mind itched to find Maeve, to discover whence Farlan had gone. Her heart misgave her.

She went farther into the kitchen gardens and the flower gardens which gave her so much pleasure and stood for a few blissful minutes, eyes closed, breathing in the warm perfumed air and listening to the sounds of her garden. Her brain ran through possibilities.

The crunch of gravel: Asphodel started and turned, but too late.

A large hand plonked itself over her mouth and nose, rendering her unable to cry out, or even to breathe. Two rough hands grabbed her waist. She caught the ripe smell of unwashed man and then someone tied a dirty rag around her mouth, a hessian sack went over her head, her wrists were tied behind

257

her, and she was tumbled and dragged along the grass and through several hedges. She fought, struggled, and kicked but only elicited a harsh laugh and a punch in the kidneys for her trouble.

She was thrown roughly onto a high firm surface, which immediately commenced moving. A cart. Her body bounced along with the movement, bruising her hips, shoulders, and right elbow. Her head smacked on the bottom of the cart each time the equipage went over a bump in the track.

Acid curdled in her guts; she could hardly breathe through the gag and the sack. Terror tumbled and coiled within her like poison, paralyzing her normally quick brain and her limbs.

Who could this be? Where were they taking her? Why were they taking her?

Another pulse of fear smote her. Was it a positive sign that they hadn't just killed her and thrown her body into the beck? Or did they have some equally fell plan to commit under darkness or far from help at her hotel?

Who could this be? Would Dougie really stoop to such extremes of behavior?

Dark, scream-wracked images of the asylum pushed into her reluctant mind.

No, please. Not again. They would hide her away in a solitary cell, and even Farlan would not be able to find her.

Asphodel wrenched her mind away from fear piling upon fear. Such piling, roiling thoughts did not help her. She must keep her wits at all costs. Nobody was coming to save her.

She must save herself.

Asphodel attempted to roll herself onto her knees.

If she could get to the side of the cart…

There! With an effort, she hauled herself to her knees, swaying with the bumps of the cart, and shuffled to the edge of the contraption. She waited a few seconds—could she afford to, or would her captors look around and spy what she was about to do? She took those few seconds to listen to the echoes around her, assess the air.

They could be rattling along a high ridge with a crashing descent on either side, but by the mineral smell of the air and the way the noise of the cart resonated, they were likely lower, perhaps enclosed by the brow of the moor.

Do or die time.

She gulped a quick brave breath and…

…Threw herself over the side. For a long moment she was airborne: she had no knowledge if she had leaped from a bluff and would fall blindfolded many yards below, breaking every bone in her body. Never to wake again.

She crashed to earth, the breath slamming from her body, the fall jarring every bone. Her head felt thick and muddy; bruises stung from shoulder, hip, thigh, and knee. She wiggled her fingers and toes. She managed to sit up and put her head between her knees, made a few desperate contortions, and there! She pulled off the sack using her knees. Blessed sight returned!

She staggered to her feet and began to run, anywhere, so long as it was away, her hands tied behind her, the gag tight between her lips, scoring the tender sides of her mouth.

A shout went up.

Terror surged, and she stumbled but righted herself

directly. She risked a look over her shoulder; the men were pulling up the cart. Two large men lumbered down toward her.

The countryside sloped down around her; a sweet beck sparkled just below, through thick ash and willow and alder. If she could just make it that far, she could disappear amongst the trees.

Asphodel's legs were rubbery and refused to run properly. The gag tasted thick and greasy in her mouth, and she sobbed with the effort of sucking in air.

She was almost at the beck—oh, sweet deliverance—when a gasping wheeze rattled behind her and the earth shook with heavy pounds of booted feet. She stumbled, regained balance, and put on a desperate surge for the trees.

Not fast enough. A thick heavy hand clamped on her shoulder and hauled her to a stop. More hands grabbed her waist. As she struggled, the man reached her. She saw the raised fist and ducked, but the heavy blow caught her temple. The landscape melted and shimmered and danced topsy turvy all around her.

Then everything went black, and she knew no more.

****

Asphodel came to with a splitting headache, a foul taste in her mouth, and muscles screaming with pain. She was blindfolded again and being manhandled somewhere, her legs dragging along. The place smelt industrial, the air heavy with the resinous scent of wood and the warm fibrous smell of wool and cotton. Cold pulsed from brick walls, and sound echoed as though in a large indoor space.

The heavy hands pushed Asphodel through a

doorway. She fell on a hard cold floor. A door clanged shut.

Asphodel forced herself to sit up and put her throbbing, beating head on her knees for a moment, trying to regain her senses. Nausea swirled in her stomach, and bile coated her tongue. At least they had removed the gag and she could breathe. Her hands. They were no longer secured behind her.

As she put her hands to her face to tug off the blindfold, a rustling and shifting sound emanated from the opposite side of the space.

Her hands froze.

Something, or someone, lurked in here with her.

Chapter Twenty

April 1881—Industrial Yorkshire

Asphodel's body was absolutely paralyzed with fear. Her hands shook so badly she couldn't at first remove the blindfold. She swallowed against a thick, dry throat and fought to mentally settle her churning stomach.

"Come on, Asphodel Quick," she murmured in her grandmother's voice. With both hands, she tugged and twisted at her blindfold until she was able to tear it from her face and fling it across the room.

The room was spacious, the darkness as thick as treacle, pierced only by a thin beam of light emanating from a narrow upper ventilation shaft. Red brick walls chilled the air. It looked like an industrial storage room of some kind, like those attached to a mill or factory. It smelt of textiles overlaid with a fresh acrid note.

To reinforce the notion of a storage room in a mill, wisps of cotton and wool fiber still adhered to walls and lay on the wooden floor. A dull thumping suddenly shook the floor. Her heart seized in terror, a flash of heavy hands grabbing her person tormenting her mind.

The thumping continued in a regular pattern and came no closer. Mechanical. Weaving looms?

A mill? Why was she taken here? Who…?

A scraping sound in the half dark. Something

shifted.

She peered through the dimness to the far edge of the room. Who or what was in here with her? Another jolt of terror.

A pile of old fabric at the end of the room moved. Asphodel watched, her eyes starting from her head. If it was a dog, she could talk to it and settle it. She hoped. What if the dog was fierce, and starving, and mistreated, and she had been put here to be…?

The creature that sat and looked at her was starving and mistreated, but it wasn't a dog.

"*Maeve?*"

Asphodel struggled to her feet. Her entire body shook. Her dirty, damp dress clung to her form. Mud streaked her clothes and body. She had a shocking thirst, and her head banged and pounded in her skull like a drum. The room whirled around her, and she sat abruptly before she fell.

A weak groan issued from the end of the room.

Asphodel kept to her hands and knees, careless of what she touched on the floor of the room.

Poor, poor Maeve. Nameless filth coated her exposed skin, and her clothes were streaked in dried mud. Her face was scraped and crusted with blood. Bruises and cuts bloomed on her hands and forearms. Her fingernails were torn and filthy. Her hair hung around her in witchlock clumps.

"Asphodel?" A mere thread of sound.

A water jug—dry—stood near an empty metal plate. A pail over to one side explained the acrid scent in the air.

Asphodel drew the smelly bundle to her and rocked her in her arms. "What is the meaning of this?" she hissed. "What do they want?"

"The papers. Dougie wants the papers. He never did want me."

Asphodel's rocking stilled. Maeve had kept the documents hidden away? She had withstood this treatment rather than hand them over?

Maeve's nose was running against Asphodel's sleeve. "That lobcock has shown his true colors. He tried it on again wit' me, but I weren't havin' owt."

She hardly dared ask. She kept a strong, comforting hand planted on the shaking girl's back and breathed, "Where did you hide the documents, Maeve?"

"In the—"

Heavy footsteps pounded along the corridor outside. Maeve buried her face in Asphodel's sleeve once more.

"Quick, Maeve!"

Too late. The door clanged open. Dougie's face leered in at her. "My men said there were voices." He minced into the room. "How do you like your new accommodations, my lady? I anticipate your—or rather my—enjoyment of the washroom, in particular."

Asphodel looked involuntarily at the pail in the corner. She valiantly repressed the pulse of fear.

She met Dougie's smirking countenance with a full glare. "Have you quite lost your wits, Great-Uncle?" she demanded. She smiled, nasty as she could make it, as Dougie jerked, his shoulders wilting.

He glanced at his two thugs glowering in silence behind him. He pasted a fulsome smile on his face, as treacherous as winter sunshine. "Now, now, my dear, no need for that."

"*No need?*" The fury boiled up in Asphodel. Her

heart banged in her ribs, and her stomach clenched. "I have been manhandled, mistreated, assaulted, and slammed in here. What can you mean, *no need*?"

His mouth turned down at the corners, his "baby about to tantrum" expression. "You must see reason, Niece."

"Great-Niece."

Dougie winced. "A very young great-uncle. I will have you marry me, willing or no. And we shall do it today by special license."

Asphodel glared. The man was mad. "You need my guardian's consent for legal marriage."

"Not if he is incarcerated, my dear. Then your care devolves to your nearest and dearest. Me."

Asphodel did not know if this was law or not. Why hadn't she checked such a simple thing? She clearly was no match for her uncle in deviousness.

Let the truth slay him. "I will never marry you, Dougie."

His face purpled, and his jowls shook. His fist waved at her. "I can compromise you, here and now."

"You can try to assault my person, but such an attack will not necessitate marriage, Dougie McDonnell. As well you know. I am more than a mere society miss, whose pure reputation is her prime asset. I am valued as a businesswoman and hotelier."

She watched him think about this, trying not to reveal how utterly revolting was the thought of him forcing his person on her. Who knew, he might do it solely for revenge.

"You clarty scum, Douglas McDonnell!" Maeve decided to contribute to this edifying conversation. "You make promises to an innocent woman, and now you shame me to my face!" Her voice was a scream. With her matted hair and filthy face, she looked like a bedlamite.

Dougie's eyes widened in panic.

"Let her go, Great-Uncle," Asphodel said in her calmest voice. "Your fight is not with Maeve."

He stared in disbelief. "The little witch betrayed you! She showed me your hiding places and told me your secrets."

"And yet, she is on my staff and under my protection. She has not been dismissed, as she was led astray by you."

Dougie scoffed. "Exactly the kind of softhearted nonsense you get when a female tries to be the boss. No stomach for it."

Asphodel struggled with herself. This was an argument she longed to have, with Dougie, with the world, with herself. She knew he was wrong, and *she would prove it*. But now was not the time. "Release Maeve. You gain nothing by keeping her here."

"She has the papers I need."

"She has told me where they are," Asphodel lied. "Let her go."

Dougie's eyes narrowed, and his mouth flattened. "I'll release her when you sign the marriage deeds."

"No."

"Very well, you will give me the Black Hart Hotel, signed away in my care, as you are young and incompetent."

A piercing pain lanced Asphodel's heart, which stuttered and froze for one dreadful moment. Her throat thickened, and she had to force the words through. "I cannot give you that. My hotel, the Black Hart Hotel, is

Isabella's legacy to me. Her passion and her life's work. Her great gift."

Dougie strolled forward. Asphodel misliked the evil grin wreathing his features like a mask. He put a fat finger under her chin and pushed it up. His voice slithered like a summer snake. "I will hunt down that fraud and imposter who calls himself Farlan Blackitter and get him consigned to the blackest dungeon, followed in due—humiliating—course to the gallows, or at the least, transportation."

All the blood rushed from Asphodel's head and chest. The room spun. Black spots floated in front of her eyes. She put out blind hands for support and found herself clutching Dougie. She let go as though his sleeve had burned her.

"Agree to sign the contract," he repeated. He waited.

Asphodel sank to her hands and knees. Her legs could no longer support her. Perhaps it was the blow she had sustained earlier. She was never normally this weak. "Let Maeve go," she gasped, "and I will look at your contract."

He jerked his head at his men.

Maeve stared in shocked disbelief. She ran to Dougie and smiled up at him, blinking away tears. "Oh, my lord, thank you." She sank and kissed his toes. "I will do anything you ask." Dougie gloated at the maid bent over his feet. Then he kicked her in the rump. "Get that filth out of here."

His men hauled Maeve to her feet and marched her to the door. She was still bleating and crying to Dougie, "Thank you, thank you, my lord."

Really, Asphodel said to herself when Dougie, his

men and Maeve had gone, I thought the girl had more spine. She sank back against the wall.

She was utterly and completely alone.

As always, she only had herself to rely on.

How would she ever extricate herself from this mess? Marry Dougie? No, and no! Sign away the Black Hart Hotel? More pain lanced her. She bent over. It would tear her in two to let them wrest her legacy away from her.

But what other choice was there?

If she did not sign it away, Dougie would ensure Farlan was arrested and incarcerated, never to see freedom or the light of day again.

What was the Black Hart Hotel compared to a man's freedom?

She loved him.

She loved Farlan Blackitter, Baron—or not—of Blackleech.

She knew it now, if she didn't before.

Farlan's liberty, his very life, mattered more to her than bricks and mortar. She would never be happy again if she allowed them to take Farlan. The Black Hart Hotel was her lifeblood, her heart, but it was just a business. She could make another business. Her grandmother had bequeathed business-smarts as much as the physical rendering of a hotel.

A terrible choice lay before her, but much as she suffered, she knew the choice was already made.

It would be Farlan.

She would *always* choose Farlan Blackitter.

She just hoped she would set eyes on him again in this earthly life.

Asphodel closed her eyes and fell to remembering

every detail, every touch, every kiss of their lovemaking. Thank all the old gods of knoll and fen she had not been missish; she had allowed herself to experience him fully.

No matter what happened to her next, she had loved Farlan Blackitter. She had given him love and joyfully, gladly taken his love for her.

And nobody could take that away from her.

She stirred. Farlan had already sacrificed everything to rescue her from the asylum. She sat up straight.

What on earth would the man do now to risk his neck? *To save her*?

She had to get out of here!

****

Farlan stalked through the glowing interior of the Black Hart Hotel. Where could Asphodel have got to? Unease grew like a canker within him. His instincts screamed. Everything in him wanted to be with her, near her, basking in the *Asphodel-ness* of her. But if something wasn't badly wrong, he had never been one of Her Majesty's scouts in the New Zealand wars.

He sought the garden—Asphodel might be seeking a moment of solitude and beauty in between setting her hand back firmly on her hotel. If not the garden, then the tower room. Farlan battled the surge of lust which enveloped him as he pictured Asphodel in his arms, alone together on the high vistas, in her private chambers…

"Sir! Sir! *Lord Blackitter.*" The high-pitched voice came from the shrubbery. Farlan stilled. What new devilry was this? As something of an expert in chicanery himself, he was alert to lures and dodges, fakes and frauds.

"Please, sir! Dougie has Miss Asphodel."

Caution blew out of his brain with the speed of a bullet. One stride, two, and he was tearing the shrubs apart to be confronted by a sorry spectacle of a filthy ragged urchin, staring up at him with dirt and tear-streaked eyes, inexplicably clutching a sheaf of official-looking documents.

Not an urchin. Maeve. The Black Hart maid.

Fear smote him like a crack of lightning. He had to resist the overwhelming urge to choke the truth from her. To give some thought to her own distress. "Are you well? What has happened to you? May I assist?" he ground out. Unable to wait for any kind of answer he demanded, "And for all the gods' sakes, tell me what misadventure has befallen your mistress!"

Maeve thrust the papers at him. "Miss Asphodel never let me down. I am ashamed of my behavior and want to make right."

His whole body locked still as he held them. The accursed papers, which would reveal him to be fraudster or lord, baron or bankrupt. "Thank you." His voice was a crust of sound. He coughed. Shoved the documents in his inner pocket. "Thank you, Maeve. Come. You appear to need food and a bath. While I assist you inside, you will tell me what has transpired."

A thought smashed into his mind. He halted. The entire world stopped with him; stopped spinning, stopped breathing. "Your mistress—Asphodel—she is hale?"

"I left her well, sir. But for how long, I dare not say."

They walked toward the kitchens, Farlan

supporting Maeve's weight. He rapped out, "Where? Where is she?" Again, he had to use every ounce of willpower not to shake the truth from the grimy maid.

"Textile mill over to Pickering. I never went before, but I guess 'twas the McDonnell works. Trouble brewing there, weavers shouting on the picket lines." She swallowed, her thin frame shaking with sobs.

Farlan fisted his hands against his sides and gritted his teeth.

Maeve wiped her nose on her arm. "That false-promising turncoat Dougie and his thugs were strutting about. They did this to me; Lord only knows what they will do to the mistress."

"How did you escape?" His men would have known to pay attention to his quiet tone.

The maid sniffled.

"Maeve—I can see you have suffered. Thank you for giving me the documents. But pull yourself together! Do you want me to save Asphodel? Help me!" Maeve looked up at him, and her face turned crafty. She blinked through her tears and dirt—and smiled flirtatiously. A red mist built in Farlan's mind. Perhaps Maeve intuited something like, because her face blanked and the flirting expression was replaced by a serious one. "I betrayed her for that overstuffed lounge cushion, and she made him let me go. She said—"

"Yes?"

"She told Dougie she would sign over the Black Hart Hotel. For me, and for your freedom too." Fresh tears cascaded down her face, making new runnels through the dirt. Farlan pushed Maeve into the kitchen doorway, commanded the staff inside—a faceless blur to him at present—to look after her, and strode off to the front bar.

"Wragg! Quick man, where is the weavers' strike? Somewhere in Pickering."

"Weavers striking everywhere about, my lord. Them's all striking. Pay's too low to keep food on the table. Them biddies only paid by piecework—ye can only mistreat a woman for so long before she rises up agin ye. And mistreatin' a whole bunch of 'em...?" Wragg shook his head.

"I don't want your philosophy, Wragg. Give me the location of Douglas McDonnell's mill."

Wragg took the pipe from his mouth. His old eyes, bright with cunning, examined Farlan. "Ye'm don't want to be goin' there, Baron. You'll never come back to what is yorn. Dougie'll have the beaks on you afore ye can say 'transportation.'"

"He has Asphodel!"

Wragg dropped his pipe into the ashtray and stared in wrinkled dismay. "That's bad, Baron. Very bad." He studied Farlan, his shrewd old eyes roving from head to foot. "Happen they'll be somptin in those papers in yon pocket might help. I guess Maeve gave em to ye?"

"What do you mean?" Farlan stared and then hoicked the papers from his pocket, sifting rapidly through them.

Farlan Blackitter, Certificate of Birth, Born on this Twenty-Second Day of November in the Year of Our Lord 1852 to Fairley Edmund Blackitter and Lavinia Blackitter. Legitimate! A surge of elation spiked, then crashed. Asphodel. He had to get to her.

McDonnell Woolen Mills and Tweed Manufactory. Proprietors Donal Angus McDonnell and Forley

272

Goforth Blackitter, Third Baron of Blackleech.

"The manufactory—I hold a fragment of the matching document—" Things clicked together in Farlan's carnival brain. "No wonder Dougie wanted me arrested, after I lifted the papers from his coach! They don't belong in his sweaty hands. Donal was Isabella's husband. Therefore Isabella inherited the textile mill. The mill is not his. It belongs to your mistress."

"And yer own, Baron, through the third baron hisself."

Farlan shoved the papers back in his pocket. "I shall give him my share of the mill in exchange for Asphodel." With no hesitation. After all this seeking and hunting for documents, he hardly cared to even read the things. None of it had any meaning without Asphodel in his life.

He added, "If Dougie is lucky, that is. When my men arrive, please be so kind as to tell them I am in Pickering at the McDonnell mill and I await their presence. Bring weapons."

Wragg shook all over and made a series of ominous creaking sounds, which Farlan interpreted as laughter. "Glad to have 'ee back, Baron. Fangmoor Beck and Castle Blackleech ain't the same without a wild Baron Blackitter to keep things interestin'."

"I'm honored you approve," Farlan replied. He grinned at the old reprobate. "Well, I'm off to liven up Pickering. I'll be back with your mistress. Thank you, Wragg."

Farlan marched to the stables and threw a saddle on Black Bran, who neighed at him in welcome. Farlan tossed his leg over and galloped away, the wind tearing his hair and the skin on his face, and his dread tearing up his insides.

He wished he was as sure of the outcome as he pretended.

He urged Black Bran to greater speed and rode like the wind to Pickering, praying to the old gods and the new that the center of his heart, Miss Asphodel Quick, yet lived.

Chapter Twenty-One

April 1881—Woolen Mill, Pickering

The room was twenty-three large paces by thirty-seven and brick-walled. The wooden door was solid as the waiting time before spring. Weak sunshine slanted down in bars as insubstantial as sunbeams from the ventilation shaft high above, barely penetrating the dark of her prison.

Asphodel paced off her frustration and growing fear. The pacing helped her thinking, and that was what was needed now.

She could sign away her hotel—*as a last resort*—only when all other options were exhausted. *Think! Think, woman.*

Dougie had imprisoned her in Harrowlick Lunatic Asylum. She refused to permit herself to be captive, to be restrained against her will, ever again.

Noise. Every time the door had opened and shut, she had heard noise outside—shouting and yelling, women's voices. If she was in a mill, something was happening. She could use that chaos, whatever it might be.

Could she surprise the guard as he opened the door? Hit him with the—she cast a frantic glance around the room. With the…pail? She wrinkled her nose and grimaced. A horrid prospect indeed.

For a time, she practiced crouching near the door, head on her knees, curled in a ball as though in the very pit of despondency, and then leaping up like a spring deer. In her imagination, she hurled the pail as well. That could give her the seconds she needed to burst from the door and sprint away.

People were outside and perhaps in the building somewhere. Even with the door shut, she caught fragments of sound. Fragments…she surveyed the pieces of cotton and woven wool scattered around the floor and drifting in her eddy as she walked. She stopped. Perhaps…

Asphodel sat and methodically ripped a wide strip from her fine white petticoat, like peeling a long strip of apple skin, ripping around and around. First she tried writing on it with mud, which merely crumbled and smeared. She gave a small scream of frustration.

Oh! She unhooked the tiny pearl brooch from her bodice. Inhaled. Pricked her finger—after all, the textile workers in this very building often injured their fingers until they were scarred with weavers' marks—and squeezed out a drop of blood. Scratched her improvised quill against the fabric, shaping blocky red letters into the wide ribbon. H-E-L-P M-E.

Now. How on earth to get the message to fly from the ventilation shaft? She needed something to weight the fabric so it could fly through the narrow vents. If her aim was true.

Her boots were way too large. She needed something small and heavy. Asphodel felt around on her person. The only thing she could find was—

—Farlan's heavy gold ring. It was small enough to get through the shafts.

But it was his evidence that he was the baron. Biddy Birkenshaw had kept the ring safe all these long years, and she planned to throw it from a window? If it got into the wrong hands, or was stolen, or simply found by a lucky person, where was Farlan's claim then?

She stood, the HELP ME ribbon in one hand, the heavy ring in the other.

Dougie could still find it on her. And she knew, without any doubt whatsoever, that Farlan would want her to use it.

Blast it. It was only a ring.

She tied the ring to one end of the fabric and then drove herself almost mad enough to need to go to the asylum in any case, with throw after throw toward the ventilation shafts. Some she pitched too weak; harder throws landed on the shafts but pinged off back to her waiting hand.

And then, suddenly, when she had almost given up, her throw fueled with anger and despair, the ring flew gracefully through the narrow shaft, her message streaming out behind it.

The large hairpin and knot in the fabric she had secured to the other end stopped the fabric from completely streaming through. With luck, the message fluttered in a stiff Pickering breeze, issuing from a window in the mill. White to attract attention, and the words HELP ME in giant red letters.

"Good work, Asphodel!" she said aloud and went back to practicing her leap of surprise for when the door opened.

****

Farlan barely registered the desperate ride to

Pickering. He and Black Branwell fused into a single being, leaping stones and fences and tinkling becks, bent over gasping and ploughing up steep hillsides, thundering down dales. He forgot time and place and once again pounded up the shale-covered hillsides of the Ballarat goldfields, rode like a demon through deep forests of New Zealand, important messages held only in his head.

He snapped back to the present as he reached the cobbled streets of Pickering, Bran's clattering hooves striking sparks from the flint paving. Farlan slowed his manic pace to a steady, more civilized demeanor, in case secrecy was paramount.

He heard them long before he saw them. A long waving snake of furious women and their menfolk, waving placards and yelling, cordoned off the main entrance to the McDonnell Tweed factory.

"Fair pay for fair work!"

"End to piecework."

"A living wage for weavers."

"Standard fixed wage for all!"

The din was incredible. Many had saucepans and metal spoons and banged them like drums. Others blew horns and whistles, and yet more set up unified chants which rang through the lengthening day.

Farlan walked Bran up and down near the striking weavers. Children and youths, no doubt also employed at the mill, swelled the ranks of the protestors.

"Here," he said to a gangly youth. "Will you walk and rub down my horse?" Farlan showed a bright shilling, and the youth took the big steed with alacrity. Farlan waited a moment. The tall young man talked to Bran in soothing tones, and his hands showed they knew how to care for a horse.

"I'll tek him to the Fiddlers Arms," the boy said in a strong local accent. Farlan nodded, patted Black Bran, and turned toward the strife.

He began asking random women, "Have you seen a young woman, long red-gold hair, Asphodel Quick?…Do you know Asphodel of the Black Hart Hotel? I fear she has been taken prisoner here."

Blank stares met his enquiries. Sympathy, frowns, teasing jokes.

"How would a lass be taken through here, sir?" one woman asked. Farlan's heart dissolved within him. It was true. If not here, where would Dougie have taken her?

He kept ploughing doggedly through the crowd, pushing through the front, his ears ringing from all the noise and shouting. He was right in the midst of it now.

Suddenly, a middle-aged weaver woman accosted him. "Miss Asphodel Quick?" she yelled in his ear. "You think she is prisoner here?"

Farlan said, "You know her?"

"Miss Asphodel is always kind to me. Come, I will take a selection of weavers, and we will storm this compound. If she is here, we will find her, sir!"

The neat, calm woman tapped seven other women on the shoulders and shouted in their ears. All nodded and bunched around her and Farlan, then they moved off with purpose across the picket lines and around the rear of the factory.

"What's that?" shouted Farlan.

There before them all waved a long white ribbon of fabric, issuing forth from a high window around the back of the factory. Every time the breeze caught it, the banner flattened out, and the message was plain to read: *HELP ME.*

"It's her!" roared Farlan and led his newest troops off to the fray.

****

The shouting rang louder now, within and without her prison. The waiting would kill her before Dougie's henchmen even got their hands to her. Surely someone could see her fine banner? Perhaps no wind stirred, and the fabric merely hung limp down the side of the building—very likely she paced the confines of the McDonnell Tweed Factory. The chanting could well be unhappy workers demanding better conditions. If she ever got out of here, she must investigate that too.

Where was the man? Hadn't Dougie threatened to return so she could sign away the Black Hart Hotel?

Asphodel alternated pacing her confines with practicing her squat and leap. The pail was positioned near the door, the pungent tang of urine floating over her in snatches.

Time seemed frozen. She was trapped in a half-lit world where nothing ever changed.

And then, with the force of a summer storm, it did.

The yelling of many voices suddenly resounded closer within the mill. Heavy footsteps stamped down the corridor—several sets—and the door flung open. In the moment before Asphodel sprang to action, Dougie's corpulent form exploded in her vision.

He stepped into the room, a twisted sneer on his face, which turned to puzzlement when he at first did not see her. At the very moment he did, she sprang out of her crouch, grabbed the stinking pail, and tipped the contents over him. Dougie leaped back with an agonized yell. Asphodel pushed him hard into his nearest thug and burst from the door like a cork from a bottle.

The second thug made a grab for her, but she danced and weaved like a butterfly in the other direction, and then she ran.

A wall of noise came around the corner of the corridor; she barely had time to register Farlan running, leading a gaggle of furious, placard-bearing women, marching in a determined fashion toward her.

"Asphodel!"

"Farlan!"

She ran straight into his arms. For a long, blessed moment, she wallowed in his strength, his solidity, the safe harbor that was Farlan Blackitter. His heart beat fast and strong under her cheek where it pressed to his chest. His hand cupped the nape of her neck, the back of her skull. She would never have to worry about anything ever again.

She stuttered, "I find myself in need of a wild man with military experience. Farlan, Dougie captured and imprisoned me. His henchmen are coming any second."

Farlan put her at arms' length, retaining his hold on her, so he could study her face and person. "Are you harmed?" His voice would have splintered an ancient oak. "Did that...*toad*...hurt you?"

"He is coming. He wanted me to sign away the Black Hart."

"You didn't?"

"Not yet. Farlan, he wanted me to sign it away in exchange for your freedom. How did you escape?"

Farlan laughed, low and bitter. "He never had me, my Asphodel. It was his last play, a desperate bluff."

He opened his coat, showed her a sheaf of documents in an inner pocket. "Maeve gave me the papers. You are embracing Baron Blackitter, Lord of Blackleech Castle."

"Oh, Farlan!"

One of the women interrupted. "Did you say Dougie McDonnell is here, miss? He is wanted outside!" Her grin was pure mischief.

Asphodel turned to the woman and recognized her word-picture client. "Leda! How lovely to see you. Dougie is just behind me in the corridor. I have enraged him further, I fear, by tipping the slop pail over him as he entered the room in which he had me imprisoned."

Farlan let out a roar of laughter. "That's my fierce moors queen. Irrepressible!"

"We saw your banner, miss. Very clever!"

A pang of guilt smote Asphodel. "Your ring, Farlan! That's how I weighted the banner. We must retrieve it."

"Hang the ring. If it led me to you, I am content." Farlan's deep silver eyes glowed like molten mercury. They were as soft as a cygnet's gray fuzz and full of emotion. Asphodel, spellbound, gazed back. Sound dimmed. Time stopped. There was only Farlan, Farlan looking at her with all his heart and soul, all his fear, all the wild boy and damaged youth. All the strong, fearless, determined man.

"Grab him!" shrieked Dougie's voice, shattering the spell. Two thugs came pounding down the corridor, followed by a furious, wet, and reeking Dougie. The weavers yelled in glee and rushed forward. The thugs pushed them aside and made to grab Asphodel. Farlan punched one of the thugs in the temple and chopped his neck. The man fell like a stone.

The weavers had Dougie and were dragging him out to the pickets to mete out a rough justice. Asphodel couldn't find it inside herself to care. Instead, she called, "You must answer now for your mistreatment of women, Douglas McDonnell."

While she watched Dougie, another thug reached Farlan. Farlan scooped her into his strong side and began to run.

"The papers!" yelled Dougie. His man made a grab for Farlan and pulled him back by his coat. Like an eel, Farlan slithered free, so he was in his shirtsleeves and vest, barely breaking stride.

The thug stood, holding Farlan's coat, the documents bulging from an inner pocket.

Asphodel struggled against Farlan, looking back over her shoulder. "No, Farlan! The documents! You cannot let Dougie have them now!"

"Hang the documents! I must get you to safety, Asphodel Quick."

Asphodel halted. "Leda," she called. "We need those papers Dougie's man is holding. Let Dougie go if he returns the papers."

"I don't know about that, miss," Leda called. "There are three hundred women outside want to have a word with Dougie McDonnell."

Dougie emitted a high-pitched scream. "Niece! Tell them to release me! I've done nothing…I've done nothing…"

"It's appalling, watching a grown man sob like a child," Asphodel observed to Leda. "But I would not deprive you of your natural justice. Come, then, Baron Blackitter."

Three women dragged Dougie away. Four of the group marched up to the thug. He quickly thrust the papers at them, turned tail, and fled away along the opposite direction.

"Here, miss," said Leda. "The brutes were not brave enough to try to intimidate several angry women together!"

Farlan remarked in dry tones, "I don't blame them one iota."

Asphodel laughed and said to Leda, "Thank you! Farlan, I think we should go and watch this. These are our people, and I am ashamed a McDonnell has mistreated honest working women so."

Farlan kept a solid, warm arm around Asphodel as they followed the women and their captive back out to the front of the mill.

The women held Dougie in front of the chanting mob. He struggled and pushed to make a break, but several women surged forth from the picket line and blocked his escape. Each time he attempted to flee, he was held back.

Finally he stood, a drooping, dejected picture of misery, as the women made speeches about their right to a living wage, no more piecework, sick pay, and holiday leave.

The speeches finished with rousing cheers from the crowd, which was growing larger as word spread. Dougie McDonnell was answering for his crimes. Finally, the crowd relieved their feelings by pelting Dougie with rotten vegetables, eggs, clumps of mud, and other more malodorous farm substances.

Dougie stood, orange mash and slimy green cabbage sliding down the side of his face. His hair clumped thick with horse manure and raw eggs. His fine clothes were obliterated with a medley of offensive soft rotten food and dung. Tears traced down his face, making tracks in dirt and more eggs.

Farlan had been flicking through the papers, scanning some, frowning over others.

Farlan stepped forward and held up his hand for silence. Such was the presence of the man, the crowd fell silent in a great wave, rolling from the front right through the crowd to its last observers, craning their heads and standing on fences and fenceposts.

Farlan's voice rang out. "I am the lost heir, the fourth Baron Blackitter, Lord of Castle Blackleech." The crowd shifted, muttered, and held its collective breath to hear more.

"These papers I hold in my hand say I am in fact the hereditary owner of this mill. In my first act as the fourth Baron Blackitter, I will restore a living wage to all workers at the renamed Blackitter Textile Mill!"

Asphodel listened, astonished.

Farlan's voice carried strong and clear to the back of the crowd. A soldier's voice, a leader's confident tones. "Equal pay, reasonable holidays, sick leave…"

The crowd went mad. Applause and chanting greeted Farlan's every word. Someone began a chant: "Baron Blackitter, Baron Blackitter!" The crowd took it up.

Several carriages drew up, accompanied by uniformed men on horseback.

Oh no! It was the magistrate. "Farlan!" Asphodel hissed. "Wilbur Westgarth is here. You must flee!"

Farlan laughed, his eyes and teeth gleaming, his head thrown back. Something tense in Asphodel dissolved; this was the real Farlan, a leader, a devil-may-care, a chancer who also cared deeply about people.

Chills gripped her spine with icy fingers. The man disembarking the second carriage—Master Shuttlestick from Harrowlick Asylum. Horror screamed in her mind. She pressed her body close to Farlan.

The magistrate, closely followed by the asylum master, began barging their way through the crowd, which had gone silent and cautious. A few bodies faded away back to other chores and other duties. Many of the women bunched up together in two solid lines, eyes determined, arms linked, making an impenetrable barrier in front of their baron. Dougie wilted off to one side, terrified of leaving the safety of proximity to Asphodel and Farlan.

Leda put her chin up and addressed the magistrate and his thin, poisonous shadow. "You have no business here, sirs."

Shuttlestick hadn't lost any of his coldness. The sight of him made Asphodel shiver and quiver inside as unwelcome memories of the asylum flashed through her brain. Farlan pulled her to him. His warmth was an anchor, a rock, a mountain to shelter within. His steadiness made her feel safe—and surprisingly, so did his astounding courage and unpredictability. He was not afraid. He was *never* afraid. He never feared what *could* happen but dealt instead with what *was*.

Farlan grinned at the magistrate. "Come for your erstwhile friend, the dishonest Douglas McDonnell? What does such a friend say about a man?"

The crowd began catcalling and whistling. The magistrate looked around uneasily. Even he could feel the mood of the crowd poised to pivot on a word or a misstep. The master stood stiff and wary, nostrils flaring and thin lips curling. His pale eyes widened as he recognized Asphodel, then lit with savage hatred.

Farlan pushed the urine-soaked, vegetable-smeared Dougie straight at the magistrate. He proclaimed, very loudly, ensuring everyone heard, "For the sake of my affianced bride, I will release her great-uncle. I am the owner of this mill. The strike is over, as I have promised to instate much better working conditions."

Dougie lost his head for a moment. He turned to Farlan and sneered, "You won't make a bean that way! You will be bankrupt in a fortnight." The crowd rose on its toes and began shouting and throwing well-aimed missiles at Dougie. Some matter landed on the magistrate, who ducked and threw himself behind several of his officers, who stolidly took the brunt of the slime. A huge pat of sloppy dung hit the asylum master on his cheek. He completely lost his cold composure, flailing his arms and crouching behind the magistrate's men.

Asphodel laughed.

Farlan held up a hand. Like a miracle, the crowd settled. "Ah, but I have all my goldfields riches behind me, you see. I will be restoring Blackleech Castle and renovating my businesses and properties. There will be increased employment for all around, from York to Pickering, Ravenscar, and beyond. I will need masons and carpenters, plasterers and blacksmiths. Weavers, seamstresses, cleaners, gardeners, cooks, maids, stable hands…"

The crowd was in ecstasy. The noise was phenomenal. Asphodel stared at him with her mouth open.

Farlan and the magistrate engaged in a very male, and public, staring match which lasted for many long minutes. Farlan was smiling, a devilish, daring grin taunting the magistrate.

The magistrate's jaw clenched tight. His lips were so thin they were a white slash in his angry face. Temper smeared his cheekbones.

"In fact," Farlan shouted, and the crowd immediately quietened, waiting for the next delightful shock. "I am taking up my rightful duties as magistrate of this county here and now. I thank Wilbur Westgarth for his years of honorable service." He grinned at the magistrate. "You, sir, are now officially relieved of formal duty."

Could her eyes open any wider?

The crowd was laughing, demanding Dougie and Wilbur Westgarth.

Wilbur Westgarth made one last try. "You have no proof," he shouted. "This man is an imposter and fraud!"

At that moment, a woman smuggled herself behind Farlan and Asphodel and tucked something in Farlan's hand. Farlan looked at it and kissed the woman on her cheek. She clapped a hand to her face, blushing rosy pink.

Farlan held his hands up and theatrically placed the ring on his right hand. He shouted, "By my grandfather's seal, I claim my inheritance." He waved the documents. "By these papers, I claim the Blackitter lands and Blackleech Castle. By the blood in my veins, I claim custody and care of all who dwell within my demesne."

The crowd surged forward as one beast. Some of them took Dougie, calling about washing him in the Pickering lake. Others grabbed the magistrate and carried him off to a similar fate, pulling at his clothing and rubbing messy substances over his face and hair.

Asphodel had whispered to Leda, who directed a team of angry strikers to grab the asylum master as he cravenly crept away. He was not cool now, swearing and shouting and struggling. The movement of the crowd brought him near Asphodel.

They locked gazes. "Help me," Shuttlestick begged her. His face scrunched in a mask of misery. Under the smeared dung.

Asphodel stared back at him impassively. "I cannot pity you. You will not be hurt, only stripped of your dignity. You will suffer some humiliation, it is true." She put her face closer to his. "But when I consider all the unfortunate women who have been your victims, losing their freedom and dignity for *years*, I believe you will get off lightly."

The crowd dragged him away.

Meanwhile, the uniformed men had been staring from Westgarth to Farlan. They recognized a leader, and perhaps they were relieved to no longer answer to the ex-magistrate. With one accord, they moved to protect Farlan.

But their protection was unneeded.

A group of burly farmers hoisted Farlan, fourth Baron Blackitter, onto their shoulders, and carried him through the crowd, to the adulation of all.

Asphodel linked arms with the weaver, Leda. "A good day's work, Leda, my friend!"

"Your man is full of surprises, Miss Asphodel. I've

never had such an entertaining day. As good as a circus!"

"Come, Leda, we are friends, are we not? Enough of the *miss*. As for 'my man,' we are yet to see about that. Come now, and bring your lieutenants, and we will enjoy food and drinks in the Black Hart Hotel. All welcome!"

Leda gleefully relayed the news; soon a large contingent of women and their menfolk were walking, riding, or driving pony traps and small carriages the seven miles to the Black Hart Hotel.

It was a grand day for celebrating.

Chapter Twenty-Two

April 1881—Black Hart Hotel

Asphodel pulled open the pantry doors, handing out rosewater and jars of currants to Mrs. Kell, her cook, who kneaded and rolled out yet another massive sheaf of her famous pastry, flour coating her from nose to knee. Two kitchen maids and a barmaid shoved the mixings of curd tart into pastry cases while whipping up more Yorkshire puddings and fat rascals. Four of the Blackitter Textile Mill weavers assisted in the crowded kitchen, indiscriminately slapping together enormous platters of potted game, forced rhubarb, biscuits, and cheese. The laughter and gossip were deafening, with the favorite topic being Baron Blackitter, fourth of his name, and his famous speech and even more famous promises.

Wragg and Tebbs bustled in and out, giving Asphodel reports as to beer and ale supplies, climbing up and down the cellar stairs, and lugging heavy barrels with them.

It was the party to end all parties.

Asphodel was putting it all on for free, to celebrate the re-emergence of the lost heir and the lifting of the curse of the Blackitters.

She hadn't had a chance to even smile at Farlan, surrounded as he was by his adoring public.

Asphodel slung herself out to the back garden, just to get some air. She rested her hands on her knees and inhaled the comforting, familiar scent of her kitchen garden.

"Ye don't want to marry the baron, lass."

Asphodel jerked upright.

The disbarred lawyer, Sean Donegal, blew another smoke ring and appraised her with his shrewd old eyes. He'd been sitting on the bench so quietly, dressed as he was in russet and green, that he had simply faded into the garden background.

"Who says I want to?" She hadn't meant to snap.

Weariness dragged at her, wrought from a long day of excitement, and…yes. She felt ignored. For the first time, she realized she wasn't Farlan Blackitter's main focus. Normally, she was a magnet, Farlan's attention burning into her like a brand. Now?

"I'm just getting myself sweaty and mucky in the kitchen, keeping the crowd fed and watered, while he entertains his adoring…*subjects*."

Sean laughed. "Then he's more foolish than I warranted, leaving such a splendid woman as yourself to feel slighted. Come, Miss Quick, sit yourself down and bide here for a while. Tell me about the crowd and the speeches."

Asphodel, who had been about to accept his invitation and sink down beside him, halted. "Sean! Not you too! Why don't you go along inside and ask him yourself? There are many souls in there repeating the story, blowing it bigger with every telling." She paused and plucked a stem of rosemary, smelling its pungent herby scent. "He is a natural leader, one who draws people to him."

Sean said, "Hold fast there, Miss Quick. He'll come out, all charming and reckless, cutting a dash through your sweet lovely heart soon enough. Listen to me now while you've had a few stars fall out of those beautiful eyes. Let an old reprobate feast his old peepers for a while on your sweet beauty."

Asphodel laughed as Sean twinkled at her. "You are incorrigible, Sean Donegal! But go on. Through all that blather, you've obviously got something to tell me of some importance."

"I'd offer you my hand and heart myself if I thought for a moment a beauty such as you would have me."

"Sean! For shame! I'm sure I heard you say that very line to Maggie two weeks past."

He laughed again. "I need to keep in practice, Miss Asphodel Quick. What if the woman of my dreams did stroll into the bar of the Black Hart Hotel one fine day? You wouldn't want me to be stuck without my lines, now, surely?"

"Well, Sean, for sure she would have to be drinking in my bar, for you never go anywhere else! Now—enough blarney and nonsense. My spirits are quite restored, thank you. What did you have to tell me?"

"Just this. Wait a little until you marry. There's lawyer's talk that married women will have more rights in property and income next year. The new laws are being drafted as we speak. The first Married Women's Property Act in 1870 didn't go far enough to truly free women such as yourself, and many strong women are not happy. As the law stands now, you would still have to gi' him the business and all the profits and get his permission to sell the old Black Hart or change it."

Asphodel was silent while she absorbed this. "This is why Dougie McDonnell was so desperate for me to marry him now—before the new Act. He would own the Black Hart business and all the income and have rights over how I managed the property."

"Yes, my love, and the wicked baron will have the same rights under this current law. Bide a little. String him along. It will do the man good."

Asphodel smiled at the old lawyer. "You knew he was the baron from the start, didn't you?"

"Yes, my darling. The estimable Wragg told me. The spitting image of his grandfer."

"Farlan seems very happy. I've only seen the documents once, in the most cursory examination, but I know one of them is his birth certificate. For a long time, Farlan believed he was born on the wrong side of the blanket. Illegitimate."

She studied Sean and said, "You know, I think the baron is entitled to his celebration. He has had a life of danger and uncertainty, with only his grandfather and no other family, and uncertain family stories, never knowing if they were truth or fable. He never really had a home, as such. And then he came here only to be wanted by the law, then risking his neck, literally, to pull me from that asylum. I was sleepwalking until I met Baron Blackitter, and now I am alive and fully awake."

The old lawyer patted her leg. "Don't be in too much of a hurry. Single, no man can wrest this establishment from you. Married, you lose all agency." His twinkle became brighter and his accent more lilting. "If you must *love* the man, then do so! You can do *that* single. The married state is for the patriarchy to maintain its control over women."

"Sean! You are a shocking rebel."

"But take my illegal legal advice and don't marry him—not for a year or two."

"You are waiting for me yourself, are you, Sean Donegal?"

"You've seen right through me, with those lovely, clever eyes of yours. You are too intelligent for me, Miss Quick. You'd run rings around even an old lawyer like me. Maybe that baron is the man for you, at that. His brain functions fast and well. Now, the night air is chilling my old bones, and speaking law gives me a terrible thirst. Particularly as you are giving it away free."

He wrenched and creaked up from the bench. "Mind you don't give the whole thing away free by marrying too soon."

Asphodel remained seated, staring blindly at her garden. Same old, same old thing. "What do you think, Isabella?" she said out loud. "You won't be happy if I just hand it over, gorgeous, handsome, debonair, titled baron though he is."

****

Everybody was present in the Black Hart. Everybody Farlan could want celebrating with him, except those who lived only in his memory. The blood raced in his veins, and his mind shouted. Triumph! Victory! Mad happiness and wild energy sizzled and danced, radiating into the crackling air around him.

He was home. He had claimed his birthright. Even better, his birthright—all these people here—*had claimed him.* He was theirs, their Baron Blackitter, back to oversee the health and prosperity of the whole community.

His grandfather...his grandfather. How Farlan wished his grandfather was right here at this moment. How he wished he was there to hear him speak today. Maybe he was there. The words flowed from somewhere. He claimed his birthright, his inheritance, his barony. He claimed his father and grandfather, Blackleech Castle.

And he had claimed the best prize of all... As he laughed and jested and shook hands and kissed cheeks, he kept an eye on Asphodel. There—a flick of her citrine hair as she darted down a passage. There! A slice of her dress as she dashed into the kitchen and remerged, handing a full tray of warm fruit pastries to one of the barmaids to pass around.

Hands slapped Farlan's back. Other hands replaced his empty pint with a full one. Voices clamored for him to tell more adventures of his riotous life. He laughed and joked and talked and laughed some more. He was dizzily, conqueringly happy.

Or he would be when he had Asphodel back where she belonged. At his side.

Farlan plonked down his empty glass. "Thanks!" he said politely to the willing hands filling it up once more, but he had no intention of imbibing more. It was time to find the proprietor of this establishment.

He shrugged off the people dogging his footsteps by walking down the passage, darting into the kitchen, and then through another door.

He ventured into the garden. He knew she loved the garden; perhaps she had sought some air and peace there. He sniffed. The faintest drift of her flower perfume hung on the breeze.

If not here, then she must be in the tower room.

Good. If she was there, he could show her the papers.

Farlan walked up the worn stone steps with a stealthy tread. Yes, a hint of her perfume tickled his nose here too. His heart rate picked up with the notion of Asphodel alone in the tower room.

Perfect.

His mind exploded with images of Asphodel, clean and dressed in fresh clothes, perhaps getting changed into something special to enjoy the party properly. Farlan let his mind play over her sweet face, her plump lips. He imagined kissing that sweet curvy mouth, the soft skin under her ear, down, to the swell of her breasts…her lithe and athletic body under all that fabric.

He picked up the pace.

He arrived at her door. He turned the latch, slowly, carefully, and gave it a little push. The door gave. He looked down at himself and smiled ruefully. He would scare a wanton with the rod in his breeches. No matter. She had seemed to like it last time, out on the bluffs. He groaned. That image just made it worse.

Farlan breathed in and pushed the door wide.

Firelight flickered golden in the darkening room. Streaks of vivid sunset strobed the circular room in red and gold, as though Asphodel's vivid hair was flying through the sky outside. And there, half dressed in filmy lace, as though she had changed her mind in the middle of dressing, her exhilarating fire-opal hair curling around her in a nimbus, bare toes outstretched to the fire, sat the center of his heart, of his very existence. Miss Asphodel Quick.

She didn't smile. She didn't look at him. Her voice, when it finally came, was low-pitched and over-calm. "Did you manage to shed your adoring public, before broaching my private sanctum?" Cold, even.

"Asphodel, what is this?" He came toward her and crouched near her. He stroked a strand of her lovely hair and curled it around his finger. She still didn't look at him.

He heard the catch in his own voice, the break in it, as he said, "Has something hurt you?" A tide of anger swamped him, and he leaped to his feet. "Who has importuned you now?"

She put out a hand. Wait. Looked up at him. Her eyes shone deep blue in the firelight. Her hair crackled red like a fire. Her body—in that almost-but-not-quite see-through lace—

He sank down to her. "Asphodel, you drive me mad with desire." He touched her plump lips, but she twisted them away from him. "What has happened?" He touched her again. She tensed, but she didn't pull away, so he pulled her tight into an embrace. She remained stiff for a few long moments, and then with a soft exhale, folded herself into him. He hugged her tight. She was so sweet, so curvy, so warm. He couldn't believe how lucky he was to have found her. It was the best find of all.

"Asphodel. Please. I thought we were friends as well as lovers. Will you tell me what distresses you? I will slay any dragon, fight any foe, build any bridge if you ask it!"

A muffled snort of laughter emanated from the region of his embroidered vest. "No dragon. Missing you."

"My love!" He tickled the back of her neck under her hair and stroked the underside of her wrist.

She nestled into him. "I've been wondering. Why did Isabella not give you the Blackitter inheritance papers when she gave you the guardian documents?"

"I believe your safety was paramount in her dying mind. When I returned to Fangmoor Beck and she summoned me and bade me be your guardian…she could die in peace, in the knowledge you would be protected. Always."

Her lovely curves melted into him as she gave a delicious sigh. His cock stirred. Pulsed. He cleared his dry throat. "Isabella knew you would find my papers."

"I interrupted you both! 'Twas the first time I saw you—a tall, mysterious, silver-eyed stranger."

"And I you. A scantily clad siren with a cloud of yellow topaz curls—and intelligent eyes searing me. My brain and heart shattered and reformed in that instant." He traced her rounded shoulder. "Then on that lonely track, I encountered your whiplash tongue. And my adoration was sealed."

She rasped a palm over his bristly jaw. "You love my tongue."

He coughed. "Yes."

Asphodel said drowsily, pressing against him, "Strange. I had your papers and you rescued mine—the title deeds to the Black Hart and my birth certificate."

"Fated. Two shapes that fit together."

He was a shameless opportunist.

He couldn't really help it. Her lacy garments enticed and half-concealed. He stroked the lace over one nipple and smiled as it jerked and hardened to a bud.

"What was that?" he asked, voice deep and low, just a murmur next to her ear, his fingers tasting her shiver. He selected a lock of hair and tickled the nipple with it. She wriggled her hips against him and made a small squeak in her throat. He bent and picked her up and sat down on the high bed, Asphodel nestled in his lap, her soft plump bottom right on his rock-hard cock.

She wiggled. He retaliated by grasping, with his whole hand, her right breast and giving it a firm jiggle, then he pinched her teat. She bounced up and gasped and sat back on him. Farlan was losing control. He put both hands on her fine plump breasts and gave them the squeeze they deserved, then bounced them in his hands.

Farlan couldn't play any longer. This was serious. He bent over her and touched her lips with his own, asking, exploring, waiting. She moved toward him, seeking him. He plunged his lips down on hers and kissed and kissed her, his heart flying away over across the moors as his hands and mouth and tongue loved her and caressed her. She wound her arms around his neck, ran her fingers through his hair, rubbed his body, his chest, neck, back, arms, shoulders. She touched his groin, and he moaned and pushed into her hand.

While he kissed her, she used her clever nimble fingers to undo his breeches and freed him from his confines. She gasped as she held his thick length, admiring, beautiful eyes wide.

Farlan allowed her to stroke him, then flipped her over and gave her pleasure with his fingers until she made high yelps and writhed beneath him.

Asphodel's eyes rounded as he finished himself off.

And then they lay together, embracing, warm, content, all well with their world.

"We must wait until we are wed," Farlan said into her neck. She did not reply. "Mmm, sleepy," he teased.

She sat up. He almost missed what she said as he was mesmerized by her naked breasts right in front of his face. Slowly, her words trickled into his bedazzled brain.

Farlan sat up and threw off the covers. "What do you mean, *you cannot marry me*?" He leaped to his feet and grabbed his clothes. He flung them down again. Naked, he paced the room, thoughts whirling through his mind. A kind of vise of grief and panic had him in its steel jaws. Red exploding patterns smashed and jangled in his brain.

A thought hit him. Fool! He had never properly, romantically proposed to her.

Naked, he knelt before her on one knee. Clasped his hands in prayer position. "Asphodel, you are one in a million, a trillion women. I love you, heart and soul. Will you do me the honor, and give me the greatest joy I have ever known, and agree to become my wife?"

She stared at him. There was a kind of quirk hovering about her mouth, pressing in. Her eyes glowed like a summer sky. An expression akin to pain crossed her features.

"What?" asked Farlan.

Asphodel's generous mouth opened like a flower, and she burst out laughing. "I have never had a proposal from a buck-naked man before!" she trilled. She laughed so much she fell on the bed, spilling lush curves from her half-undone lacy clothing. She looked abandoned. She looked delightful.

****

The laugh took hold of Asphodel like a bubbling river through her consciousness, melting all care, all weariness away. She peeked at Farlan's face. Oh dear. He looked hurt and crestfallen, so crushed it was comical. His expression made the belly-laugh burst forth from within her again. After a while, she was just laughing. Laughing away her trauma, shock, and fear.

"Farlan," she gasped, "is that the naked truth?" She collapsed in giggles once more.

He stood, leaning over her, and waggled his very erect manhood close to her face. Her eyes grew wide. His smile flickered back. "You are a businesswoman. Best you see the goods before you buy." She dragged her gaze away and studied his face. His lovely mouth stretched in an evil grin, and his eyes were lit silver.

"Farlan, come here. Listen, you are apparently my legal guardian. I do seem to have a surfeit of guardians, for a woman who really has no need of one, let alone two!"

"Lucky I am, as it turns out." He leaped nimbly over her and settled himself on the bed next to her, half upright, propped up by the wall and the pillows.

Asphodel sat up and faced him. "Unfair! Reminding me of your gallant rescue."

The smile had run away from his face. He looked frowning and earnest now. The chiseled planes of his cheeks and jaw glowed in the firelit. He touched a finger to her left hip and traced a gentle circle. Asphodel's skin thrilled all over. Her breath caught in her throat.

His voice was low and serious, the bass notes sending delicious shivers through her to her toes. "I cannot bear the thought that anything would happen to you, Asphodel Quick. And it does, with alarming regularity!"

"Only since I met you, Farlan Blackitter, adventurer and wild man!"

"You are speaking to your baron, miss."

"Ha to that! Prior to you stealing my ring, I was a staid and prosperous businesswoman."

"I told you, I will give you a better one. Asphodel, my heart, will you permit me to put a ring on your finger?"

"A ring, a corset, a straitjacket—it's only a matter of degrees with you men, isn't it? Anything to keep us under control." Asphodel joked, but indeed her words pricked with truth.

Farlan's heavy black brows snapped together. His cheekbones ridged pale. An atmosphere of thunder crackled around him. He made a supreme effort, reaching for lightness. "Women are not to be suppressed for too long, as your valiant weavers have shown this day."

He gripped her hip with his whole warm, strong hand. "Asphodel, answer me. Yes, I am your guardian, but see me! I am Farlan Blackitter, adventurer and wild man, yes, but also the man who craves your love, who yearns for—finally—a settled home and—family." His voice cracked on the words. "After travelling the wide world, to my surprise I find my heart's desire right here where I belong: a woman of extraordinary courage, of conviction, of the most incendiary beauty, sprung from the very soil that made me."

She could listen to him all day. Such poetry and passion in this proud, brave man! And poor Farlan. To

be denied home and family for all those long years…
She brushed a tear away from her face with a brusque
hand.

"Asphodel, I beg you. Explain your feelings to me.
I want to hear you. I want to know you."

She pressed her lips together and swallowed the
lump in her throat. Yes, she owed him this.

She took a deep breath and huffed out her fears. "I
will try to explain, but Farlan—don't be angry!"

He growled deep in his throat. "I could never be
angry with you, Asphodel of the moors, flower of the
wild places."

His fingers began a lazy circling of her hip, her
side, her arms. His touch calmed her. She gave him a
tremulous smile. "Not only are you my guardian—
which is an obstacle, but perhaps not insurmountable—
but you must understand, as a single woman, I own this
hotel. I own the property, I own the business, and the
income is mine. If I marry you, you will own the rights
to all this. I could not sell it without your permission or
change anything. You will own all the income deriving
from the business. You will have the legal right to make
all decisions concerning this."

Farlan sat up and gripped her face in both his
hands. "Hang the Black Hart Hotel!"

She wriggled in his grasp, but he merely tightened
his fingers and said in ferocious tones, "I will give you
Blackitter Castle, and gladly! I will sign the lot away
over to you. There! Now will you marry me, you
recalcitrant wench?"

Asphodel laughed. "So romantic, Farlan," she
teased. "From dainty flower of the moors to wench in
barely a sentence."

He barked a laugh and released her, rubbing a frustrated hand through his dark curls and rasping along his black-stubbled jaw.

"Just wait, is all I am asking," she said. "Sean Donegal—you know, the old disbarred lawyer—says they are writing new laws as we speak, that will give women the full rights to their property and income. When that law is passed, perhaps we may have this conversation again. Should you still want to. You may of course have found a less recalcitrant and more willing wench by that time."

Farlan's expression darkened. She waited in some mix of trepidation and anticipation. What would he respond to first?

He climbed over her and strode around the room, his tall muscular figure rimmed in red and gold like an angry god. "That interfering old saddle mouth!" He came over to her and leaned over the bed, staring down at her. "But you are right, of course. It is right you should be informed of these matters, which affect you so directly." He paced again, lithe and frustrated like a caged untamed beast. "Asphodel! Cannot you trust me? Can I not sign papers which give you your rights, now and in perpetuity?"

"I don't know." She rose from the bed and washed herself from the jug on the washstand. She peeked over her shoulder. "You are very silent."

Farlan was staring at her with darkened eyes, watching every movement of her hands as she wet her skin and rubbed in the places which most needed washing. He swallowed. "Would you allow me to assist you, madam?" He came over and took the soft washcloth from her hands. She stood, shivering with delight as Farlan carefully, delicately, dipped the cloth in the water and smoothed it over her body. He traced the curving line of her hip and waist. He dabbled under her arms, watching hungrily as her breasts rose up as she obligingly held her arms over her head. He ran water over her breasts until they glowed wet in the flickering light and tingled with sensation.

Farlan dipped the cloth in the water and trailed the warm water along her thighs, and finally dabbed her right on her aching apex. Standing, Asphodel parted her legs so he could wash her, the roughness of the cloth rubbing against the bud of sensitive flesh. Her legs quivered. Sensation shot through her body like fireworks. Just as she could no longer stand, or bear the exquisite torture of Farlan's administrations any longer, he scooped her up against him and laid her on the bed. He covered her with his warm, strong, muscular, safe form, and Asphodel gave herself up to pleasure.

A while later, as she sank into sleep, Farlan's gravel tones thrummed against her cheek. "Fine, my love. We wait."

Chapter Twenty-Three

June 1881—Two months later

How Asphodel loved summer on the moors, even though it was one of the busiest times for the Black Hart Hotel; but these days, when wasn't it a busy time? She hoped Isabella would have been proud of her. "I trust your spirit resides here somewhere still, Isabella McDonnell, for you would love what the Black Hart Hotel has become." Patrons came from miles around, for the good mood, the quality ale and bitters, and the unsurpassed, stunning vistas. And they came for Evie.

Evie Lovelace had proved to possess a rich variety of talents. Singing, dancing, burlesque. Teaching the maids and male staff how to play a part in a lunchtime or evening show. Some patrons were shocked, but even their rapacious and salacious gossip just garnered more curious customers.

This lovely June morning, Asphodel had permitted herself a rare long amble over jagged crests and down dales. A fresh dawn pinked the tips of hill and heather. She swung her arms as she strolled, inhaling brisk peaty air. The sky brightened from dark turbulent gray to washed-out baby blue. Drifts of fluffy lamb-clouds dotted the sky like peaceful grazing sheep. A solitary star still blazed overhead. The day announced itself with a smear of rich apricot and gold to the east.

Her heart skipped and sang.

She bent and touched her namesake, bog asphodel, the bright yellow star-like flower of the fens.

"Hello, lovely life!" Asphodel called, surprising a family group of ducks from their tiny pond. "Hello, moors! You birthed me. This is where I sprang from and where I belong. My very cells are made from your mineral soils and sweet air, like the black lambs that graze on your grasses, the vegetables cossetted in your unforgiving soils. We are the biting air, the broad great skies, the stories, and the secrets—and the pain and death."

A pure surge of joy swelled and spilled over, her beating heart pumping the elation through her body like a fever in the skin. She danced around for a few minutes. Putting a protective hand on her belly, she bent over a little to catch her breath.

When she straightened, her land had given her the answer, as she knew it would.

There was no need for words here. One just listened to the birds and the wind, the sound of tinkling water in the tiny becks and the calls of native creatures who called this rich, desolate place home.

It was time.

Asphodel indulged in five more hearty breaths of the pristine, peaty air, and then she made her way back to the Black Hart Hotel. As she approached her beloved pub, a woman's voice soared out over the hills, the notes tumbling and liquid, but the tone decidedly naughty.

Evie Lovelace was limbering up for the midday dinner crowd, who often stayed long past dinner to enjoy her singing and to be deliciously scandalized by her latest outrageous show.

Even Asphodel never knew what the pageant would be. It depended on Evie's volatile moods. One day she would simply sing, Gentleman Jack offering a surprising and pleasant bass counterpoint, leaning over Evie, peering down her cleavage, and turning the pages as she tinkled out a tune on the pub piano. Every man in the place was always transfixed, wishing they were Gentleman Jack for the duration of the song.

Another day would bring dancing, either demure or quite eye-wateringly naughty, Evie alone or with Maeve, Maggie, and even Wragg and Tebbs, if the show needed a little comedy.

Sometimes they would act a scene from Shakespeare, though Evie always bequeathed the scene a title of her own invention. Few of the farmers and goodwives recognized the source.

Asphodel opened the side door to the little back bar and let the chanteuse's lovely voice wash over her. The soaring, untrammeled notes matched her mood. She waited in the bar, swaying her hips as her friend trilled. Gentleman Jack spied her there and rushed to offer her a chair. "Greetings, Jack," she said. The poor man wore the dazed expression he always had while listening to Evie sing.

The dashing diva broke off mid-warble.

"Darling!" Evie kissed both Asphodel's cheeks. Singing lit her face with passion. Her brown eyes lured like melting peaty pools. Her dark chocolate curls artfully framed her painted visage. Her vivid red spangled dress, as always, was two sizes too small—in all the right places.

Asphodel gave her an affectionate hug. "What

treasures are you inflicting on your unsuspecting but adoring public today?"

"A little bit of song, and a *lot* of dance," said Evie, widening her eyes, fluttering her lashes, and pouting her bright-red painted mouth.

Asphodel laughed. "You'll give those poor yeomen heart failure."

"The Blackitter Textile Mill workers have been given a half-day holiday," her friend announced. "So I am giving them a show to remember—" She sashayed her hips and shimmied her fine shoulders and breasts. "—and you, my darling, must know that I have spoken with the adorable and wonderful Mrs. Kell and ordered triple the number of dinners and delights from your kitchens."

Gentleman Jack's eyes glazed as the diva shimmied. Asphodel tried not to laugh at the poor entranced man. She did laugh at her friend. "Mrs. Kell? *Adorable?* Oh, you are funny, Evie. No one has called that terrifyingly organized woman adorable in her life."

"Precisely, my love. We all need someone to believe we are adorable. Her food certainly is."

"Manna from the heavens," confirmed Gentleman Jack, finally coming to and grinning at Asphodel.

"I'm not even going to try to ask you not to shock the York goodwives, Evie," said Asphodel mock-firmly.

"They love me, Asa. I wager they go home after one of my shows and hunt out a scrap of spangle here and a trick of tinsel there, and who knows what they get up to under those staid dresses? I'm sure their husbands are smiling more than they used to."

"Well, you bring me in a pretty penny, that's for

sure. I'm so very grateful." Asphodel clutched both of Evie's hands. "If it wasn't for you in that terrible place…"

"Now, now, my love," the diva crooned. "You sent your handsome fellow here to pluck me from that place like a ripe fruit…" She gazed at Gentleman Jack from under her thick black lashes. "Pplluuckk," she repeated, making the most of the tongue movement and lip pout occasioned by the word. Jack changed color and cleared his throat.

"I'll leave you to it!" said Asphodel. Well content, she went on her way to check every aspect of her business: kitchens, pantry, bars, dining rooms, guest rooms, garden, dairy…

****

Rapid footsteps followed her to her tower room. She sped up and, laughing, made it to the top of the stairs and did her best to slam the door, but Farlan Blackitter—for it was he—reached the door almost as soon as she did and stuck a thick, muscular arm across her, barring the way.

Asphodel squeezed her lips together to trap her mischievous giggle, but all unwilling, her face stretched in a wide, happy smile. "The Wicked Baron returns."

He leaned in, taking her space and her air. He grazed her lips with the slightest of kisses. Making his voice throaty and sinister, he replied, "Come to ravish the lonely young orphan, who knows not her own startling and glorious beauty. A Yorkshire moor treasure, hidden away in a tower."

Asphodel held his gaze and deliberately unfastened the top two fastenings of her bodice. "Is it hot in here?" she gasped theatrically. "I must remove some of this intemperate clothing."

Farlan growled in his throat and tumbled Asphodel through the door. He pushed it shut. He embraced her, kissing her thoroughly, and then tore himself away.

He took her to the window seat, where they could both look out over the landscape. "Asphodel," he said, and this time the gravel in his voice was real. "You must not taunt me so. I am becoming desperate—" Here he kissed her lingeringly again. "—to love you. To make love with you properly. With everything I have to give you."

Asphodel gazed into his beautiful clear gray eyes and stroked the emphatic line of his strong jaw. "I want you too," she said softly.

Farlan put both hands on her shoulders and squeezed. "Then marry me, curse you!" He tore his hands away and rose from the seat. "Sorry. Another year, three months, two weeks, two days, fifty minutes, and thirty seconds to wait. I know."

"You cannot know when they will pass the new law?"

"How many times have I asked you to marry me now? One thousand, at least."

"Do you tire of asking me, Baron?"

"No!" Farlan paced the room. "I tire of waiting. I tire of wanting you until my head, my skin, my heart, and mind are exploding with need. I want you for my baroness, Asphodel Quick. I am running out of patience. I cannot wait like some moony hero in a ridiculous poem that only sapskulls read. I am a man of action, not of patience."

"Well, man of action, why do not you take me and show me all the works you have been doing at

Blackleech Castle?"

Farlan paced the room moodily. "Yes, my castle is almost fit for a baroness. It will be ready long before my chosen wife!"

Asphodel put her hand on his arm. He would not meet her gaze. "Come now, Farlan Blackitter, I want to see what you have done. There is certainly no chance of my marrying you while the castle remains in disrepair."

Farlan whirled, his face alive. "What are you saying, my Asphodel? That if the Castle Blackleech is habitable…?"

"Take me there to see it first. And then we will talk of ifs and buts."

Farlan groaned and ruffled up his disordered black hair, which Asphodel smoothed with a calming hand. He caught her wrist and pulled her to him, kissing her with all the want and need in his kiss. Familiar desire snaked and curled in her belly. She pulled back, laughing.

"Almost you seduce me, Baron Blackitter, kissing me until I am dizzy and wanting."

He held her tight to him for a long moment. "Come then," he said, his voice muffled in her hair. "Come and I will show you your new home, if you will have it."

****

Blackleech Castle reared up like a broken sword from the jagged landscape. Asphodel loved its bleakness like she loved the moors. She rode Whicker, and Farlan cantered on Black Branwell. By the time they reached the castle, they were both rosy-cheeked and laughing.

A bevy of gardeners swarmed over the grounds. The tangled trees on the long drive had been clipped

313

and pollarded back into an avenue. The drive itself had been relaid with fine gravel. Garden beds surrounding the approach to the castle bloomed with scented roses, grand specimen shrubs, colorful summer flowers of all kinds. Asphodel gazed all around, wide-eyed, making sounds of approval, of surprise, of admiration.

As they approached the castle, a delighted shriek tore from her throat.

They dismounted. Farlan gave the horses into the care of a stable hand who rushed up upon their arrival. Farlan took Asphodel's hand and led her along the broad drive toward his ancestral home.

Blackleech Castle still towered majestic in its grounds, but now its stone walls had been stripped of thick ivy and shone with mellow welcome. Golden sun kissed crenellations and battlements. The roofs had all been repaired. Mullioned windows sparkled with tiny rainbows. They walked up the grand front steps, hand in hand.

"Farlan, it's gorgeous," Asphodel enthused. "You must have been working night and day!"

"Wait until you see the inside." His voice was curt, but Asphodel heard how proud he was, how excited, to be the Blackitter who restored the ancestral castle. It meant so much to him.

Farlan showed Asphodel through room after room which had been cleaned and polished, hung with elaborate tapestries, and carpeted with thick warm rugs of gigantic dimensions.

"Where on earth did you acquire these fabulously luxurious carpets?"

"I had them made. I met many friends on the goldfields. A Turkish rug-maker amongst them."

"Oh, Farlan, it's all so beautiful!"

"Come. I will show you the baroness's rooms. They are habitable, but naturally my baroness will choose and alter as she wishes. I have merely begun to make a comfortable home."

They walked up two grand staircases, a smaller one, down several corridors, and at last scaled a tiny curving staircase.

"A tower room! With views right across the moors. Why, there is the Black Hart Hotel! How sweet and quaint it appears at this distance."

"I spend many a long lonely day here staring over at that establishment."

"Nonsense! What shocking lies you do tell."

Farlan grinned at her. "It is the truth."

Asphodel faced him. "How delightful you have made it. Furnishings and luxury from around the globe." She turned away and squinted into the sunlight at her pride and joy, her hotel, her legacy, her fight.

"One day, your children will play here. The Blackitter curse will be faded and exploded by your energy and love."

Farlan was silent. She turned and regarded him.

"It is the dearest wish of my heart." His voice cracked on the words. His shoulders tensed. His brilliant silver gaze locked on her face. "Asphodel, my heart, my love, I cannot wait another year. If I learned anything in my dangerous and active life, it is this: *Life starts now*." He reached for her and kissed her gently on her lips, leaving them tingling and wanting more. "Asphodel Quick, will you do me the honor and make me the happiest man alive, by becoming my wife?"

"Yes!"

"Asphodel, I... *What*?"

"I said yes, I will marry you. Tomorrow, if you like."

"Do you mean it? You aren't teasing me—no, you wouldn't, not when it means the absolute world to me. Asphodel, are you sure?" He studied her face, and what he saw there made his light up—then flame red-cheeked with passion.

"You do mean it!" he said wonderingly. He grabbed her and squeezed her tight and then kissed and kissed her in a frenzy, as though they were soon to part and never set eyes on each other ever again.

Finally, at last, when Asphodel's lips were swollen and she had almost melted into a puddle of soft lust, he managed to draw away.

"But why?" he said. There was no fooling Farlan, or at least not for long.

"I had to make sure all would be ready."

Farlan frowned. Asphodel took his hand and placed it tenderly on her belly. "Those children you mentioned. Your family. The Blackitter clan. On the lovely moors, that day we rode away from Biddy Birkenshaw... We have already started on the heir. I would prefer he is indeed the legal heir, Blackitter curse or no."

Farlan resembled a man struck by a bolt of lightning. "You mean...?" His voice was a harsh, almost painful whisper. He stared, like one entranced, then he sprang into action.

Of course. He was Farlan Blackitter.

"Call the banns!" he yelled at the top of his voice. He jumped through the narrow window onto the castle battlements, waving and capering until everyone far below stared up at their lord in confusion. "Call the banns! Pry the priest from his drinking! Ring the bells!"

Crowds of workmen, gardeners, artisans, masons, and castle servants were massing far below and craning their heads up.

Asphodel joined him on the top of the castle. "Careful!" Farlan hissed. "There is still the Blackitter curse to consider!" He put a protective arm around her.

He called out to the world, "Call the musicians! Muster the poets! For Asphodel Quick has finally agreed to marry me!"

The crowed below all began a great cheering and clapping. Some of the castle servants embraced each other.

"Farlan Blackitter has finally come home!" Farlan yelled. And then, in full view of everybody below and for miles around, he caught Asphodel in his arms and kissed her.

"I never told you the rest of the Blackitter curse," he said.

"What? There is more? What can be worse than the heir dying or disappearing in every generation?"

"The Blackitter curse says—and obviously it happened to my grandfather too, given the situation with your grandmother, Isabella—the Blackitter curse says a Blackitter will only find love when it is too late."

Asphodel's heart twanged with pity. "And I kept putting you off." Then her courage and strong practical streak reasserted itself. "Well, Farlan Blackitter, we have broken that rotten old curse right open! Blasted it to smithereens!"

Farlan held a triumphant fist in the air.

All his people cheered.

****

Much later, Farlan escorted Asphodel—his soon-to-be bride!—back to the Black Hart Hotel, and there, most reluctantly, after a prolonged bout of kissing and caressing in the tower room, bade her farewell and rode back over the high track toward Blackleech Castle.

As he rode Black Branwell into view of the castle, the setting sun caught fire on the castle battlements, and the castle stood out against the harsh landscape as a black silhouette. His home! His ancestral castle and lands.

Asphodel said yes.

His heart flooded with happiness; a triumphant orchestra jangled in his brain in a wild dance of jubilation and immense gratitude.

His wily, mad old grandfather had sacrificed his home and his love of the moors to save them all. Farlan stood in his stirrups and yelled out a loud, echoing call of thanks to the old man. How he would have loved Asphodel's fire and passion, her good sense and calm way of dealing with all life threw at her.

She was carrying his child. Every protective instinct in his body clamored for him to turn around, race back to the Black Hart, scoop her up, and bear her back to Blackleech Castle so he could care for her and protect her. His blood thundered in his veins.

As the black night fell over Blackleech Castle, Farlan strolled restlessly in his grounds. Snatches of boyhood memories still teased the edges of his consciousness. The dark green bitter smell of the yew walk, the strange blue poisonous berries on the old trees. The dart of English birds in an English twilight garden. The peaty, heathery smell of the desolate peaks drifting on the teasing wind.

That ten-year-old boy Farlan danced and ran ahead of him down the dark walk. A fierce pain stabbed his chest, and memories flooded in, an avalanche of sound and shape, like the thundering, terrifying collapse of the Ballarat goldmine. Except—this time nobody needed to be saved—only himself. He opened his mind and heart and allowed the memories to run through him, cutting him with their fresh, sharp edges.

The piercing pain of remembering, of belonging, surprised him with its power to hurt. He had kept it all trapped inside, deep down. His deep love of his home. All the happy memories of childhood. Buried beneath rough times on the goldfields and the trauma of war in somebody else's land.

He belonged now to many places and many people. Pieces of him were scattered over the wide world, from the southern hemisphere to the northern. Memories, loves, friends, fear, near-death, and trauma, over and over again. Adventure, excitement, danger, and finding that fearlessness and joy of life within, despite all.

And then he stole the ring and the valiant heart of a red-haired moors witch—the cleverest thing he had done in his entire worthless life. Asphodel Quick pulled all those scattered pieces together and taught him to become himself: Baron Blackitter of Blackleech Castle.

His baroness and his child—children, the old gods willing. In the dark, Farlan sat on the old yew walk bench, child and man bound back together, and cried for sheer happiness.

Chapter Twenty-Four

July 1881—One month later, Blackleech Castle

When the Baron Blackitter of Blackleech Castle finally married his baroness, all of Yorkshire came to Fangmoor Beck to celebrate. A carnival set up in the Blackleech Castle grounds, and acrobats, jugglers, fortune tellers, and proclaimers thronged the castle walls for a week.

The Black Hart Hotel bulged with patrons, visitors, and paying guests. Mrs. Kell quadrupled the kitchen staff and brought in provisions and delicacies from the surrounding homesteads and villages. Wragg and Tebbs took on four new apprentice bar staff, and even Iain and Malcolm were training up local lads and lasses in keeping a large hostelry running smoothly.

Evie and Gentleman Jack entertained the crowds with singing and dancing every night. Even Rose Robin appeared with her wife and Romani clan, who settled out on the plain near the hotel, adding to the festive air with nightly spirited Romani music and their fierce clapping dances.

The wedding itself was the greatest event for a century. Asphodel would have been content with a modest wedding, perhaps out on the untamed moors, but Farlan insisted that all the people of his barony should know their lord had finally secured his bride.

Farlan married his Asphodel in the courtyard of the restored castle. Asphodel wore a white dress covered with silver gauze and spangles, and sweet wild roses in her braided red-gold hair. Flowers were everywhere, covering the arbor under which the couple said their promises and vows, along the walls, in tubs and pots and perfumed bunches in every alcove and nook.

Evie and Gentleman Jack sang naughty songs at the wedding, written especially for the bridal pair, and entertained the crowd mightily. The feast was ridiculous and profuse; the speeches profound and amusing.

The Romani band struck up whirling tunes, and all that could fit into the castle grounds danced the night away with passion and joy, none more so than their mad baron and their wild moors baroness.

Asphodel found a moment to hug Evie. "I am so happy, Evie. When I met you, I was in such extremity. And now I have a husband, who is the sun and stars in my firmament, and I have a close and beloved friend in you."

"I'm so glad to see you happy, Asphodel Quick— Blackitter. I have had a fine old time in the lovely Black Hart Hotel. But I wanted to tell you, my dear, I shall only see you about once per year now."

Asphodel studied her friend's face. The singer's grin sparkled, and her big brown eyes glowed like golden lamps. "Tell me then. What mischief are you brewing, Evie Lovelace?"

"Gentleman Jack and I are starting a traveling theatre troupe. We will bring shows and entertainment to all the tiny villages across the bluffs, down in the dales, and along the coast. Any people longing for adventure or see to the world shall join us."

Asphodel embraced Evie and wiped away a few tears. "I'm not crying, not really. I knew I would not have you forever, my lovely friend. Your courage and desire for adventure will always lead you into interesting ways. I'm so glad you have Jack to care for you."

"He is a fine man, my Jack." She gave a naughty wink. "He is plenty man to keep me well content for many a year!"

Gentleman Jack sauntered up then and gave Evie a smacking kiss on the lips. "She only wants me for my educated accent," he drawled, but his grin could have lit up the castle by itself.

"My perfect romantic hero," Evie breathed theatrically, and then Jack whirled his diva off into the dance.

Maeve approached then, holding the hand of a young man who appeared quite dazzled by her. The maid curtsied.

Asphodel grabbed the girl's hand and drew her up. "No need for formality, Maeve! I'm still your Asphodel."

The maid shed a few tears herself. "I thank you again for all you have done for me, Baroness. You saved me from a dreadful future with that tyrant. I must have been mad to…"

"And you saved us, Maeve, by giving the papers to Farlan. You will always be welcome here at Blackleech Castle."

Asphodel glanced over at Wragg, sitting on a bench under the great wall of the castle, with Tebbs and other gnarly moors folk.

He pulled his pipe from his mouth and saluted her. "There will allus be a Blackitter at Blackleech Castle," he intoned. "And by the looks, there be more comin' very soon." He laughed like a creaking gate, and Asphodel laughed with him.

She came close to him and bequeathed him a kiss on his leathery old cheek. "Yes, there is an heir on the way," she whispered. "How can you tell?"

"I got eyes in me 'ead," he responded and grinned enigmatically. "Best of luck to ye, Asphodel Quick, for old lady's sake and yer own."

"Thank you, Wragg. You have always stood staunch by my nana and me."

****

The night was turning into day by the time Baron Blackitter led Baroness Asphodel to the tower room. They sat, fingers entwined, and stared out over the great sculpted landscape. The dark sky was lightening in the east. A tremendous streak of golden red burgeoned over the slash of horizon. Asphodel rested her head on Farlan's strong, steady shoulder.

"What if our baby is a girl?" Asphodel said. "Will you be unhappy, Farlan?"

Farlan turned to her, and the fierce joy in his face made her heart pick up its beat. "I will be the happiest man alive, my love, joy of my heart." He kissed her lingeringly, with all the time in the world now to love her properly.

"I have been thinking of this," he said. "And of the Black Hart Hotel. If we are so lucky as to have a girl first—and I still can hardly imagine holding my own child in my arms, in my ancestral castle—and I have you to thank for all my happiness, Asphodel

Blackitter—"

Asphodel kissed him, and they did not speak for a several passionate minutes. As her husband explored the fastenings of her dancing gown, she held his hand still. "Mmm, Farlan? Yes?"

"I suggest we write into law that the eldest girl of every generation shall inherit the Black Hart Hotel outright. It shall be hers in perpetuity, in memory of Isabella McDonnell and Asphodel Quick, who fought hard and successfully against the wrongful laws of their time, made by men, upheld by men, enforced by men."

"Farlan, yes! It shall be exactly so. Have I told you I love you?"

"And now we have made provision for my daughter, it is now time we worked on the Blackitter heir!" Farlan kissed her again with feverish passion.

Asphodel laughed. "I don't think it works like that, my darling!"

"Show me, then, temptress of my dreams. Show me how it works." Farlan's voice was gravel—but his incandescent joy lit up Blackleech Castle and streaked like a comet across the wide moors sky.

A word about the author…

Maryanne Ross is totally addicted to reading. She adores writing sparkling historical romances with lively heroines and intriguing heroes.

She has a science degree in horticulture and sets many of her award-winning stories in gorgeous wild landscapes.

When not writing, she loves bushwalking, taking flower photos, and travelling with her partner Graeme. An unforgettable visit to the gothic, brooding North York moors inspired this story.

She works as a PR and development consultant for an Aboriginal organisation.

Connect with Maryanne at
https://www.maryanneross.com/
and https://www.facebook.com/MaryanneRossAuthor.

Thank you for purchasing
this publication of The Wild Rose Press, Inc.

For questions or more information
contact us at
info@thewildrosepress.com.

The Wild Rose Press, Inc.
www.thewildrosepress.com

www.ingramcontent.com/pod-product-compliance
Lightning Source LLC
Chambersburg PA
CBHW070044030726
47506CB00002B/325

* 9 7 8 1 5 0 9 2 4 0 4 6 3 *